D0295719

Conjugal Rites

By Paul Magrs and available from Headline Review

Never the Bride
Something Borrowed
Conjugal Rites

Conjugal Rites

PAUL MAGRS

headline
review

Copyright © 2008 Paul Magrs

The right of Paul Magrs to be identified as the Author of
the Work has been asserted by him in accordance with the
Copyright, Designs and Patents Act 1988.

First published in 2008 by HEADLINE REVIEW
An imprint of HEADLINE PUBLISHING GROUP

1

Apart from any use permitted under UK copyright law, this publication
may only be reproduced, stored, or transmitted, in any form, or by any
means, with prior permission in writing of the publishers or, in the
case of reprographic production, in accordance with the terms of
licences issued by the Copyright Licensing Agency.

All characters in this publication are fictitious and any resemblance
to real persons, living or dead, is purely coincidental.

Cataloguing in Publication Data is available from the British Library

Hardback ISBN 978 0 7553 4641 7
Trade Paperback ISBN 978 0 7553 4642 4

Typeset in Garamond by Avon DataSet Ltd,
Bidford-on-Avon, Warwickshire

Printed in the UK by CPI Mackays, Chatham, ME5 8TD

Headline's policy is to use papers that are natural, renewable and recyclable
products and made from wood grown in sustainable forests.
The logging and manufacturing processes are expected to conform
to the environmental regulations of the country of origin.

HEADLINE PUBLISHING GROUP
An Hachette Livre UK Company
338 Euston Road
London NW1 3BH

MORAY COUNCIL LIBRARIES & INFO.SERVICES	
20 25 54 07	
Askews	
F	

For Steve Cole

A Familiar Voice

The ladies were poised over their walnut cake and morning coffee in their favourite café, The Walrus and the Carpenter. The café was in the oldest part of town, at the foot of the 199 steps that led up to the ancient abbey.

Inside it was small, cramped and chintzy. Effie was petite and hardly noticed this, but Brenda was on the large side and today she felt a bit squeezed in. As they talked, their voices blended with the tinkling of spoons and crockery and they weren't aware of the young waitress eavesdropping on their every word as she dithered about the room.

Brenda was saying, 'I don't see how you ever make any money out of that junk shop of yours.'

Effie's eyes bulged slightly. 'Junk! That's nice, I must say.'

'You know what I mean. Knick-Knacks.'

'Antique collectables, I'll have you know, Brenda.' Effie looked her friend up and down. What would Brenda know about taste?

'Hmm. What I mean is, you're hardly ever open. Only about two hours a day. And you absolutely hate browsers, don't you? You don't exactly encourage them.'

Effie shuddered. 'It's true. I can't stand the way they just . . . loiter about.'

'How do you survive?' All Brenda knew was that in order to make a living out of her own establishment, the cosy guest house right next door to Effie, she had to work her socks off all the time.

'I have my means.' Effie pursed her lips and sipped her coffee. 'Anyway, money is overrated. I don't have many wants.'

'Oh, I do.' Brenda smiled. 'Besides, I like to be up and doing. I like work.'

'Well. It takes all sorts, doesn't it?'

Effie looked up sharply then as the young waitress pounced on their table and, with a great clatter, started to clear their used dishes on to her tray. There was something odd about her manner. Effie had noticed the way the girl had been hovering around their table.

'And how was that, ladies? Anything else I can get for you, is there?'

'No, indeed,' said Effie. 'That walnut cake was rather less moist than we're used to.'

The waitress said cheerily, 'Changed our supplier, didn't we? And we're not very satisfied, either.'

'See, Brenda? Everything's slipping. Hell in a handbasket is the phrase that comes to mind.'

Brenda was pulling her old woollen coat back on. 'Well, we'd know about that, wouldn't we?'

As the ladies were standing up to go, it was as if the waitress could hold herself back no longer. 'Excuse me,' she burst out. 'It's Effie Jacobs, isn't it?'

Effie frowned. This young woman was new to The Walrus and the Carpenter. The regular staff all knew Effie and they would never behave so oddly forward. 'It is. What of it?'

The waitress grinned and gave a slight squeal. 'I thought I

recognised your voice! Oh my God! You're famous! You're a celebrity!'

Effie experienced a moment of alarm. She picked up her handbag. 'Don't be ridiculous.'

'But you are!'

'My dear, I—'

'Wait till I tell the others . . .'

Brenda was completely confused by now, looking from Effie to the waitress and back again. 'I don't understand! It's just Effie. We're in here every week and no one ever notices her. Why's she suddenly famous?'

The young waitress stared into Brenda's perplexed face. 'What? Don't you know?'

Now Effie was trying to bustle them both out into the street. 'She's being ridiculous, Brenda. Let's go.' She ushered Brenda to the door, horribly aware that they were being stared at by ladies at the other tables.

The waitress wouldn't stop. She called after them: '*The Night Owls*, that's why! That's why she's a celebrity now. Isn't that right, Effie?'

Effie thrust open the café door. 'Come along, Brenda,' she said firmly.

Brenda was wedged in the doorway. 'But I . . . Effie, what's she on about?'

'She's quite clearly off her rocker. She's probably on some form of recreational drug. What's Whitby coming to?'

The young waitress could see by now that for whatever reason, she had embarrassed Effie. Strange. You'd have thought the old woman would be proud of her new-found fame. The girl shrugged and picked up her heavy tray. 'Oh well. Bye then, Effie. I'll listen out for you! You'll be on again, won't you? On *The Night Owls?*'

Effie tossed her head and slammed the door behind her. *Crash, tinkle*, went the bell.

You Don't Need to Know

They were out on the chilly cobbled street, clip-clopping down the hill towards the harbour. As they mingled with the mid-morning crowd, Effie was the more purposeful. Brenda felt that she was being rather furtive and cross.

'What was that all about?' she asked, willing her friend to slow down a little.

'She was quite clearly mixing me up with somebody else.'

'She seemed very sure of herself. And she knew your name.'

Effie gave a short sigh of impatience. 'Never mind, Brenda. It's nothing.'

Here they had to pause at the bridge as the crowds surged back and forth. The gulls were wheeling and screeching and the Esk was a startling sheet of blue. It was a brilliant morning. Brenda thought Effie looked pinched, worried and somewhat exhausted. She appeared even older than she usually did.

'You've gone and got yourself involved in something, haven't you?'

'Now stop it, Brenda.'

A gap opened in the shoppers and sightseers, and Effie darted into it. Brenda wouldn't be put off and dogged her heels across the bridge. 'What is it, some new investigation? You really love it, don't you?

You're never happy unless there's something spooky you can go shoving your beaky old nose into.'

'I like that!'

Brenda was glad to have irked her. Now they were plunging into the warren of shopping streets on the west side of the town. Effie was really hurrying along, forcing Brenda to call out at her back, louder than she would have liked: 'What are the Night Owls?'

'Hm?'

'The waitress mentioned the Night Owls. Twice. What are they?'

Effie was the picture of exasperation. She clutched her bag to her and the two ladies stood glaring at each other on the pavement. 'Oh, nothing, Brenda. Just leave it, will you? Now look, I've an appointment at Rini's for a shampoo and set. I'm saying goodbye to you here.'

Brenda felt as if she was being dismissed. She raised her eyebrows and said in a very level voice, 'See you later, then.'

Effie softened somewhat. She looked up into her friend's trusting face and quietly murmured, 'Look, I'm not being secretive. It's just . . . it's not a mystery. It's not something spooky. You just don't need to know what it is, Brenda.'

'I see.' She wasn't in the slightest bit mollified.

'Bye then,' Effie said, with a tight smile, and darted into a back alley that led to a quick way to Rini's Salon.

A Feeling in Her Water

That evening, Brenda was playing hostess in her attic rooms to another good friend. Robert was a young man who worked up at the Hotel Miramar. Brenda found him to be handsome, funny and good company. She rather liked it when Effie referred to him as 'your young man'. Tonight was one of their gentle, gossipy nights, with Brenda pouring out sherry with a sweet glug-glugging noise, the fire crackling and some soothing bluesy numbers playing on the old-fashioned stereo.

They were considering Effie's queer evasiveness that morning. Brenda felt rather gloomy about it. 'It's a cult, isn't it? That's what she's got herself into.'

Robert smiled. 'Oh, I don't think so. Can you see Effie joining a cult?'

'Yes, quite frankly. She comes from generations of Whitby witches. We don't know what she might be inclined to join.'

'If it was anything important, she would tell you about it herself, Brenda. She trusts you. You're her friend. She hasn't got many of those.'

Brenda went to turn over the record. She came back with the sherry bottle and topped them up. 'I know. You're right, Robert. You're always right. So level-headed.'

'I don't know about that.'

'I do. Effie and I would have come a cropper a couple of times in our investigations if it hadn't been for you.' A series of lurid memories flashed through her mind at this point. It was true, Robert had been very helpful and loyal to them.

'I just help out when I can. I can't let my best friend get into danger, can I?'

They grinned at each other and chinked sherry glasses. 'Don't you think it's strange – a young man like you having an old woman like me for a best friend?'

'Not really. How old are you again? Two hundred and six?'

'Hush. No, really. I *do* depend on you, lovey. And I feel like I'm going to do so even more in the coming weeks.'

'How's that? Don't tell me. You've got a feeling in your water. Something wicked this way comes.'

'That's right. I have.'

He could see now that she was being very serious. 'I've learned to trust your intuition about these things. I'll be there to help, Brenda. Whatever happens.'

'Cheers, sweetheart. Now. More sherry?' She filled them up again. As she sat back down, she realised she was feeling a bit swimmy.

Robert suddenly perked up. 'I meant to ask. Have you got any of these convention people staying at yours?'

'What convention?'

'Something Mrs Claus is holding at the Christmas Hotel. We're getting the spillover guests up at the Hotel Miramar. I wondered if you had any staying with you.'

Brenda dreaded to think what kind of affair it was that Mrs Claus was putting on. 'Any what?' she asked.

'The convention is for people who . . . dress up. As . . . things.'

'What kind of things?'

Robert pulled a face. 'I'm not sure what you'd call them.'

'Goodness. No, I don't think I've got any of those booked in. When is it?'

'This weekend. We're swarming with them up at the Miramar. I've seen some very funny sights, going about in their skin-tight Lycra and their masks.'

Brenda sighed. 'I still haven't got over the last Goth weekend.'

'I think this weekend is going to be even weirder than that.'

Brenda clicked her fingers. 'Maybe that's what Effie's up to.'

Robert settled back on the green bobbly armchair and said musingly: 'The Night Owls.'

'Hmm?'

'You said the waitress said something about The Night Owls.'

'She did. Familiar, is it?'

He frowned very deeply. Endearingly, Brenda thought. Then he said, 'It rings a bell. Somehow . . . The Night Owls . . .'

Everyone Listens

Robert was a love.

Brenda still felt like she and Effie had let him down somewhat over that terrible affair with his poor Aunt Jessie. There was nothing they could have done to stop her turning into a primitive apewoman-zombie-type thing last spring. And then, to compound matters, Brenda's gentleman friend of the time had shot Robert's aunt in the head and . . . Well, suffice to say it was an awful do all round.

She thought that Robert understood, though. He knew that Brenda and Effie were steeped up to their eyebrows in funny goings-on here in Whitby. Often quite satanic and insalubrious goings-on.

Brenda still had a strange wave of foreboding going right through her the following afternoon. She nipped down to the grocery store on the ground floor of her guest house. Owners: Leena and Raf. Both very obliging and friendly – and very, very nosy. Leena, of all people, would surely know what the Night Owls were.

The shop was swarming as usual with a thousand aromas: fenugreek, coriander, garam masala. Wooden boxes were stacked perilously in each of the aisles, and that very busy Bollywood music was playing over the speakers as Leena watched a movie on the closed-circuit TV.

Brenda leaned over the counter to ask her a few questions. Leena looked at her, amazed.

'You mean you've never heard of it?'

Brenda stammered, 'I thought it was maybe a weird secret society or something . . . Hang on! You mean, you *have* heard of them?'

'Of course!' Leena grinned with triumph. Any excuse to show off. 'I've even been on the programme!'

Now Brenda didn't know what she was talking about. 'Programme?'

But Leena was yelling into the back room, where her husband was busy with his pricing gun. 'Raf, listen to this! Brenda hasn't heard of *The Night Owls* . . .'

He gave a short laugh. 'Where's she been?'

Brenda cried out impatiently: 'Tell me what it is!'

Leena sighed and tutted, loving the moment. She carefully unfolded a copy of the local paper, *The Willing Spirit*, and opened it to the radio listings page.

'Here, look.'

'Whitby FM? I never listen to that . . .'

'Look carefully. From eleven p.m. till six a.m. every night of the week.'

Brenda peered down the page, following Leena's finger. My eyes are getting worse, she thought. And then she saw the title. Ah. There it was. *The Night Owls.*

Leena stared at her. 'Are you saying you're never tuned in?'

'Never even heard of it. Should I have?'

'But . . . everyone listens! Everyone!'

Now Raf came out of the back room, dusting his hands. He looked as amazed – and as tired, Brenda noted – as his wife as he said, 'We've been up all night, every night for the past three weeks.'

'You do both look a bit worn out,' Brenda said. 'I just thought you were working too hard.'

Leena smirked. 'And so does Effie. She looks tired all the time too, doesn't she?'

Raf flourished his pricing gun airily. 'So do loads of people in Whitby just lately. Haven't you noticed?'

Brenda gasped. 'Now that you mention it . . . yes, they do. I thought there was maybe a bug going round. Me, I tend to be impervious to stuff like that.'

'Everyone is staying up all night,' Leena said. 'Listening to their trannies in bed.'

Raf put in, 'She means wireless radios, rather than cross-dressing friends, of course.'

'Of course.' Leena rolled her eyes.

'But what is it? What is this show?' Brenda was still none the wiser.

'You must listen!' said Leena. 'You must tune in!'

Brenda started squinting at the tiny print of the radio listings again. 'It doesn't say much about it here, except . . . Oh.'

'Problem?'

A horrible queasy feeling was going through Brenda at that moment. 'The host,' she said thickly. 'Mr Danby.'

'So?' Leena expertly started folding *The Willing Spirit* back up.

Brenda found herself actually shuddering as she explained why her blood was suddenly running cold. 'It's a name I know of old. I hope it's not the same smarmy, wicked old man.'

Leena looked at her dreamily. 'Oh, he's wonderful. He's ever so good at putting his guests at their ease.'

'He would be,' said Brenda, narrowing her eyes.

'I think you should listen and judge for yourself.'

'I will,' Brenda said, stern with sudden resolve. 'And while I'm here, I'll have a box of spicy tea, please.'

Cod Almighty

At first it almost sounded innocuous. Just a radio talk show. Just everyone in town listening all night to some folk blethering on. But once Brenda knew the truth, after her visit to Leena and Raf's shop, she started looking more carefully at the denizens of her adopted town. That day as she went about her usual business she took careful note of the faces around her, and they were indeed etched with fatigue. They were worn and wan. Haggard with concentration.

What was being said on this late-night show? What was so fascinating and compelling as to keep everyone up all night?

The name Mr Danby didn't inspire much confidence in her. Not after their last run-in. That dapper, evil little charlatan with his shiny comb-over and his twinkly eyes, and that insinuating purr of his . . .

That night, when Brenda and Effie went for a fish supper, Brenda decided to tackle her friend on the subject of *The Night Owls*. They were at their favourite restaurant, the very modestly priced Cod Almighty, bang on the harbour front.

'I never mentioned it to you, Brenda, simply because I didn't think it seemed important, that's all.'

Brenda gave the menu a cursory glance. 'Hmmm . . . I think I'll have whitebait.'

'You always have whitebait. I don't know why you even bother reading the menu.'

'Followed by a crème de menthe knickerbocker glory. You're a bit tetchy this evening. Behind on your sleep?'

'As it happens, I am.'

Brenda shook her head. 'I never thought you would be taken in by a fad like this.'

'A fad?' Effie's eyebrows were as high up her forehead as they could get.

'That's what it is, isn't it?' Now Brenda was folding and pleating her napkin.

'It's a very interesting show,' Effie said. 'People talk about all kinds of things. There's no set agenda. The DJ gets them saying all sorts of fascinating nonsense. Secrets. Surprising things.'

'Does he now?'

'You will have to listen in.' Effie gazed levelly at Brenda.

Brenda burst out: 'But Effie . . . *Mr Danby*! Didn't that ring any alarm bells for you?'

Now Effie lowered her voice. She looked almost furtive for a moment. 'Well, maybe at first . . . but he's all right really. He's very good at what he does on that show.'

'What about when he opened that beauty parlour last autumn, eh? The Deadly Boutique. What about that? Promising to take decades off the age of all those foolish, gullible women who flocked there to have him experiment on them.'

'I know! I was one of those foolish women.'

Brenda wafted her napkin. 'Well, he was up to no good, wasn't he?'

'He's changed his ways,' Effie said. 'I'm sure of it.'

Brenda wasn't having it. The smell of everyone else's dinner was making her feel hungry, and when she was hungry she became less tactful. 'Look what he did to poor Jessie! He sucked all the life out of her. Turned her into something from the dawn of time. That's where all of poor Jessie's problems began, wasn't it?'

'Look, Brenda, what harm can he do simply hosting a phone-in show?'

'I can't believe I'm hearing this. He should be locked up!'

'Just because he ran a dodgy salon for a while . . .'

Brenda stared open-mouthed at her friend. 'Don't you remember the night he trapped me and you down there? When he locked me in his Deadly Machine and had a go at regressing *me* right back? And how we had to have an almighty punch-up, just to get away with our lives?'

Effie leaned in. 'Ssssh, Brenda. You're raising your voice. Do you want everyone to overhear about the scrapes we get ourselves into?'

'I don't care. I don't have anything to hide.'

'Oh, you don't, do you?' Effie ostentatiously rearranged her silverware and gave Brenda a significant look.

'Hmm. Well, obviously I *do* have quite a lot to hide. My true nature and so on. But you know what I mean.'

'I'm afraid I *don't* know what you mean, Brenda. I rather think you're overreacting to this whole business. It's only a phone-in. It's only a bit of fun! Now, shush up. Here comes the waitress to take our order.'

Brenda Tunes In

Brenda knew Effie was wrong. It wasn't just a bit of fun. She knew there was something more to this. But she didn't push the point just yet.

Later that night, tired and replete, their heads swimming with vinegary fumes and crème de menthe, they crossed back over the harbour bridge and wound their way through the streets to home, waving goodbye outside Effie's tatty junk shop.

Brenda let herself in to her own place and was quiet as could be, going up the side staircase, thinking that some of her current guests might already be abed. Mr Timperley, booked into room number three for a full week, was rather old and fragile-looking. He didn't want to hear his landlady galumphing about after a night on the town.

In her gorgeous, sumptuous attic rooms she soon made herself comfortable with a pot of spicy tea and a little fire going. She had a fiddle with her battered old radio, tuning it in to the local station.

There were some moments of whining and buzzing static, and then she got a voice that was indistinct at first, but still chilling in its familiarity.

It was twenty past eleven and his show had already begun. Brenda sat back in the bobbly green armchair to listen, cradling her mug of tea. She was tuned in to *The Night Owls* and ready to hear what it was that had put her friend Effie – and much of the rest of the town – under such a strange spell.

'Well, my friends,' Mr Danby was saying as the signal sharpened into absolute clarity, 'as ever, I have no idea what it is we will be talking about between now and the early hours. We have midnight and all the dark hours before dawn to get through first. Don't you just love that thought? That we will be here together all that time, and we can talk about anything we like. Anything at all that occurs to us. Let us hope there will be some surprises coming our way before morning breaks over the North Sea . . .'

He's so slimy, Brenda thought crossly. Really, if I didn't have to, if I didn't feel compelled to, I certainly wouldn't stay up like this, listening to him going on.

Now Mr Danby was getting ready to welcome his first caller of the evening.

'Gloria's waving to me from the control room. Line two . . . Here we are. Good evening . . . Sheila, is it?'

A tremulously soft, feminine voice joined Mr Danby on the programme. Brenda's eyes widened as she listened in. 'That's right, Mr Danby. I'm a first-timer on *The Night Owls* tonight. I've never phoned in before, but I've listened for weeks, every night. I think it's a fantastic show. I love your way of talking to people.'

'Oh,' said Mr Danby modestly. 'I just give them a little respect and listen to their woes and all their funny little stories, Sheila. It's surprising how grateful people can be. We are so used to being neglected and unheard, aren't we? Someone listening, just listening at the other end . . . well, that can be a wonderful thing, can't it?'

'It can indeed, Mr Danby,' Sheila warbled.

Sheila, what are you doing? Brenda thought. How can you take him seriously? He's so smarmy. Brenda felt that she could happily throttle him.

'And what is it you would like to talk about this evening, Sheila?'

'Oooh, I'm quite nervous, actually. I've never . . .'

'Just you take your time, my dear.'

Brenda reflected that it wasn't at all like the formidable Sheila Manchu, glamorous owner of the Hotel Miramar, to sound as nervous as this. What was the matter with her? Brenda was used to seeing Sheila wafting about in something clingy and being the centre of attention. Why was she going all daft with Danby?

'All right, it's like this,' said Sheila breathily. 'I own a hotel in a rather select part of Whitby. It caters for a younger and perhaps slightly racier crowd than do some of the old-people-type hotels out on the sea front. We have a nightclub in our basement and barbecues in the beer garden and all manner of exciting attractions . . .'

'Sounds like an advert, Sheila.'

'Oh, that's not what I meant, Mr Danby. I never phoned in to blow my own trumpet. What I'm really calling about is another hotel. The Christmas Hotel, right on the Royal Crescent, on the cliffs overlooking the harbour. That's one of these supposedly respectable places, crowded with old-age pensioners.'

'I know it very well, my dear,' simpered Mr Danby. 'When she was in better health, my poor old mother used to go there often for a Christmas knees-up.'

'Because it's Christmas every day at the Christmas Hotel. Yes, I know.' Sheila sighed huskily. 'And it's run by that terrible harridan Mrs Claus. Her with her ruddy cheeks and broken veins and getting pushed around in a bath chair by her staff of willing boys all dressed as elves. Well, what I've got to tell you all tonight is that she is pure evil. Do you know what she puts in the meat pies on pie and peas supper nights?' Sheila's voice had turned rather shrill by the end of this. Mr Danby felt he had to interrupt.

'Erm . . . you do realise that what you're saying might be defamatory, don't you, Sheila?'

'Of course I do,' she snapped.

'Oh, good. Carry on, then.'

'Dead human bodies,' Sheila said, with the utmost relish. 'That's what she puts in the pies. She has people murdered. Even some of her own elves who escape from her control. She butchers them and serves them in pies to her ancient guests.'

'That's very interesting,' said Mr Danby. 'And she's your biggest rival, would you say, as a hotelier?'

'That's not why I'm making this public. I'm saying it because she needs to be stopped. She has a stranglehold on the media here in Whitby. You may know she owns the local paper, *The Willing Spirit*. Plus the entertainment supplement *The Flesh is Weak*. She even seems to have the police force on her side and in her pocket. I thought your show would be a good way of letting the whole town know—'

'That she's evil? Well, you've certainly managed to alert the town to your views on the impressive Mrs Claus. But don't you fear for your safety, Sheila?'

'Why no. What can she do to me?'

Mr Danby gave a very dark little chuckle. 'I imagine she can do quite a lot.'

Brenda realised at this point that she was clutching both arms of her chair in shock. What was Sheila playing at? How could she

20

suddenly be so indiscreet? Brenda, of course, had no time for Mrs Claus at all, but she would never have dreamed of casting aspersions around the place like that. It seemed like a very unwise thing to do. Mrs Claus was indeed powerful in this small town.

Now Mr Danby was saying, 'Next up this evening we've got . . . well, well. On line one, it's Mrs Claus . . .'

A harsh voice boomed out of the wireless. 'Yes, and I'll have your listeners know that Sheila Manchu is talking out of her hat. That blowsy old drunk, what does she know? She can talk anyway. She was married to a criminal for all those years. A master criminal from London. So that hotel she's got, she got that through blood money, you see . . .'

'Oh dear,' sighed Mr Danby. 'You ladies are pretty riled up tonight.'

Mrs Claus went on in her stentorian tones: 'And Sheila needn't think she can do me down and take away my business. She's just jealous because I'm hostessing the Vintage Costumed Hero Ball this weekend.'

'Ah yes,' put in Mr Danby. 'I've heard about this. Do tell, Mrs Claus, is it true that this weekend will see the biggest gathering of retired costumed superheroes ever in the world?'

'Well, I don't know about that, Mr Danby. But I do know they are hard work to look after. I've got ninety-four pensioners running about my establishment, and all of them have some kind of superpower. All of them in costume. It's an unholy ruckus, it is. I wish I'd never accepted the booking. And another thing . . .'

And so it went on. Brenda was thinking furiously as Mrs Claus rambled on. She was followed by another Whitby local, and then another. Each had their axe to grind and most had peculiar things to say about fellow residents. With a curious candour and a worrying lack of discretion, Mr Danby's callers went murmuring and railing through the night. What could be making them talk like this? Saying things they would never dream of saying in the daytime or to people's actual faces?

And then a very unexpected voice piped up.

'Hello? Mr Danby?'

Brenda jolted upright in her armchair. *Robert!* What was he doing calling in? Oh, help, she thought! Everyone's at it now. She shifted closer to the wireless to hear what Robert was going to come out with.

'I'd just like to say that what Sheila Manchu was saying earlier this evening, before midnight, it's all true. Before I worked at Sheila's hotel, I was an elf at the Christmas Hotel. And Mrs Claus had us drugged, all us elves. We were her slaves because she used to pop noxious substances in our cocoa. I was lucky to get away from that hideously festive place when I did.'

'This is very interesting, Robert,' Danby broke in pompously. 'And do you also back up Sheila Manchu's wild claims of real human flesh in the meat pies?'

'Oh, yes, indeed. We went investigating there, me and my friends Brenda and Effie, at the end of last year, when my Aunt Jessie went missing. And we found dead bodies in the walk-in freezers. We found some pretty revolting stuff, actually.'

Brenda found herself yelling at her radio: 'Robert, what are you doing? You can't go saying that on air!'

Mr Danby snickered. 'Investigating with your friends Brenda and Effie, you say? Would that be Effie Jacobs, by any chance? The delectable Effryggia, who has become such a stalwart of this very same humble show?'

'That's her,' Robert said. 'Though she's more Brenda's friend than she is mine. Effie can be downright sniffy about people, and she looks down her pointy old nose at me, as it happens. But I don't care. She's a witch, you know.'

'Come, come, Robert,' laughed the host.

'No, I mean it. She's got a house stuffed with ancient grimoires and all that. All her family were witches, going way back.'

Brenda was on her feet, pacing up and down, asking her room at large: 'What's going on? Why is he saying all these things?'

Then she was brought up short by Robert saying: 'But my real friend, of course, is Brenda.'

'Yes,' purred Mr Danby. 'Effie herself has mentioned this mutual friend once or twice on my show. What is it about this Brenda, Robert, hmm? What's the low-down on her?'

'The low-down!' snorted Brenda crossly. 'I like that!'

There was a pause then, a moment of dead air. Robert wavered and made a kind of umming noise. It was as if he was coming to his senses, live over the airwaves.

'Come along, Robert,' urged Danby. 'All of Whitby is waiting. Go on. Tell us all what it is about Brenda that's so amazing. So fascinating. Tell us her secrets.'

Robert sounded strange. Half hypnotised. He was struggling to make sense. 'Brenda's . . . secrets? No, I can't. I . . .'

'Oh, you can. We're all friends here.'

'I won't. I . . . I must go now.' Then there came the decisive clunk of Robert's phone being put down. There was another hiss of dead air on Whitby FM.

'Oh dear, listeners. I do believe we have lost young Robert there. Just as he was about to tell us something I believe might have been rather juicy. There's nothing we like more, is there, than a good bit of juicy local gossip? Never mind. There's still time for the secrets to come tumbling out. Next caller . . .'

Good old Robert! thought Brenda jubilantly. Thank Hecate he had managed to come to his senses! She sat back heavily in her armchair. But what on earth had happened to him? Had Mr Danby managed to hypnotise him over the phone lines? Was that what was happening to everyone who rang in?

She sat there fuming, incandescent with rage. She just knew that, once more, Mr Danby was up to no good. He was poking a big stick into the murky-bottomed waters of Whitby's social whirl. And he was dredging up the muck. There'd be trouble, she could tell.

But what for? What was it all for? Why couldn't everyone be like her, and just relish the idea of an easy life, a quiet life? Why go raking up trouble?

At least, Brenda reflected, nothing further had been said about her. She gave a huge sigh of relief, then had to have a nightcap to steady her jangling nerves.

And she slept. Having uneasy dreams, there at the top of her guest house, in her sumptuous attic.

Quick as a flash, first thing in the morning, she was up and doing her exercises – star jumps and jogging on the spot. Probably she put the fear of God into poor old Mr Timperley, whose room was directly beneath the attic. But she had to be up and doing.

She had business to attend to.

Not Everyone is in League
with the Devil

Effie came blearily to answer her door. 'What is it, Brenda?'

Brenda was shocked to see her friend standing at her doorway in her nightie. She had never seen Effie looking so dishevelled. She'd obviously not slept a wink. 'I listened to that programme last night,' Brenda said, frowning.

'What, *The Night Owls?*' asked Effie, with a nonchalant yawn.

'Of course *The Night Owls*. And I was appalled! Look, can I come in, Effie? It's freezing out here.' It was true. Since first dawn the winds had been stiff across the bay. The morning was one of those dreadful soggy ones at the start of autumn, when there was no turning back. The leaves were a gingery mush in the gutters and Brenda's boot soles were claggy with crushed conkers.

Effie let her in with, Brenda couldn't help imagining, less than her usual enthusiasm. The junk shop was dim and felty with dust. It was hard to make out what was on display in that unwelcoming room of heaped and battered tat. As the door slammed behind her, Brenda made her way to the back and Effie's galley kitchen, where they usually sat to chat. She flinched at her own lumbering reflection in the glass witch balls and flyblown mirrors. Dozens of aged clocks ticked arrhythmically, as if determined to induce heart palpitations. Brenda had never found Effie's home a very comforting place.

Once they were sitting on stools in the back room, Brenda waded into the subject in hand: Mr Danby and his indiscreet programme. 'He's got everyone under his spell. Even Robert! Did you hear him last night? He was talking away like the rest of them.'

Effie filled her kettle crossly. 'So? That's what people *do* on *The Night Owls*. That's what it's for. Getting things off your chest.'

Brenda watched her narrowly as she clicked on the gas ring with unnecessary force. *Whoosh* went the blue flame. Brenda made her voice gentler. 'I thought it was horrible. Dangerous, too.'

Effie tossed her head, and her salt-and-pepper hair fell even more messily about her shoulders. Now she looked more witchy than Brenda had ever seen her. 'You *would* feel like that. Did you listen *all* through the night?'

Brenda passed her the tea caddy. The kitchen was so small it was like sitting aboard a tiny boat together. 'I dropped off around three, but I heard enough.'

'Oh . . .' Effie sighed, peering into a cake tin and producing a mould-spotted wodge of Battenberg. 'So you never heard me?'

Brenda blinked. 'When were you on?'

'Around half five. I believe Mr Danby feels bereft if I don't make my appearance on his show. So I don't like to disappoint him. He was very interested in you, as it happens, Brenda. He was asking all about our friendship, and our little adventures . . .'

Brenda waved away the offer of cake. She stared appalled at her friend. 'No! You never told him anything, did you?'

'What do you take me for?' Effie slammed the cake tin away as the room filled with kettle steam.

'I don't know,' Brenda muttered. 'You can be pretty easily led sometimes, Effie. Look at that business last spring up at the Hotel Miramar, when everyone was worshipping that bamboo voodoo god from another dimension. Goomba. You were completely sucked into that.'

Effie mashed the tea savagely with a silver spoon. 'I was possessed, along with everyone else. This is different.'

'I'm not so sure,' Brenda told her.

'I know what I'm doing. It's a bit of harmless fun. Just chit-chat.'

'But it's Mr Danby!' Brenda burst out. Effie handed her her tea. It was too strong. 'He's bound to be up to no good!'

Effie perched herself on her own kitchen stool. 'I think you misunderstand him, Brenda. When he started up The Deadly Boutique, it was with the aim of bringing joy into the lives of the women of Whitby.'

'And it all went to the bad. Never forget that, Effie.'

'You won't let me, will you? You always look on the darkest possible side of things, Brenda.'

Brenda balked at this. 'I do not!'

'Poking into shadows. Thinking the worst of people. Not everyone's got ulterior motives, you know. Not everyone is in league with the devil!'

Brenda glowered. 'I know that.'

'What is it, Brenda? Your own shrouded, miserable, Gothic past? Is that what makes you suspect the very worst about every-one?'

Brenda slammed down her cup and saucer on Effie's dirty work surface. She opened her mouth to speak, but thought better of it. Instead she hoisted herself up and turned, with great dignity, to sweep out of Effie's antiques emporium.

I Think She's Been Subsumed

Brenda stomped up their sloping street, fuming. Absolutely livid. Wondering why it was that she and Effie could never get embroiled in an adventure without having a massive stand-up row. It happened every time. Anyway, she thought, it was unfair of Effie to bring up the past like that. She was privy to very secret, very tender and distressing facts about Brenda's past. Hardly anyone else knew the truth.

Brenda was starting to dread the thought that Effie might get on the radio and broadcast the whole lot. She could imagine her closely guarded secrets being spread, like a seeping mantle of mist, across the Whitby rooftops in the middle of the night. Everyone listening, aghast, appalled, as Effie blew her cover. Disinterring the true tale of Brenda's nature. Her terrible supernature.

Brenda popped into Woolies for a big bag of pick 'n' mix. Just the thing to cheer her up. It never failed. She crunched minty bonbons and strawberry fizzers and hunks of cinder toffee as she yomped up the hill to the Hotel Miramar, where Robert was off duty for the morning.

When she got there, she gave him a very stern look. He gulped and said, 'I really don't know what came over me.'

'I was a bit surprised, to say the least,' she said.

'But I was compelled. I was in my room and I just had to phone in . . .'

'At least you jolted out of it, when he got too nosy. But what's he trying to do? What's to be gained from everyone spilling their secrets over the airwaves?' Brenda sighed and poured their tea from the aluminium pot. Ugh, aluminium. She always had proper china in her guest house, but she knew Sheila Manchu's standards at the Miramar weren't quite the same, though she'd never be rude enough to point that out.

They were sitting in the bay window of the bar at the Miramar, with a view of the rooftops above the harbour. Rain was coming down steadily now, and the sun was struggling to break through. Brenda sipped her tea and found it metallic and stewed.

Robert was looking gloomy as the shadows of the rain ran down his face in thick grey stripes. 'There are a lot of secrets in this town,' he said quietly. 'We've all got them, haven't we?'

'Of course,' Brenda hissed. 'And the way we manage to rub along from day to day is by keeping a tin lid on them. All hell could break loose, what with some of the people who live round these parts.'

'And you say Effie won't see sense?'

Brenda tried adding sugar to her thick orange tea. She nodded sadly. 'I think she's been subsumed.'

'She's not been the same since she went into that coma last spring.'

'Don't. I still feel guilty about that.'

He swiftly changed the subject. 'What do you want to do?'

I need to be decisive, Brenda thought. I need to spring into action. She said, 'I want to find Mr Danby. Beard him in his den.'

'You want to go to the Whitby FM studios? We could get to him there.'

Brenda squinched up her face in concentration. 'Shame we don't know where he lives. He's a slippery customer. Last time we met, he was doing everything he could to keep his mother alive. She was a tiny, wizened old thing. A miniature nun whom he carried around in a suitcase like an old vampire.'

'Jesus.'

Brenda glanced at her friend and for second thought how nice and smart he looked in his desk clerk's uniform. Much nicer, at any rate, than the elf outfit he'd been forced to sport when he'd worked at the Christmas Hotel. She nodded firmly and told him, 'Let's go tonight. You're not working, are you?'

'Nuh-uh. Luckily. But it's been a bit hectic here, with the spillover from the Vintage Costumed Hero Ball.'

For the past few minutes Brenda had been vaguely aware of people coming into the bar area and standing about chatting. She had been so absorbed in her conversation with Robert that she hadn't fully taken in their array of strangely colourful costumes. 'Of course,' she said, peering about at the early drinkers at the bar. 'That's what all these people in Lycra are here for. I wondered.'

Robert nodded, following her glance. 'Quite interesting lives, some of them. See her, over by herself at the bar? That's Mrs Midnight.'

There was a plump, frizzy-haired woman in a blue satin cape trying to get the barman's attention. She wore a kind of tiara effect in her white hair.

Robert continued to explain: 'In the sixties, Mrs Midnight single-handedly rescued the men on the first failed British Mars expedition. She's got superpowered lung capacity or something, I believe.'

Brenda had fallen into a reverie. The sixties seemed such a long

31

time ago. Such adventures! The Mars expedition, of course! And here was Mrs Midnight now, right in front of her. Brenda flattened herself back on the banquette. Would the old woman with the frizzy hair and the cape still remember her? Best not to chance it. To Robert she said lightly: 'Yes, I remember Mrs Midnight. Reading about her escapades in the papers and so on. Hasn't she let herself go? She shouldn't have tried to fit herself back into her old cossie.' Mrs Midnight was getting served now. Fortunately, she had moved across to the other side of the bar, to be with a gaggle of skinny old men in even odder outfits than hers.

Lucky escape, Brenda thought. But would she still blame me for that Martian fiasco? All these years later? Surely not. Some of the details were quite hazy in Brenda's mind, but she seemed to remember that she and the plump superheroine opposite hadn't exactly seen eye to eye back then.

'That's the point of them all getting together.' Robert smiled. 'Getting back into their old cossies. The convention this weekend is the only time and place these oldsters get to wear their superhero outfits.'

'Who's she with?' Brenda was craning her neck. 'Who's this who's come in after her?'

A tall, stooped figure clutching a Campari and soda had pursued Mrs Midnight to her secluded corner. He was extremely aged and sporting a skintight lime-green costume topped off by what appeared to be a yellow motorcycle helmet with ears.

'That's Harry the Cat, from Salford,' Robert said. 'He was big back in the fifties.'

'He's definitely shrunk.'

'Lime-green Lycra's not a good look even on the young and pretty.

What does he look like? Well, at least Mrs Midnight seems glad to see him.' She was hanging off Harry the Cat's neck and kissing the visor of his helmet. This he removed, revealing a lined and cross-looking face that made Brenda gasp.

'I'll tell you who he looks like!' she cried. 'My guest in room number three! That's Mr Timperley, in the thigh-high boots and the little cat ears! My goodness! Mr Timperley!'

'Shush, Brenda!'

She couldn't quite believe it. Mr Timperley, with his tweedy sports jacket and his careful tread on the stairs. He had seemed such a quiet soul! And all the time he was Harry the Cat, scourge of the Salford gangs!

Robert gave a knowledgeable grimace. 'That's how it is with secret identities, Brenda.'

'Well, I'm amazed,' she said, and set down her teacup. For a few moments they continued to stare at the multicoloured personages at the bar. There was something rather pathetic about them, Brenda decided. The British superheroes were never like the American ones, she reflected nostalgically. Rather than being gleaming and buffed up and patriotic like their stateside counterparts, the more homely heroes of the British Isles were a dishevelled and sometimes ineffectual breed. In Brenda's experience they were more of a hindrance than anything else when it came to adventures. She sighed, and hoped none of them would recognise her this afternoon. She turned back to Robert with a warm smile: 'Anyway, I'd best get back and have a tidy round and prepare myself for this evening's rigours.'

'You do that.' Robert watched her gather her things together.

Brenda gave a last glance round as the bar continued to fill up.

She was careful to stay out of sight of Mrs Midnight. 'A whole townful of ancient and ineffectual superheroes! Ha!' she grinned, buttoning her woollen coat. 'And I thought Goth weekend was weird. Ta-ra, lovey.'

All Togged Up

Early evening was coming down when Effie went over to Brenda's. She gave a worried-sounding knock on the door in the side passage.

'Brenda, I've come to apologise.'

Brenda looked her friend up and down. Effie was in her oldest, dowdiest coat and hat, and she looked suitably contrite. 'Oh, you have, have you?'

'The way I went on at you before, it was unforgivable.'

'Hmpf. Well,' sighed Brenda, peering out of the passage at the gloomy blue of the lowering skies. 'Isn't it a bit late for you to be out? Shouldn't you be listening to your tranny?'

Effie looked completely miserable at this. 'I don't care about that. You're right. I was addicted. I was saying things I shouldn't. Behaving appallingly.'

'Well. Never mind.'

Now Effie was looking closely at her friend, and realising that she too was in her outside clothes. 'How come you're all togged up? Where are you off to this late?'

Brenda smiled fondly. 'Aha. You can always tell, can't you, when there's some investigating going on?'

Up went Effie's eyebrows. 'What? You were going off alone? Without me?'

'Not quite alone. I'm meeting Robert. I didn't think you'd want to be involved in this affair. We're going to the studios of Whitby FM. I'm going to have a word with this precious talk-DJ of yours.' Brenda was fiddling with her keys, as if impatient for the off.

'You're going to see him!' Effie looked thrilled.

'Well, you needn't sound so alarmed. He's just a man. Just an ordinary person.'

'I'm coming with you,' said Effie firmly. 'You're not leaving me out of this.'

Brenda never said a word. She simply stepped out into the passage and locked her door behind her. The shadows were gathering, and by the time they stepped into the sloping street with their arms linked, the baleful blue darkness was almost complete.

The first thing they did was bump into Robert, down on the sea front, as Brenda had arranged. He was in his fleece-lined flying jacket and thrumming with anticipation at their adventure.

'Evening, Brenda, Effie.'

Effie surveyed him with her usual mistrust. 'Good evening, young man. I see you've managed to involve yourself in our business yet again.'

He gave a happy shrug. 'Whatever, Effie.'

Now Effie had turned her attention to the passers-by on the harbour. Various brightly coloured promenaders had drawn her incredulous gaze. 'Will someone please tell me who all these funny-looking people are? There are some atrocious sights wandering the town this evening.'

Brenda told her, 'They're retired superpowered heroes, Effie.'

'I don't believe it.' There was a whole gaggle of them outside Cod Almighty and the amusement arcades. Effie peered closer.

'They come from some kind of do at the Christmas Hotel,' Brenda added.

'There'll be more to it,' Effie said darkly, 'if Mrs Claus is behind it.'

Robert chimed in: 'Quite.'

Brenda was amused by the whole superhero thing. And she was still amazed by her elderly guest in the cat ears. She told Effie, 'It turns out that Mr Timperley, who's staying at mine for the week, he's one.'

'Heavens protect us. This town gets stranger by the day.'

Now it was time to get on with their own business. Brenda turned to Robert. 'Where are the studios, then? Robert, you said you knew.'

'Not far,' he said, tugging up his collar against the brisk sea wind. 'On the harbour front. The redeveloped bit. With the luxury apartments.'

'Up the swanky end of town, eh?'

'Where else?' said Effie. She experienced a little flutter inside at the very thought of visiting Mr Danby at Whitby FM Towers. It wasn't that she was starstruck at all. She wasn't sure what it was. But she was all agitation, just thinking about seeing him at work. At the very centre of his web of chat.

Succumbing

The studios were something of a let-down. The three adventurers had followed Robert's directions all the way through a bleak industrial estate, and now they were gazing at the side of a one-storey building with matt-black windows.

'Looks like a pretty ordinary office building to me,' Brenda said. 'Or a warehouse or something.'

'What do you expect it to look like?' asked Effie, who, truth be known, was the most disappointed of the three. She had expected something rather more glamorous.

'No one's about,' Brenda observed. She led the way to the dark doorway. The only doorway they could find. It seemed a very obscure entrance. She buzzed the entry box and called into the speaker: 'Hello? Can we come in?'

A very distant, tinny voice replied, 'Yes? Hello?'

'We'd like to come in, please. We've . . . um, got an appointment with Mr Danby.'

Robert shook his head. 'This'll never work.'

The security guard sounded irritated. 'He's on the air! You can't see him now!'

Effie sighed and clutched Brenda's arm. 'We've gone about this the wrong way.'

'But we must see him!' insisted Brenda. What did they have to lose by causing a scene? 'I demand to come in!'

'Go on, Brenda,' urged Robert. 'You tell him.'

'Will you open these doors? Or do I have to get my shoulder behind them?' She was quite prepared to. Brenda had knocked down a fair few doors in her time.

'Look,' squawked the man from security, 'who is this?'

'My name's Brenda, buster, and my dander's right up.'

'Here we go.' Effie smiled, at her back.

There was a pause, and then, to their amazement, the tinny voice told them, 'I'll buzz you in.'

Effie couldn't believe it. 'What? They're just letting us in?' When she had gone to Leeds to appear in the audience of *Nancy!* – that dreadful talk show – there had been all sorts of security measures. But here were the metal doors giving a sharp buzz and swinging open freely before them.

'Here goes,' Brenda said. 'Seems the direct approach pays off.'

Gallantly Robert stepped through the dim doorway first. 'Huh. Looks pretty dark inside. I can't see where—'

'Ouch!' yelled Effie. 'You watch who you're shoving, young man. Oww!'

'Keep still!' hissed Brenda. 'Don't move! I don't like this!'

'Neither do I. I think it's a—'

'Do you think it's a—'

Now that all three were standing in the dark interior, the door gave a huge clang as it slammed behind them.

Brenda howled, 'A trap! Yes, I do!'

'We're shut inside! Oh help! Oh no! I'm—'

'Keep calm, ladies. Let's not get in a flap yet. Let's—'

Robert stopped abruptly. The three seized each other as another noise – a terrible hissing noise – filled the dark room. It was getting louder, and more insistent.

'What's that?' Brenda cried.

'What?'

'Gas! It's gas!'

'Noooo! They can't! Let us out!'

'Ooh, Brenda,' said Effie, swooning nastily. 'I do feel a bit funny . . .'

'Effie!'

There was a petite, demure thud in the darkness as Effie dropped to the concrete floor.

Robert was coughing and choking. 'Brenda, I . . .'

Brenda raised her voice, railing against their unseen enemy. 'Where are you, Danby? You can't do this to us! You can't . . .'

But it was too much even for her. She heard Robert collapse close by her, and then she started to see luminous spots in front of her eyes, blotting out even the blackness. She felt herself slipping, and succumbing to the foul-smelling gas.

As the hissing grew louder about her, and she felt the rough concrete against her face, Brenda lay there clinging to her consciousness for just a few moments longer than her friends.

And she could have sworn she could hear the mocking laughter of that toad Danby issuing poisonously into the room.

The Punch-Up

Mr Danby was precisely as Brenda remembered him. He was a dapper man with an eerily broad skull and a conniving manner. He wore evening dress with a silk cravat and was giggling gently as the three intruders slowly came to.

Brenda heaved herself up to her knees and watched him rubbing his tiny pale hands.

'Oh dear. Dear oh dear,' he simpered. 'How I dislike having to resort to such tactics. Oh dear.'

'You!' Brenda growled at him.

'Yes, I am sorry, my dear Brenda, if you find yourself alarmed at being captured like this.'

Now that the room was a little brighter, Brenda could see that they were locked in a grimy and denuded storeroom. Mr Danby was standing with his back to the interior door. She heard a groan and realised that Effie and Robert were regaining consciousness. She stooped to help them. Poor Effie was delirious.

'Auntie Maud? Auntie?'

Brenda stroked her hand and helped her up. 'Ssssh, Effie. It's all right. Calm down.'

A fit of panic seized Effie as she remembered what had happened. 'Help! Brenda! Gas! It's—'

'It's all right, Effie. We're—'

Beside them, Robert was on his feet. 'Owww, oww. My head.'

Mr Danby sounded so calm, so soothing. Just as he did on his nightly show. 'The fog inside your heads will vanish in a few moments. I regret that I had to render you unconscious. It's just that you looked so fierce. I quite feared for my safety.'

Brenda rounded on him and found her fingers twitching. She was dying to smack him one. 'You've got some explaining to do.'

Mr Danby ignored her, fixing instead on the shaky Effie, who had risen to her feet by now and still looked confused. 'Effie Jacobs!' he cried. 'We meet in the flesh once more.'

Effie refused point blank to be charmed. She focused on him and gave one of her deadliest scowls. 'Mr Danby. I thought you had changed your ways. I thought you were such a smoothie on the radio. A reformed character. But Brenda was right about you.'

He shrugged helplessly, as if that had little to do with him. 'I dread to think of what she's been saying.'

Now Robert became all gallant, stepping forward protectively to demand: 'What are you going to do with us? You can't just go taking prisoners. We'll be missed.'

Mr Danby sighed and gave him a disparaging glance. 'More's the pity. And I can't just kill you either, much as I'd like to be rid of you. You ladies brought my glorious Deadly Boutique to an ignominious end last year.'

'Let us go, Mr Danby,' said Effie, in a very steady voice. She had been rattled by his mention of killing. She wasn't sure what this oleaginous fop was capable of, and she wanted out. 'We promise we won't tell anyone what you're up to with your talk show.'

Brenda put in, 'How could we? We don't even *know* what it is he's up to.'

'And that's the way it'll stay.' The little man glowered at them. 'You don't need to know.' A red lightbulb above the doorway gave a sudden fierce buzz. 'Now,' he said, 'if you'll excuse me, that's my signal to be back on the air. The adverts are finished. Will you be comfy enough in here?'

'Oh, yeah,' snapped Robert sarcastically. All three captives were staring at the door, which had opened behind Mr Danby, revealing the presence of a gaggle of figures as short as he was. They gathered about him protectively, like terrible bouncers, and escorted him from the storeroom. The door clanged, leaving four of these curious guards behind.

Effie backed away. 'Ugh. He's got his primitive cave-women people looking after him again. Awful man.'

It was quite true. The security women were tiny, naked women from the dawn of time. Mr Danby seemed to use them for all his dirty work. They were staring at the captives with their feral yellow eyes burning in the dark.

Brenda sighed. 'I could have done without another punch-up with the primitive apewomen,' she said. 'But . . .'

Actually Effie suspected that Brenda rather enjoyed having the excuse for a good punch-up. She had once told her she found it an enormous stress relief, especially if the people she was fighting really deserved it.

Soon the dim and squalid air of that empty storeroom was ringing out with the cries and slaps of an unholy tussle. Brenda started it. She went barrelling towards the four hirsute guards with both hefty fists flying. Effie and Robert had no choice but to back her up and join in. Any compunction Robert had about punching a lady (even one with fangs and unopposable thumbs) vanished as the primitive women fought back viciously with sharp teeth and savage claws. He concentrated on pushing the women away and trying to urge Brenda and Effie back to the main exit, which he had found hidden in the shadows of the far corner.

They soon realised what he was yelling about, as he kicked the door open with a great metallic screech. Brenda and Effie turned tail and ran while they were winning, leaving the scene of the dreadful fist-fight behind.

As they pelted through the bleak wasteland of the industrial estate – knowing full well that the slave women would not follow them too far – Brenda cried out to the others in a rueful bellow: 'That's yet another less-than-successful investigation.'

They reached the waterfront. Effie had to pause and ease away the stitch in her side. 'Why is it,' she gasped, 'that so many of our adventures involve us breaking in somewhere, having a fight, and running away again?'

'Don't know,' said Robert. 'And why does Mr Danby have apewoman security guards?'

'I think he's kinky,' said Effie decisively.

Brenda shuddered. 'We're well out of that one, I think. You don't know what might have happened while we were in his power.'

Bacon Sandwiches

Brenda wasn't happy till they were safely in her attic sitting room. They went thundering through the deserted streets, and shooting up her side passage. They made a ghastly noise running up the side stairs. But at last they were in Brenda's rooms at the top of the guest house.

She urged them to sit as she retreated to her open-plan kitchen, wielding her blackened frying pan with aplomb. 'Spicy tea and bacon sandwiches! Just the thing when you've had a nasty run-in!'

Robert collapsed on to the paisley two-seater. He realised he'd come out having had no supper. 'Brenda, you're a marvel.'

Effie eased herself on to the bobbly armchair. She still felt the lingering traces of that knock-out gas floating around her addled head. She pursed her lips thoughtfully and conceded to Brenda, 'Well, you've certainly proved you were right, ducky. Mr Danby is clearly up to his old nefarious and wicked tricks. I was too stupid to see. I was mesmerised by his charm, entranced by his chat.'

Brenda smiled kindly. 'Do you both want tomato sauce on your bacon sandwiches?'

Robert was leaning across to her cluttered mantel, tuning her wireless. There was a squawk of static, making Effie shield her delicate ears.

'Sorry,' he said. 'I'm trying to get *The Night Owls* on Whitby FM. See what he's saying . . .'

Brenda swished the spitting, quarrelsome bacon in the pan and mused: 'We must figure out what he's playing at. Do you think it could be he's trying to take over the minds of everyone in Whitby? Using some kind of subliminal messages . . .'

Effie harrumphed. 'No tomato sauce for me, Brenda. Wretched, gory-looking stuff.'

And then the smarmy tones of Mr Danby came to them through the crackling medium of Brenda's tranny. They all paused, ears cocked to listen.

'. . . earlier tonight, dear listeners, I'm sorry to report. Who would have thought a convivial little show like this one would make enemies? I'm sure I never thought such a thing was possible. But there you go. You try to bring a little light into people's lives . . .'

Brenda switched off the gas ring and brought their heaped plates into the sitting room. The smell of the bacon was driving the ravenous Robert mad. 'What's he saying?' she asked.

Robert seized his plate. 'I think he's talking about us!'

Effie jerked upright. 'What?' Then she looked at the mammoth doorstep Brenda had cut for her. How was she going to manage that, with her little mouth?

Mr Danby was still broadcasting to Whitby at large. He sounded so woeful and righteous, Brenda felt her fingers tingling once more with incipient violence.

'It sounds strange, I know,' Mr Danby sighed, 'but I really got the sense that these people hated me and everything my show stands for. And what do we stand for? Just people speaking their minds. Free speech! Well, I suppose there are always going to be people who want to spoil that. Weirdos and fanatics. I tell you, Night Owls, when they came breaking into these studios, making their violent protest tonight, I really – for a moment – felt in fear of my life.'

Effie just about choked on a piece of bacon rind. 'The devil!'

'I want you to watch out for these three people, Night Owls. Make sure you give them a wide berth. The two old ladies are not as benign and harmless as they may seem. One or two of my colleagues here are going for medical attention this evening, after their fracas with our vicious intruders . . .'

Brenda felt a hot shiver of dismay pass through her. 'He's trying to turn the whole town against us.'

'. . . one pale, skinny old woman. I thought she was a friend of this show. She runs a junk shop right next door to the B and B of the thickset woman I believe to be the ringleader. And a young man who lives and works at the Hotel Miramar. Whitby is a small town, and you will know who I am talking about. You will recognise your enemies when you see them next . . .'

'Crikey!' said Robert. 'Can he do this?'

Effie set her unfinished supper aside. 'I think he just has.'

'Switch it off,' urged Brenda. 'I can't listen to any more of him. Eat your supper, both of you.' She realised that both her friends were looking at her.

'What's going to happen, Brenda?' Effie asked.

Brenda sagged down on to a kitchen chair beside her breakfast bar. Could Danby really turn the whole town against them? Just by saying these things on his radio show? She shook her head dolefully. 'I don't know,' she said.

But she did know really. She had said it herself. Danby was

hypnotising all of Whitby with his late-night gassing. Could he really tell people what to think?

It was Brenda's own worst nightmare. Being demonised like this. In her own recently adopted town.

The three friends stared at each other for a moment, and then Brenda hastened to pour out their tea.

A Function to Attend

What happened next had all to do with the retired superhero ball being held at the Christmas Hotel that weekend. Brenda and Effie had heard a little about it, and they had observed a few masked and Lycra-clad pensioners gadding about town. Brenda even had one of the ex-superheroes staying incognito in her guest house: a Mr Timperley, who was once Harry the Cat, scourge of Salford.

'I wasn't sure you'd want to go,' Effie said, as they hastened along the frosty sea front. 'I know you're not fond of the Christmas Hotel.'

'I'm quite intrigued. Should be quite a spectacle, hordes of ancient heroes dancing about.'

Effie, too, was intrigued, not least by how she had come by their invitation. 'The tickets were in a blank envelope shoved through my door when I got back. Come to the dance. So I thought, why not?'

'Any excuse to throw our glad rags on, eh?' Brenda smiled. Effie still hadn't complimented her on her frock, which was new, from a rather select shop in town. It was a black velvety number and Effie hadn't said a word as yet.

But Effie was still focused on her precious mystery. 'Of course, it's an obvious trap.'

'Of course. Someone is inviting us here clandestinely . . . probably for a very nasty reason indeed.'

'Evidently.'

They both mused as they swerved into the back streets filled with dark and shrouded gift shops displaying starfish, sticks of rock, and Gothy bats in their windows. They began on the steep incline to the West Cliff and the Christmas Hotel.

'Still, it's all fun, isn't it?' Brenda smiled. 'Whew. Let me get my breath back.'

They paused and gazed across the picturesque jumble of slate-blue rooftops, shining in the drowsy evening. Effie stared further afield, shielding her eyes against the burnt orange of the sun. 'Look at the abbey over there. Glaring and glooming down at us.'

Brenda studied its fanged and jagged ruins. 'I know. I keep thinking about what it conceals . . .'

'Let's not think about that,' Effie said quietly.

'But it's the reason for all of it, isn't it? Why everything in this town is so weird and deadly.'

'And the reason you were drawn here in the first place.' Effie nodded and gripped her bag tighter. 'Yes, I know.'

Brenda sighed, taking in the whole vista of the bay. 'Still, I prefer it to what my life was before. Years and years of aimless wandering . . . never settling down . . . getting hounded from place to place like a monster.'

Effie briskly patted her friend's broad back. 'I'm glad you're happy here.'

'Come on, then. Don't let me wallow.' Brenda turned away from the splendid view and set her dancing shoes in the direction of the top of the West Cliff. They had a function to attend. She beamed at her friend. 'Let's go and see what's going on at the Christmas Hotel . . .'

The First Masked Hero Ball

Brenda gazed around at the interior of the grand entrance of the Christmas Hotel. It was even more ludicrously festive than ever. Every light fitting, banister, picture rail and item of furniture was bedecked, strewn and festooned with glittery trim. Holly, ivy and mistletoe nestled in every vantage point, and the most hopelessly tasteless Yuletide muzak was blasting out from the hidden but ubiquitous speakers.

Brenda had never had a nice night out at the Christmas Hotel. Something had always gone disastrously wrong, every time she came here. Tonight would obviously be the same, but for the moment, she was relishing her splendidly outrageous surroundings, and even tapping her foot to 'God Rest Ye Merry Gentlemen', which was being played to a reggae-type beat. The ancient cloakroom attendant took their outer things and they were ushered into the adjoining rooms, where the members of a huge crowd jostled and appeared to be knocking back a viscous scarlet punch.

Brenda smiled. 'Seems lively enough.'

The two of them paused in the doorway of the largest downstairs room at the Christmas Hotel – the Grand Ballroom. It was white and gold, rather like a very pale, delicious Belgian chocolate. Brenda and

Effie surveyed the rumbustious, colourfully attired crowd that was swaying and chattering within.

'Quite a bit of talent about,' Effie purred thoughtfully. She was eyeing the older gentlemen, most of whom were wearing clingy Lycra superhero outfits. Some of them filled them better than others. The whole room was a profusion of helmets, horns, breastplates, boots and swishing capes.

Brenda snagged them a couple of glasses of punch from the table and laughed. 'Effie! That's not like you.'

Effie swigged at the lethally strong drink and screwed up her eyes. 'Well, it's been yonks since a man's even been near.'

'Hmm,' said Brenda. 'Ever since . . .'

Effie looked momentarily cross. 'Since I had my terrible let-down. Yes, Brenda, no need to bring *him* up again.'

Brenda could have kicked herself. She didn't want to bring Effie down by mentioning heartbreak from the past. Certainly not when the two of them seemed on the brink of actually having some fun. 'We don't have much luck with fellas, do we?' The music was getting louder, and she had to just about bellow this down Effie's delicate ear.

Effie nodded. 'You're not wrong there.'

Brenda's attention was caught then by a gap opening up in the festive crowd. The masked and costumed guests were drawing back to let a cumbersome figure make its way across the carpet. Brenda felt herself bristle with trepidation when she saw who it was. She nudged Effie to warn her. 'Oh, watch out,' she said. 'Here she comes on her motorised scooter. Mrs Claus herself . . .'

Even the scooter was decked with holly, mistletoe, purple spangly tinsel and fairy lights. In the middle of it all, Mrs Claus was incandescent with pleasure: a gargantuan woman in red stretch Lycra and silver pompoms. Her candyfloss hair was teased up to a huge lilac cone and her ruddy face seemed more crazed and dissolute than ever before. She absolutely reeked of brandy, Brenda thought, as the old woman brought her noisy carriage to a standstill.

'Darlings!' Mrs Claus cried, eyeing the pair of them eagerly. 'What a wonderful surprise, seeing you here at my humble do.'

Effie replied in her usual mildly acerbic, dignified manner. 'It's a marvellous assemblage, I must say. I've never seen such a . . . colourful and surprising bunch.'

Mrs Claus swept one crimson talon through the air, taking in the whole roomful of guests. 'These are the unsung heroes of Britain, this lot. The secret heroes who saw us through the darkness of all those postwar years.'

Brenda put in, 'I recognise a few faces. That's Captain Lightning, isn't it? And Sparko, his boy companion?' She had noticed them earlier, under the potted palms, by the tall windows.

'Not so much of a boy any more,' added Effie.

'Yes, and the chap next to them,' Mrs Claus said, pointing in a very indiscreet manner, 'the one dressed as Marlene Dietrich. That's Marlene Dietrich Man. One of our more exotic costumed heroes.'

Effie couldn't keep the scepticism out of her voice. But she knew Mrs Claus of old. She knew the old bag didn't do anything unless it was going to be of real benefit to herself. She stared down at the resplendent proprietress. 'So you've got them all here out of the goodness of your heart, have you, Mrs Claus? Just to give the old dears a treat?'

'Of course,' said Mrs Claus, with a beatific leer. 'Why, Effie, you make it sound as if I'm always scheming and plotting.'

'Hmpf.'

Now Mrs Claus's tone became sly and suggestive. 'Mind, I'm surprised to see you two showing your faces in public this evening.'

Brenda gripped her punch glass tighter. 'What?'

Mrs Claus raised her lilac-dyed eyebrows. 'Public enemies, aren't you? According to that daft Mr Danby on the radio. It's a wonder he's not got the lynch mob after you. What were you doing, breaking into the studio?'

'We'd rather not talk about it,' Effie said stiffly, cradling her drink.

'But we're convinced that something is afoot,' Brenda added.

'Yes, well,' Mrs Claus said, and lowered her usual hectoring tones. Brenda and Effie had to crouch somewhat to listen. 'Did I tell you, I've even been phoning in myself. I can't stop myself! It's a compulsive need in the wee small hours. I pick up that receiver, and next thing I know, I'm chatting live on air, slagging people off! Saying the most awful things! Sheila Manchu and I had a dreadful go at each other the other night.'

'I heard,' Brenda told her.

'I'm the same as you!' Effie exclaimed. 'It feels like I'm mesmerised.'

'It's like when he ran that Deadly Boutique.' Mrs Claus shook her coiffed and frosted head. 'He exerts a strange kind of power over us females, that dapper little man.'

Brenda frowned. 'What can he be getting out of it? Stirring up all this bad feeling?'

'I don't know! But I'm sure you two will work it out.' Then Mrs Claus returned to her usual jocular manner. 'Now, if you'll excuse me, I'm calling out the bingo numbers in the main lounge . . . Oh, by the way, have you met Harry here? He was saying that he knew you, Brenda.'

Brenda turned to see who Mrs Claus was talking about, and as she did, the proprietress revved her motor and the scooter trundled past them.

Brenda drew in a breath. There before her was her guest from the room directly below her sitting room. Mr Timperley was standing there in all his heroic glory. 'Brenda?' he said, gazing in admiration at her black velvet gown.

'Oh, Mr Timperley. How are you?' She was quite startled, seeing his shiny Lycra and buffed-up helmet this close to. 'I hardly recognised you . . . in your costume.' She turned to her friend, praying that Effie wouldn't start her off laughing. 'Effie,' she said, 'this is Mr Timperley. One of my guests this week.'

Mr Timperley fetched off his cat-eared helmet and grinned at them. His silver hair was awry and Brenda was alarmed to note that he was wearing false fangs. He was saying, 'And I am so very glad to be staying in your establishment, Brenda, rather than here in this tacky dump.'

'Sssh!' gasped Brenda, even though Mrs Claus was well past hearing range now. One of her servile elves might be close. It didn't do to speak too openly at the Christmas Hotel, as Brenda well knew.

'Well, it's true,' said Mr Timperley scathingly. 'It's all very festive and glitzy on the surface, this place. But there's something rank and nasty beneath the skin of the Christmas Hotel.'

Brenda was transfixed by his outfit and his glinting cat fangs, but Effie was nodding in steady agreement with him. 'You're quite right, Mr Timperley. I've always said just the same. It's like finding a dead mouse in the Christmas pudding. I'm Effie Jacobs, by the way, Brenda's neighbour.' She thrust her hand at him and he shook it warmly.

'Charmed, Ms Jacobs. But while I'm in costume, you must both call me Harry the Cat.'

Brenda smiled. 'Scourge of the Salford gangland killers. Yes, I remember your reputation, back in the sixties. How amazing it is to meet you like this.'

Mr Timperley shrugged with fake modesty. 'I was quite a terror. Hopping across the back-to-back rooftops. I miss all of that.'

'I suppose everyone here misses their days of crime-fighting,' said Effie, glancing around the heaving ballroom.

'Time moves on,' the old man sighed, and rubbed a smear off his green visor.

'For most of us, yes,' said Effie. 'Not for Brenda here, though. She's been the same age for nigh on two hundred years.'

Brenda was alarmed by this. That lethal punch must have gone straight to Effie's head. She nudged her friend sharply. 'Oh, piffle. Stop it, Effie.'

Now the rather un-catlike old man was giving Brenda a good survey, making Brenda very uncomfortable. He said, 'She's a very handsome woman. You both are. I hope you'll both do me the honour of a dance later this evening, once the band gets going.'

'We like a nice bop,' Brenda said, deciding that there was no way she'd take to the floor with this little scrap of a man on her arm. They'd look a right pair!

Effie was pushing herself closer to Mr Timperley. Brenda couldn't tell if she was serious or not, but she was fluttering her lashes a little and saying to him, 'Tell me, Harry, what did your special superpowers consist of?' The old thing looked mightily flattered by her attentions, and, while they were making super-hero small talk, Brenda gently excused herself and wandered off into the crowd, on the pretext of looking for the lavvy.

She wanted to slip away because she was having a presentiment. Every now and then she got one, and they always led to trouble, she found. As she wove through the party-goers she was having the most curious feeling that things were about to take a sudden nasty turn.

It was because she was very psychic and sensitive, she was thinking. At least sometimes she was. Being built of body parts from many different sources, as she was, and having been brought to life by lightning and necromancy, as she indeed had been, she was quiveringly alert to nuances. To all sorts of funny things coming through the ether.

Brenda went to the lavvy and found it empty. Her new shoes echoed sharply on the sparkling tiles underfoot. The dripping ambience of the place filled her ears with foreboding. Something wasn't right. Something filled her with tingling horror as she advanced into the ancient loos.

One stall was occupied. The room was devoid of any human activity, but one wooden door was closed tight shut. Brenda called out, 'Hello? Hello?' And no answer came. Whoever was in there ignored her. She pressed her ear against the varnished teak of the door and couldn't even discern a single breath.

She braced herself. The door was heavy, but she could break it down, if need be. She was strong. She girded her loins. She prepared herself for what she'd see. She gave the door an experimental push.

It was occupied, but it wasn't locked.

The heavy door swung open with an embarrassed creak. Brenda jolted backwards at the sight within.

Mrs Midnight was slumped on the lav. She was in full aquamarine superheroine cossie, bursting at the seams, frizzy hair all over the place and her tiara dislodged. She was dead as a doornail.

Brenda let out a squawk of dismay.

She had been strangled oh-so-festively by festoons of – what else? – Christmas tinsel.

Conflab

As soon as they were allowed to leave the Christmas Hotel, the two ladies did so. The corpse in the ladies' lavs had put the kibosh on the evening's fun.

Brenda and Effie linked arms and clipped quickly home on the cobbles, down the West Cliff, through the mostly deserted streets of shops, towards home. They were gabbling like mad all the way about this vile new development.

'I know what you're going to say, Brenda. You've been bridling all the way down the hill and along the prom.'

'What am I going to say?'

'That it's every time. Every single time we go to the Christmas Hotel, something horrible happens.'

'That's quite true.' Brenda thought back over several past adventures. She shivered at the thought, as the mournful hooting of the gulls and the boats entering the harbour reached their ears.

'And,' Effie went on, 'every single time, the evidence gets brushed under the carpet. Mrs Claus has her servile elves come dashing in and clearing up the mess. The police are summoned and sent brusquely away again.'

Brenda's expression darkened. 'Mrs Claus likes to clear up her own messes.'

'Quite. So the most outrageous things can go on, but somehow Mrs Claus is never herself implicated.'

Brenda looked at her friend with interest. 'Do you think she's responsible for the strangling of Mrs Midnight?'

'I don't know. She's strong enough, even if she's not particularly mobile. But she was standing there talking to us for much of the time.'

'Hmmm. I wouldn't put it past her. She's a wicked old woman.' Brenda reflected sadly that she hadn't had a proper chance to show off her new dress. She hadn't had a full night's wear out of it. And she certainly hadn't had a turn on the dance floor. Even the excitement of a murder didn't make up for that.

'She certainly is wicked.' Effie exhaled a boozily sympathetic sigh. 'Poor Harry the Cat. Poor Mr Timperley.'

'He's distraught, isn't he? He would be. They've known each other since their heyday. They have survived so much. All of those costumed superheroes have. Crazed power-mad supervillains. Incursions from beyond the earth, under the earth and even other dimensions. They've seen it all.'

Effie tutted. 'For it all to end in a common, grubby little murder like this. Murdered by tinsel trimmings, of all things. Isn't it just bally awful?'

Now they were passing a street of pubs, rowdy with folk music. Not even this raucous noise could deter the ladies' deliberations. Brenda said, 'Would Mrs Claus really go to the trouble of organising a whole weekend like this? Just to assemble all of these guests . . . and then top one of them under everyone's noses?'

'She might do. If she hated Mrs Midnight enough.'

'We just don't know. Mrs Claus is so careless. So secure in her power base, here in Whitby. She wouldn't care about covering her tracks.'

'But she's got a hotel of crime-fighters and masked detectives to contend with,' Effie pointed out.

'Yes. Perhaps not the best context for committing willy-nilly homicide. Well.' She came to an abrupt halt and Effie realised they were outside Raf and Leena's grocery store and Brenda's guest house. 'This is me. Home again.'

'Off to listen to *The Night Owls*?' Effie teased.

Brenda glanced at her friend. 'I thought I might as well check it out . . .'

Phoning in

'. . . And I suspect that we will be hearing much more about this evil upheaval before the evening is out. Hello? Line two. You are . . .?'

'My name is . . . was . . . Harry the Cat.'

'Oh yes. And are you, in fact, a cat, or just a person pretending . . .?'

'Nothing like that. I was a crime-fighter, many years ago in north Manchester. I wore stretch Lycra, thigh-high boots and a helmet with pointy ears. It was all the gangland crime I dealt with, and I was, if I'm not modest, something of a legend round my own parts.'

'Were you indeed? I take it you're here in Whitby as part of the Vintage Costumed Hero Ball up at the Christmas Hotel?'

'I am that. And I can't tell you how much I was looking forward to this reunion. A chance to meet old friends and colleagues again . . .'

'That's what generally happens at these things.'

'And murder? Does that "generally happen", too?'

'Murder, Harry?'

'It'll be hushed up. But I had a lady friend. A wonderful lady who I've known for many, many years. And tonight – the night of our long-desired reunion – she has met the most atrocious end.'

'Oh dear. Is that right?'

'She was murdered in the midst of the celebratory proceedings.'

'There's been a few calls already this evening, reporting some kind of fracas at the Christmas Hotel. I'm glad to hear from someone in the know. Tell us, Harry . . .'

'The thing is, Mrs Midnight – or Sandra, as I always knew her – she could hold her own, easily.'

'Indeed.'

'She could fight her corner. She could stand up for herself. She was a real bruiser. Her superpowers . . . Do you know what her superpowers were?'

'Take your time, Harry the Cat. Don't upset yourself.'

'She didn't have any superpowers, did she?'

'Oh.'

'She had the costume. She had the look. She was a very brave woman. But she never had any special powers. She was never bitten by a radioactive insect. Or struck by cosmic rays from outer space. She couldn't fly. She couldn't even run that fast. Oh, she was quite useful in a punch-up. She could fetch you a hefty wallop.'

'But she was, on the whole, pretty defenceless?'

'If truth be told, not many of us old-time heroes have real powers. We liked to think we had. It was as if, by putting the old cossies on, we were conferring great powers on ourselves. We were gallant vigilantes in a Britain gone mad. With great powers come great outfits, or something like that. Anyway . . .'

'The Night Owls are very sorry for your loss, Harry.'

'Huh, well. The thing I'm here to tell you is, I know who did it.'

'What?'

'I know the murderess. And it's someone with real powers. Powers for true evil. Necromantic powers.'

'Necromancy? Here in Whitby?'

'Where else? And this person – this foul murderess – she is someone I know you yourself are concerned about. Someone who you think should be taken somewhere where she can't be a menace to the public any more . . .'

'Why, who is this person? Tell us!'

'I think you already know. She is a true monster. She—'

At this point in the broadcast there came an almighty thud at Mr Timperley's end of the line. It startled many people who were listening that night. Especially those in headphones, listening in the dark as they sat up in bed. The thud echoed through their heads and left a terrible pause in its wake.

'Harry? What is it? Why have you gone quiet?' The host's voice was urgent, dismayed. When Harry the cat replied, it was in a colourless whisper.

'Did you hear that? A sound outside my bedroom door . . .'

'Please, you must tell us, Harry. Tell us now the identity of the murderess.'

'Her name is . . .'

'Yes?'

A great scuffle broke out on the line then. A noise of someone scrambling quickly and guiltily to their feet. Harry the Cat was heard to yell: 'SHE'S HERE!'

Then there came the terrific bursting open of his bedroom door. Harry the Cat whimpered, and then his line went completely dead.

'Are you there? Harry, what's going on?'

His fans had never heard Mr Danby sound so disconcerted. He let a few unprofessional seconds of dead air slip by. Then he said, in a shocked-sounding voice: 'It's no good . . . he's gone.'

Accusations Fly

Brenda folded her arms and gazed at him levelly from the doorway of his room.

Mr Timperley backed away as far as he could get. The phone receiver dropped out of his hand. He switched off the radio, which was still tinnily calling his name. Absurdly Brenda noted that he was still dressed as Harry the Cat. Little good that would do him now.

'Get back!' he quavered, knocking into his bedside table. 'Avaunt! You have no right to come bursting into my room!'

She advanced further across the rucked carpet. Her tone was thunderous and her wig was off. In her dressing gown and no make-up, Brenda made a formidable sight. 'Why, Mr Timperley?' she demanded. 'Why would you do that to me? What have I ever done to you?'

'Oh, Brenda. I . . .' He was shaking as she approached, clearly expecting her to do away with him in a flash.

Brenda stopped. She tried to sound rational. She tried the voice of reason. 'You know very well, don't you, that I didn't murder your lady friend.'

Mr Timperley looked suddenly sneaky and coy. 'All I know is, I've seen some very funny things since I've been here in this town.'

Brenda snorted. 'Yes, but that's normal round here.'

The old man let out a tortured sob. He cried, 'I wish I'd never come. I've not been away from home for over twenty years. I'm not used to all this. It's too much . . .'

Brenda's heart twinged. She cursed herself for being too soft, but her first instinct was to help him, as all the force and willpower in his body seemed to sag. She stepped forward to support his weary frame. 'You've had a shock. Here, sit down.'

'Don't come near me,' he snapped. 'Don't hurt me.'

Brenda was stung. 'Don't be ridiculous! Who put these stupid ideas in your head? I wouldn't hurt anyone!'

'That's not what I hear. That's not what I've heard tell about you . . .' He sat on the bed, and the look in his eyes was so awful and fearful that Brenda had to turn away.

'People say terrible things. People gossip. But none of it's true. I wouldn't hurt anyone . . . on purpose.'

Now Mr Timperley nodded at the radio that he'd fumbled to switch off when Brenda entered. 'That Mr Danby. On the radio. He's got his head screwed on right. He knows what's what. And he reckons you're wicked. You're . . . unnatural.'

Brenda tossed her head. 'I could tell you a thing or two about your precious Mr Danby. He's no angel. Don't go listening to him.' But even as she said this, she felt horribly self-conscious in her night things. She felt herself to be unnatural and monstrous and ugly. This old man was staring at her as if she was the worst sight he had ever beheld. Brenda gripped her dressing gown lapels together, preparing to beat a hasty retreat.

'You killed her,' Mr Timperley accused her hollowly. 'You strangled her with your bare hands . . .'

'I did not.'

'And then you walked out of that place scot-free. What the devil's going on in this town? The whole place is crazy.'

She backed away. 'I think I'd better make some hot, sweet tea . . .'

'I've got to get out of here,' the old man gabbled. 'I'm at your mercy. You could do anything you liked to me.'

Brenda could see the situation was getting out of hand. Mr Timperley was hysterical. 'Oh dear,' she said, as he started working himself up into a panic again.

'I've heard you. All the commotion in the middle of the night. Sneaking up and down the stairs. God knows what you're up to half the time. Nothing good. Black magic, I call it!'

Brenda was about to remonstrate once more when they were both interrupted by the clatter and bang of the downstairs outer door. Someone had let themselves into Brenda's guest house rather urgently. Their footsteps were coming rapidly up the side stairs. Then Effie was shouting as she came tottering on to the second landing.

'Yoo-hoo, Brenda, I've let myself in! I've still got that key you gave me . . . Where are you, Brenda dear? Were you listening to the radio show? That horrid little man was— Oh!'

Brenda leaned out into the hallway, and beckoned Effie into Mr Timperley's room. 'I'm in here.'

'So I see!' wheezed Effie, winded by her dashing round.

Mr Timperley was on his feet, thrusting a twiggy finger at the new arrival. 'You! The other one. Your witchy old friend. I've heard about you too, madam. You're from a long line of nasty old hags, aren't you?'

'I beg your pardon?' Both of Effie's eyebrows shot up.

'You heard me. I've heard all about you. The pair of you. And the terrible things you get up to.'

Effie turned to Brenda. 'What's the matter with him? He was so nice up at the Christmas Hotel. Why has he turned like this?'

Brenda flapped her hands. 'Oh, that's because—'

'You murdered her, that's why. My lady friend, Mrs Midnight . . .'

Effie rolled her eyes. Brenda had never felt quite so grateful before for her abrupt good sense. 'Poppycock. You silly old fool. Standing there in your skin-tight leopard-spotted Lycra, making rash accusations. I could clobber you, I could. And phoning *The Night Owls*, too! Stirring up all the bad feeling against Brenda . . .'

The old man wouldn't listen. 'I know what you're up to in this town, you two. I know you're here for a reason. It's to do with the gateway into hell, isn't it?'

Effie was alarmed by this. 'Don't listen to him, Brenda. He doesn't know what he's talking about.'

Brenda lowered her voice. 'What do you know about the gateway?' She took a step forward. Her fingers twitched.

Mr Timperley found himself cornered. He stammered as he replied: 'Just . . . that it's the reason there are so many strange folk here in Whitby. Mrs Claus told me. There's an open, gaping wound somewhere in Whitby, and all sorts of THINGS come creeping out of the underworld, and you two are somehow mixed up in it all . . . Stay back!'

Brenda looked thoughtful. Her expression twisted in the stark bedroom lighting. 'That's true. You're quite right. We are very much mixed up in it.'

'Brenda,' Effie broke in. 'You don't have to tell him anything. This withered old fool . . . Let me at him.'

'No, Effie. He's traumatised. He needs to understand. We aren't the enemy here.'

Mr Timperley looked highly sceptical. 'Aren't you?'

'No,' said Brenda heavily. 'And you should most definitely trust us more than you trust the likes of Mrs Claus. Or Mr Danby. Can't you see? They are filling your head with poison. Manipulating you . . .'

'They are my friends.'

'They are nobody's friends,' Brenda told him. 'They are trying to turn people against me. They are trying to turn the whole town against me. They are using you.'

Effie said, 'Do you think that's what they're doing, Brenda? Is that what they're up to?'

'I do now.' Brenda nodded grimly. 'I think they won't be happy until they have me hounded out of town.'

Effie folded her skinny arms. 'We'll make sure they don't succeed.'

Brenda said, rather miserably, 'It's happened before. I've been hounded out of so many places. I never get to stay for long. I thought Whitby was different. I thought I was settled here. That I had a place . . .'

Effie cried, 'But you do have a place! You belong here! With all of us.' She felt they shouldn't be going into all of this with the treacherous Timperley before them in his catsuit, but Brenda was about to surf a wave of depression, and Effie knew she had to hoick her back.

'That's kind of you, Effie, but—'

Mr Timperley had been biding his time. Foolish women, he laughed. Easily distracted. Happier talking about their feelings. Now they're not watching me.

And he darted for the door.

'Hoy!' Effie howled, as he went by in a yellow streak of shiny Lycra. 'He's making a run for it!'

'Get after him!' Brenda bellowed.

They went hurtling down the side stairs after him. But Harry the Cat was nimble and spry, even at this age. He was used to leaping over back fences and on to terraced roofs.

'He's out the door!'

They lost precious seconds as Brenda fumbled with a rain hat she grabbed from the coat rack. No way she was running about the streets with a bald and gleaming head.

'Come on!' Effie shrieked, grabbing at her hand and pulling her out into the alleyway.

They could hear his slapping footfalls on the high street. The town was eerily quiet, and they could chase his echoes down the gentle slope of the hill to the sea front.

'Look! There he is!' Effie called, as they rounded a corner and saw his thin shape darting past Everything's a Quid.

Brenda had to pause for breath, clutching her knees. 'Reporting back to the Christmas Hotel, no doubt . . .'

'I can't believe how fast he is!' Effie gasped. She urged Brenda back into action and the two of them jogged past the rough pub on the corner and the tourist info, and then they had a clear view of the prom.

'Hang on!' Brenda hissed. 'Who's that?'

Effie squinted. Mr Timperley seemed to have been stopped in his tracks outside Woolworths. Another figure was standing there. 'Someone's got him . . .'

A kerfuffle had broken out between the two figures as Brenda and Effie hastened towards them. There came a few winded cries and then the newcomer dragged the old man down to the pavement. All at once Brenda saw who it was.

'Robert! You've got him! Well done!'

Effie couldn't help herself. 'Put the boot in!'

'No, don't hurt him,' said Brenda, as they all stood there panting, looking down at their terrified quarry.

Robert looked as grimly determined as Brenda had ever seen him. He whipped off his scarf and bound Harry the Cat's wrists behind his back. 'I've got him.'

'Let me go!' The old man wriggled and snarled. 'You'll regret this!'

'Hold his legs, Effie,' Brenda urged.

Effie was still seething with anger. 'Shall I give him a slap?'

'Get away from me, accursed witch woman.'

Robert gave a short laugh. 'Well, here we all are again. Fighting in the street in the middle of the night.'

Brenda asked him, amazed: 'Robert, how did you know we'd need help?'

'When I heard this fella on the radio, I thought – something's up. Someone's out to get Brenda.'

'They murdered my girlfriend!' Mr Timperley howled. 'They killed Mrs Midnight!'

'They wouldn't hurt anyone. Shut up, you.' Robert looked up in concern at Brenda and Effie. 'We'd better get him inside somewhere, ladies. He's making too much noise. We look a bit conspicuous, right outside Woolies, pinning someone down like this.'

'Good point.' Brenda gave him a brisk nod and prepared to hoist up their prisoner. She couldn't wait to get back indoors. Here she was, parading about in her night things and a see-through rain hat. Thank goodness all the excitement seemed to be over for now.

What the Prisoner Said

'Mind out,' Effie snapped. 'That's an antique, that is. That chair you're tying him to is worth a fortune.'

Robert doubted if the rickety old thing was worth much at all, but he tried to be a bit more delicate as he and Brenda finished lashing the old man tightly in place.

Brenda studied their prisoner doubtfully. 'He won't cause a fuss now, will you, Mr Timperley?'

Robert was gazing about at the junk shop. He was quite taken by the multiple chandeliers, swagged in cobwebs; the shelves of leering Toby jugs; the crazed glass of the flyblown mirrors and dusty lamps. 'Nice place you've got here, Effie. I've never been in here before.'

Effie wasn't easily flattered. She sniffed and nodded at the now silent Harry the Cat. 'What now? Do we interrogate him?'

Brenda shook her head. 'I think a calm chat is in order. Get the kettle on, Effie.'

Mr Timperley spat at them: 'Why should I chat with you?'

Brenda came to stand right in front of him. She took a deep breath. 'For the last time – I'll say it pleasantly – I did not murder your friend. Of course I didn't. But I believe I was meant to find the body. I believe that I am supposed to look like a suspect.' Her tone sounded so measured and polite. How could anyone not believe in her? Robert wondered.

But still Mr Timperley was gibbering and agitating. It was as if his mind had snapped. 'You're the only suspect. You're a monster. I've heard all about you.'

Robert broke in: 'Don't talk to her like that!'

Effie was coming back from the galley kitchen. 'I'll smack him, shall I?'

'Leave him be,' Brenda sighed, and sat down carefully on a musty plush armchair facing the old man. 'Who did you hear this from, Mr Timperley? Why do you say that?'

He stared at her levelly. 'The person who asked me to come here. The person who said I needed to book myself in to your guest house. That's who. Though I wish I had never bothered. I'm too old for this. I wish I had stayed at home.'

Effie asked, 'Who told you to do these things?'

'I was to keep an eye on the beast-woman. The monster-woman.'

Brenda held her breath for a moment. When she spoke again, she couldn't keep the hurt out of her voice. 'Is that what I am?'

Timperley nodded coldly. 'So I was told.'

Brenda felt herself welling up. It was the worst time ever to start up the waterworks, but she couldn't help it. She said, 'I have been kind to you, Mr Timperley. I gave you my best room. It was immaculate. I welcomed you. I cooked you breakfast. I even went across town at dawn to buy the kippers you wanted . . .'

Behind her, Effie made an impatient noise. 'You're too soft, Brenda. Look here, Timperley. Who's been saying these things about Brenda?'

Mr Timperley was talking in a much calmer voice now. A steady, accusing voice. A voice thickened by horror at what he was attempting to describe. 'She's not a natural woman, is she? She has no surname. Have you asked her? No birth certificate. No national insurance number. No family. Certainly no children. You don't really exist, do you, Brenda?'

'Leave her be,' Effie snapped.

'No,' said Brenda. 'Let him talk.'

'We're her friends,' Robert told him. 'We're all the family she needs. We know all about Brenda. Nothing you say can shock us.'

The old man went on. His eyes were mint-green with malevolence. Brenda could see now that he was quite mad, and that he was terrified of her. To him she was an abomination, that was clear. 'She has no soul. She has no real place on this earth. She was brought to life by the vilest practices. Body-snatching. Necromancy. Raising the dead.'

Effie shouted back at him: 'Who are you to judge? You go walking the streets dressed up as a cat!'

Mr Timperley ranted and raved: 'She isn't safe. She comes from evil. Every fibre of her being is infused with evil.'

Brenda shook her head. She was gazing down now. She wouldn't look him – or any of them – in the face. 'No . . . that's not true.'

'She can't help it. She draws evil and vileness towards herself. She is at the centre of a great whirlpool of malignity. She needs to be stopped. She needs removing from this place.'

Effie was bristling with fury. 'So Mr Danby . . . or Mrs Claus . . . or whoever it is pulling your strings . . . they've got you believing all this stuff.'

Robert said, 'You're trying to oust Brenda from her home. You've got it wrong. She's done more good since she's been living here than anyone has. She's saved people's lives. She's been fighting the forces of darkness, with no thought for her own safety, without ever asking for a reward . . .'

Timperley sneered at this. 'All that may be true. She might be a very nice person for all I know. But she is still, in the pit of her black and cankerous stolen heart, a thing of supernature. An evil creation.'

Brenda thrust her face into her hands. 'Noooooo,' she moaned. She lurched upwards, out of her chair, blindly reeling and clattering into the aisle.

'Brenda . . .' cautioned Effie. 'Don't upset yourself. Mind that lamp, it's priceless.'

'It's not true!' Brenda moaned. 'Stop saying these things!'

Robert went to her. He touched her arm. 'He's just trying to upset you . . .'

'Pay him no heed. The old devil,' Effie added.

Brenda sobbed. 'The things he's saying . . . they are things I think about . . . sometimes. I can't help it. I really do come from evil. I was cradled and coddled in filth and wickedness. I was made to be a bride to a monster, and there is no escaping destiny . . .'

'You've got a lot to answer for, Timperley,' Effie snarled. 'Upsetting my friend like this.'

Timperley said mildly, 'I'm merely passing on a message.'

'From those who brought you here,' said Robert. 'Brenda's enemies.'

The old man shook his head. 'You persist in thinking I was brought here by Mrs Claus and Mr Danby.'

Effie said, 'They are the ones conspiring against her.'

'Perhaps. But it wasn't they who sent me.'

Brenda's tear-stained face jerked up. She stared at him blearily. 'Who sent you? Who sent you to say these horrible things?'

'I will tell you . . . if you promise not to hurt me. Don't kill me.'

Effie threw up her hands. His cravenness disgusted her. 'Of course we won't!'

'You can't promise that,' Timperley stammered. 'I don't know how she will react when she hears who is after her.'

'After me?'

Now the cat-man was enjoying himself. He purred and preened as he made his revelation. 'You haven't seen him in ages. Many, many decades. He has been looking for you for a long time.'

Brenda took another involuntary step backwards. A precious lamp crashed to the floor, unnoticed by her. 'Oh no,' she said softly.

'You know, don't you? You can sense that he has found you. You are somehow aware that he is on his way.'

Robert reached out for her again. 'Brenda, who . . .? Who's he on about?'

Effie stared at her. 'Brenda, you've gone white . . .'

'It can't be,' Brenda mumbled. 'It can't be him . . .'

'It is,' Mr Timperley cried happily. 'He contacted me directly some months ago. He's been in the Greater Manchester area for some years. Living rough. I helped him get back on his feet. I had no idea who he was at first. I nearly died when he told me. I could hardly believe it . . .'

Brenda was halfway down the aisle now, as if some dreadful force compelled her out of earshot of the old man's tale. She said, 'He should be dead. He should be deader than dead. How much can he survive?'

Mr Timperley wouldn't stop. 'He's in rude health. He is extremely well. He is like a young man again. Vigorous, powerful. And hell-bent on seeing you again. He wants you back, Brenda.'

Effie interposed herself protectively. 'Well, he can't have her! Who is this person ... this person you say's been living rough? Brenda wants nowt to do with him!'

Just then something clicked in Robert's head. He gave a quick gasp. 'You don't mean ... He doesn't mean ...' He looked at his friend. 'Brenda?'

She nodded. 'He does. Oh God.'

'He's come back, Brenda,' said the former scourge of Salford. 'And he wants you.'

Effie was confused, looking from one to the other. 'Who's he on about?'

Brenda intoned flatly: 'My fiancé.'

'What?'

Brenda said, 'We were made for each other. Literally. The wedding never quite came off.'

'You deserve each other,' Mr Timperley said.

Robert tried to interrupt. 'Brenda, if it's someone you don't want to see again, then you don't have to ...'

'I do. I have to see him. I have to. It's destiny.'

'I still don't understand!' Effie complained.

Mr Timperley told them: 'He's here in town right now. He's found his way back to Brenda.'

Brenda stiffened. Her face was a pale mask of horror. 'What did you say?

'Face it, Brenda.' Her prisoner smirked up at her. 'Your Frank is back.'

Stitched Up

Brenda's first port of call the following morning was the police station, where she had to undergo a reasonably vigorous questioning on the subject of the dead woman in the toilets at the Christmas Hotel. She was the one, after all, who had found Mrs Midnight slumped there. Did that really make her a suspect, though?

The police didn't think so, she could tell. She had helped them enough in the past couple of years with various sticky investigations. They knew she was virtuous and reliable.

'But why did they drag you in, then?' asked Effie, an hour or so later, as they chewed things over with cinnamon toast and frothy mochas in The Walrus and the Carpenter.

'In a case like this,' said Brenda solemnly, 'they have to follow every lead.' She was feeling slightly grumpy this morning. She'd spent a sleepless night listening to the dreary rain on her attic roof, and fretting about everything.

'It's Mrs Claus they should be talking to,' Effie said. 'I wouldn't put it past her to commit murder in her own hotel, just for the sheer hell of it. She gets away with all sorts.'

'It's true,' Brenda sighed. 'That Yuletide hag has the police force of Whitby in her handbag. She can do what she wants with impunity.'

'They aren't pressing any charges against you?' Effie looked at her friend with concern. She could see how mithered Brenda was feeling.

'They've nothing on me. I'm all right. At least, as far as the murder thing goes.' Brenda shoved her unfinished toast away from her. 'As for the rest of it . . .'

'Hmmm. There's been rather a lot going on lately, hasn't there?'

'You're not kidding, lovey.'

Brenda felt like she was being demonised on two fronts, and that was a lot, even for the likes of her. First of all there was Mr Danby, the slimy late-night talk-show host who was still having a go at her across the airwaves. Last night she had tuned in, even though she knew she would never hear anything good about herself.

'This wicked and unnatural woman is dwelling in our midst,' Mr Danby had been ranting. 'She has already tried violence on me twice . . . We, the innocent denizens of Whitby, are not safe in our beds at night whilst we harbour this woman . . .'

The Night Owls was turning, night by night, into an even more seething cauldron of discontented gossip. And now there was this murder thing going on. Brenda had the distinct feeling that she was being stitched up.

Effie was saying, 'There are people here who want to run you out of town, Brenda.'

'Well,' Brenda said resolutely, dabbing the chocolate mocha froth from her lips. 'I won't let them. I've been run out of too many places in the past. I'm settled here now.'

'That's the spirit!'

'Yes, once upon a time I'd have skulked away in the dead of night. If I had thought for one second that my dearly held secrets were out . . .'

'Well, now you've got friends. You don't have to run and hide.'

Another great wave of gloom threatened to overtake Brenda. 'I'm not so sure about that.'

Effie raised her eyebrows. 'Oh,' she said, clocking on. 'You mean the other matter.'

Brenda hissed across the gingham table, 'What if Mr Timperley isn't lying?'

'He's talking rubbish, Brenda. He was trying to put the willies up you.' Effie didn't feel half as sure as her words sounded.

'Do you think so?'

'I know what I'm talking about when it comes to people putting the willies up you.'

Brenda shuddered. She thought about Mr Timperley's final words to her the previous evening. They had all stood there shocked as he spat at them and cursed.

'You monstrous woman,' he had screeched. 'You evil behemoth.'

'Behemoth indeed! Well, you're paying for the full three nights of your stay, Mr Timperley,' Brenda had warned, trying to normalise matters.

'I'll pay anything. I'll be happy to get away alive. Mrs Claus has told me all about you.'

'Oh, her. Well, she's no better than she ought to be. Go on, scram. Coming here with your accusations. And your lies.'

'Lies?' said the old man softly. 'I haven't been lying. Every word was true.'

Brenda caught her breath. 'About my . . .'

'Your fiancé? Oh yes. It's all quite true. He's working his way back to you, Brenda, with a burning love inside. And he's been after you for years.'

His words rang through Brenda's aching and addled head as she sat there in The Walrus and the Carpenter, with Effie. This was a turn of events she had never wanted to deal with.

'Perhaps . . .' began Effie hopefully. 'Perhaps he won't find you. Perhaps it'll all blow over.'

'No. He's on his way.' Somehow Brenda knew the truth of it. She could feel it in every fibre of her being. The proximity of a kindred spirit.

'I warn you!' the crazy Mr Timperley had shouted as he left her guest house last night. 'You'll get yours, Brenda! You've got it coming!'

'I think it's true. What Mr Timperley was saying.' Brenda shivered. 'About meeting my . . . Frank in Manchester. Finding him living rough. Finding him . . . and rehabilitating him. Bringing him back to life. It all rings true. He's coming here, Effie.'

'Snap out of it, Brenda. There's no point getting all aeriated.'

'You don't know what he's like. You have no idea.'

Effie had never seen Brenda as rattled as this before. She was raising her voice, too loud for privacy in this tiny café. Other faces were turning to see, to listen in. Effie leaned in close and whispered to her friend, 'Look, we can deal with anything, can't we? Just think about some of the terrors we have faced together, eh? Unbelievable things. Terrible things. Things not of this earth.'

'My Frank is worse than all of those.'

'He's just a man. We can fettle men.'

'He's a very unique man,' Brenda said.

Effie pursed her lips. 'That's as maybe.'

'You don't understand . . .'

'I understand only too well, I think,' said Effie, sitting back.

Brenda looked up and stared at her friend. 'I need your help, Effie.

I wouldn't ask, only . . . I think I need your help really badly this time.'

'Go on. Anything.'

Brenda swallowed. She had a crumb of cinnamon toast lodged in her throat, which only added to her discomfort. 'I'm going to ask you to do something I don't think you'll be happy about.'

'We won't know that until you tell me what it is.'

'I want you to use your powers.'

At first her friend had no idea what she meant. 'My . . .?'

Brenda ploughed on. 'Your powers as the last in line of a whole dynasty of Whitby witches. I know you hate black magic and all, but . . .'

Effie paused for one incredulous moment, and then she threw up her hands. 'What you're asking is . . .'

'I know. You've spent your whole life avoiding your inheritance.'

'It's not just that. Black magic scares me. You don't understand.' Now Effie was speaking in such low tones that Brenda had to lean close to hear her. Her friend's face had gone very pale.

'I wouldn't ask. I'm just . . . really worried about him, Effie. I don't want him near me. I can't let him . . . take me away.'

'All right. All right,' said Effie. 'I'll think on.'

'Will you?'

'I'll see what I can do.'

But Brenda could see that her friend wasn't at all happy about the request.

Sanctum

Mr Timperley thought Mrs Claus was the most magnificent woman he had ever met. He was relieved to be back in the relative safety of her Christmas Hotel, but he quailed inside when he stood before her. This morning, as he bent before her motorised scooter, he was wearing a mac over his Harry the Cat outfit, and still he was shivering with trepidation.

'You have been very brave, spending nights in that wicked woman's guest house,' Mrs Claus congratulated him. 'Thank you.'

'Back when I was Harry the Cat, I faced ghastly peril on a daily basis,' he said. 'But I must admit, that Brenda woman terrifies me.'

Mrs Claus reached out with one scarlet-tipped claw to pat his bent head. 'It's over now. You can stay here in my Christmas Hotel, in the bosom of my care.'

Timperley's eyes lit up at the mention of her bosom, which was prodigious. He said, 'The police haven't charged her, you know. They wouldn't be able to make the charges stick.'

'No matter.' Mrs Claus abruptly reversed and wheeled herself jerkily about her opulent drawing room. Mr Timperley hadn't yet taken in the full grandeur of this inner sanctum. He was still amazed at being admitted into her private realm. He was dazzled by the lights, by the tinsel, by the closeness of this powerful female. His head swam with the scent of pine needles, satsumas, Turkish Delight. He tried to concentrate on what his mistress was saying now.

'All we want is for the rumours to abound,' she mused. 'Brenda might be a murderess. That is all the people of Whitby need to whisper. We just want to subtly undermine her place here, and that will be enough . . .'

'Why, Mrs Claus?' asked the former Harry the Cat. 'Why do you hate her so much?'

Mrs Claus gazed out of her sitting room window, at the dreary rain on the prom and the clouds massing above the bay. 'Hatred? Who can tell? It's such a mysterious thing. It gets right under your skin. You should know.'

His face darkened. 'Indeed I should. I hated Mrs Midnight for years. Decades. I would gladly have done her in a long time ago.'

Mrs Claus watched him carefully. Then she said, 'Shush, my dear. Best not say these things aloud. Even here, in my inner sanctum.'

But the old man was off now, in a reverie of loathing. 'For me, it was the way Mrs Midnight was so insinuating. So sure of my affection. She thought we were a team. She thought I loved her back. But she never had a clue what was in my mind! Never! I hated her! I'm glad she got all choked and strung up with your Christmassy tinsel!'

Mrs Claus scooted forward a little. Oh, what had she unleashed in this man? He was clearly even less stable than she'd suspected. 'Err, right. All right then, let's think happier thoughts.' She gave him a sickly smile and took his hand. 'The second masked ball this evening, hmm? Will you be sticking around long enough to attend?'

He scowled. 'I can't go anywhere, can I? Not while you've got . . .

him holed up here. I feel like he's my responsibility. I brought him here . . .' The old man's eyes darted about. He was feeling trapped, Mrs Claus thought: good.

'You got him to do the dirty work on your old girlfriend,' she pointed out, with some malice.

'You told me to!'

Mrs Claus gave a bitter laugh. 'Funny how people just do what I tell them to. It could quite turn my head. It could drive me to terrible, Catherine the Great-type extremes.'

'Anyway. While he's here, I stay here. At your hotel.'

Mrs Claus turned brisk, rubbing her hands together in an attempt to lighten the mood. 'Well, then you will be here for my second masked ball this evening. And you will dance with me and my motorised scooter.'

Mr Timperley shivered inside his lime-green catsuit. 'If you like . . . It would be an honour, Mrs Claus.'

Note of Terror

'I think we should go there tonight, that's all.' Effie sounded determined, as they hurried through the bitter rain on the sea front.

'And have everyone looking, and pointing?' Brenda asked.

Effie stopped and looked back at her. 'I think you should be there to show them that you don't give two hoots about their suspicions. You aren't a murderess. You aren't what Mr Danby says you are.'

'Hmmm. I'll give it some thought.' What's all this going to do to my business? Brenda wondered unhappily. Are they going to drive my guest house into the ground with all their gossip? When she thought about this, she felt even more irritated by Effie's wittering.

'It's a masked ball, Brenda! You can go in disguise!'

Brenda tutted and shook her head. 'I'm always in disguise. If I'm going, I'm going as myself. In all my glory.'

Effie took this as a good sign. Brenda was reasserting herself. Surely her confidence was returning. 'Good for you! And besides, we haven't had a good look at the fellas yet.'

'Man mad, you are.'

'Hardly.' Effie rolled her eyes, secretly thinking that it might be quite pleasant to get some male attention for once.

Brenda left Effie at her junk shop and antiques emporium, and toiled up the steep incline to her own side passage. She was pretty sure she was going to cave in and go to this second ball at the Christmas Hotel tonight. It was true: however down she felt, however many complications came crowding in, she found it all irresistible. She loved to be in the thick of things when there was intrigue about.

First, though, there was something else to contend with. What's this? she thought. A letter? Jammed right under the welcome mat and all crumpled up. Nasty cheap stationery. Awful handwriting. Terrible English.

There was only one man she knew it could be.

Frank did warn you, didn't I, my love? I said I were on my way to see you again and to claim you for my one and only. So here Frank is, my love, in this town what you have made your own and hidden yourself away from me in. I can see why you came here. Something powerful here, and evil. Something that calls out to the dark space inside Frank where Frank should have a soul. You are here for the same reason. But I have come after you to claim my rites. Frank's conjugal rites as your husband as what should have been all those many years before.

Oh help, Brenda thought, closing the front door with her bum. She locked it swiftly, shakily behind her, and thudded up her stairs. She wasn't happy until she had locked herself securely in her own attic. Then she read on.

When our father made us he intended that we be one. I thought we would be man and wife. But he stopped all that. He looked upon the body he had made – your body – and he was frightened of it.

He tried to murder you, minutes after bringing you to life. Frank could never forgive him for that. I thought you were dead. For a long time I thought we had left you for dead.

Brenda shouted in her room, as if she could talk back to the letter's author: 'Shut up! Stop it! I don't want to hear it!'

Our father is long dead. There is only us two now, on the face of this earth. We should be together, Brenda. We will be together. Frank has come back for you.

Brenda hurried into her bedroom and threw herself down on the rumpled silk of her counterpane. Tears were boiling in her eyes. 'You can't have me! You won't have me!'

The Screaming Ab-dabs

Effie was very concerned about her friend. She was having a fit of the screaming ab-dabs; that was what Effie's Aunt Maud would have called it. Brenda had gone to jelly, and Effie had never seen that happen before. Not even when the two of them had faced together the demon abbess at the gateway to hell underneath the ruins of Whitby Abbey. Or fought the voodoo god Goomba in the beer garden of Sheila Manchu. Brenda took these kinds of things in her stride.

But, thought Effie sadly, now that she knows her old fiancé, Frank, is in town – well, the poor old moo is going to pieces.

What can I do to help? Effie wondered. She knew very well. Brenda had begged her for magical assistance. And Effie had decided that even though it went right against her better judgement, it was the least she could do.

That was why the two friends found themselves shut in one of the upper rooms of Effie's chaotic home that early evening, rather than having their weekly fish supper at Cod Almighty. The lights were turned down and Brenda was agog as Effie worked at a long, low table, strewn with what appeared to be a jumble of scientific and magical bric-a-brac. Tubes and flasks bubbled with vile-coloured fluids. A handy-sized cauldron seethed with some foul-smelling substance. Effie worked hard, tossing handfuls of powders hither and thither, consulting battered tomes she plucked from the overstocked shelves, and occasionally setting light to things. After an hour she was getting frazzled in the hot little room.

'Oh, I was always terrible at casting spells,' she told Brenda. She was swathed in a lilac mist at this point. 'My aunts used to despair of me . . . Ah, hang on, I've lost my page . . . Here we are.' She resumed flicking hastily through one of her arcane books.

Brenda was nodding encouragingly, as she had done all evening. The room reeked of rotting eggs, lavender and liquorice. 'It's very good of you, this, Effie.'

'Don't you fret about me, lovey,' said Effie, stirring the cakey contents of her cauldron.

'But I know you don't want to be like . . . your ancestresses. I know you don't want to be a witch.'

Effie gave a wry shrug. 'Too late for that. Oh look, the mixture is thickening . . .'

There was a horrible gloopy noise as the mixture started to expand and overflow the confines of the small cauldron. It was a sickly green colour by now and porridgey in consistency. And as it flowed across the cluttered bench, it showed no signs of stopping.

'Erm . . .' Brenda said, 'What's it meant to do, this spell?'

'Repel old boyfriends,' Effie told her, peering at the mixture and tapping a nervous tune on her teeth with her fingernails. 'Very useful in some tight corners. We make a kind of dough and bake it into little cakes. Then you eat them all and go to the masked ball with me later tonight, and even if he jumps out at you, you're protected from him.' She flipped through her book again, hoping to find a way to make the mixture stop growing. They had enough for twenty old boyfriends by now.

'I see.'

But even as she struggled to bring the cake mix under control, Effie could see that Brenda wasn't convinced. And if she was honest, Effie had little faith in her own magical abilities. Here's Brenda, she thought, afraid for her life, and all I can do is bake fairy cakes. Effie suddenly felt useless, cursing and cajoling her wayward cake mix, with her witchy forebears staring down at her from their gloomy portraits, no doubt tutting at her shenanigans.

Her aunts had always looked down upon her, she felt. She had tried to turn her back on their nefarious ways. Like Brenda, Effie had tried to live a quiet life in Whitby. But the spirits of her witchy aunts were always gathered about her. Staring through the silvery eyes of their ancient portraits. Waiting for her to turn to the magical, mystical path. Just waiting for her to go to the bad.

Perhaps, she thought, none of us can ever escape our destiny. Perhaps fate is as sticky as fairy cake mixture.

At last she hit on the right words and made the cake mix cease its remorseless growth. But not before it covered the whole of the work bench, crunching and tinkling glass retorts as it went, and some of it had spread in gelatinous tentacles to the floor.

'Even if it doesn't work,' Brenda smiled, 'at least we've got something in for teatime tomorrow.'

'Quite,' said Effie, feeling hopeless. Now to make the fairy buns, about which she felt a little more confident.

The Return of the Repressed

It had been many years since Mrs Claus had visited the cellars beneath the Christmas Hotel. There was never any reason for her to come down to this level, with its gloomy cavernous spaces, which dripped and smelled of sea salt, and seemed to open out into the vast, labyrinthine interior of the West Cliff itself.

It wasn't Christmassy at all down here. It was mouldy and tangy with fish and mildewed wine. Mrs Claus went down in a lift with Mr Timperley to meet the guest they had been keeping safe and secret here, and it was only when they reached this lowest level that she wondered whether coming alone like this had been wise. These men could do anything to her down here, and what could she do to protect herself?

Hmm, she mused. Quite a lot, really. But she wasn't used to the feeling of helplessness. She relished it for a moment or two as Mr Timperley led her tinselled chariot through a series of unfamiliar narrow corridors.

'I feel almost embarrassed now about secreting our guest down here in the cellars,' she told Mr Timperley. 'We could have given him a proper room.'

The old man shrugged. 'I don't think it matters either way to Frank. He's not used to luxury.'

Mrs Claus sighed. 'I don't suppose he is. Ah, the poor love.'

'Watch out, it gets a bit tight here. Let me help with your chair.'

They rounded a final corner and the squealing of the chair's wheels sent a shudder through Mrs Claus. She was suddenly aware of a stirring in the darkened room beyond. She could hear him breathing as he got up to welcome them into his lair. She peered intently into this den of cobwebbed wine bottles and rotting crates.

'Yoo-hoo?' she called. 'Frank? Are you there? Goodness, it's so gloomy, so filthy down here.'

Mr Timperley said, 'I think Frank prefers it like that. He's had decades . . . two full centuries of hiding in dark corners.'

Mrs Claus sighed dramatically. 'What a terrible life the poor love's had! I'm glad I've got you and him here now. I can do something to help him. Hello? Frank?'

Then he was suddenly right by them. She felt his hot, foisty breath on her perfumed neck. His cold hand brushed her arm. Mrs Claus gave a small shriek of fear.

'Frank is here,' he said. A rough voice, she thought. Rough as two bricks grinding against each other. A navvy's voice. Common as muck. 'Frank is right beside you,' he told her.

'Jesus,' she muttered, and then swivelled in her chair to get a good look at him.

Frank stood nearly seven feet tall. He had knocked into the bare bulb and sent it swinging, sending shadows rocking wildly about the room. Mrs Claus gulped. She could see him now, and to her eyes, he looked marvellous. Beautiful, even. There was a pinched, malnourished look about him, but he was still wonderfully attractive to her. He was all man. He radiated a fierce masculinity. It sent quivers right through her as she gazed up at his broad frame. He was a proper brute. A perfect bit of rough.

Mr Timperley spoke up in a nervous tone. 'Frank . . . Mrs Claus here wanted to—'

'Who?' Frank grunted, twisting his impassive features.

'Me, Frank.' She spoke up. 'I own the Christmas Hotel, up above. I brought you here.' As she spoke, she could hear the delicious music playing upstairs. Even this far down, the Christmas spirit could be heard, wafting down through the neglected levels. It buoyed her up and made her feel more confidently festive.

'You never brought me here,' the man-monster growled warningly. 'It was Frank who decided to come here, to this town. To find her. To take her. To get Brenda.'

'Yes,' said Mrs Claus, with a flash of irritation. 'But it's all my plan, dearie. It's all my doing.'

'What she's saying, Frank,' Mr Timperley said, 'is that she wants to help you, in any way she can.'

'Why?' Frank glared down at Mrs Claus on her stilled scooter, and for a second she was held frozen by those stark black eyes. He said, 'Frank doesn't trust her. Doesn't like the look of her.'

Oh God, he's thick, Mrs Claus thought. You can't have everything, can you? He's a proper dopey sod. She coughed gently. 'You should trust me. You should thank me.'

He raised his voice and barked: 'Frank thanks no one!'

Mrs Claus pulled a surprised face. 'Not even your friend Mr Timperley?' She knew now that she could twist the two of these silly men around her little finger. It was so easy. Lemon-squeezy. Men were a doddle, every time.

Frank's expression softened. 'Him, yes. Harry Timperley's a friend. But you others. You women. Never.'

She laughed. 'A woman-hater! Typical!'

'He's upset,' Harry Timperley told her. The last thing he wanted was an upset Mrs Claus. 'We're so close to success, he doesn't know what he's saying.'

'I know what I'm saying. Frank knows what's what. What Frank wants to know is, when is she coming? Where is she now?'

Mr Timperley had to pull Mrs Claus's chair back to the entrance of the room again, as Frank whirled into a fit of pique. He took out his frustrations on the manky wine bottles and splintered wood. His visitors watched impatiently as he noisily smashed stuff up.

'Hush, Frank,' Mr Timperley said. 'Don't upset yourself.'

Mrs Claus was watching narrowly as Frank hefted crates and reduced rubble to dust in his fingers. 'Ooh, he's very strong. Look at the physique on him. He's all man, isn't he?'

This caught Frank's attention. He liked a nice compliment, having been starved of attention for so many years. 'Frank's a good-looking man. Frank's a good catch.'

Mrs Claus made a moue of appreciation. 'I should cocoa, dear.'

Mr Timperley took the chance, while Frank was standing still, to tell him quickly: 'Brenda's coming here, Frank. Tonight. To the second masked ball. We will bring her to you.'

'Here? Down in this cellar?'

'Not down here. You must come up out of the shadows, my friend. You must join the party above ground.'

Mrs Claus could feel the excitement bubbling up inside of her now. It was the usual fizzing, tumultuous sensation she got right before any of her Christmassy functions. Her flesh was alive with anticipation. Even though to her it was Christmas every single day of the year, she hardly ever lost this feeling. And now the sensation was tripled. This was going to be an extra-special do. She grinned and, knowing that she was going to get just what she wanted, burst out at the monster before her: 'You've got to come to the dance, Frank. And you have got to join in with the fun.'

Frank's face creased and furrowed with puzzlement. 'To the dance? Amongst people? Amongst real human beings? Frank has . . . I have . . . never been invited to anything. Ever before.'

'But you have been now, Frank.' Mrs Claus beamed at him. In the meagre cellar light her face was fierce and hot as a blazing pudding. 'Come into our world, Frank,' she told him. 'And claim your bride.'

'It's Christmas Eve, Frank,' said Mr Timperley.

Mrs Claus giggled happily. 'It's Christmas Eve every night at the Christmas Hotel.'

Frank grunted. Now he too could feel excitement welling up in him. His hollow insides started to thrum with happiness. At first he hardly recognised the emotion for what it was. He murmured to his companions in the darkness: 'A good night . . . for a wedding. At last. Two hundred years late. My wedding night at last . . .'

With triumph clearly in sight, Mrs Claus threw back her head and screeched with laughter, rocking in her motorised chair. She howled with mirth. 'Won't Brenda be chuffed to bits!'

The Second Ball

As Brenda hurried up the West Cliff road that night after Effie, she was reflecting that one thing about her best friend was that she could be a proper morale-booster when the chips were down. Some adventures, Brenda would rather slink off home and hide in her attic bedroom. But Effie was always brave and doughty. Effie was always the one to lead the pair of them right into the heart of the deadly goings-on. And so here they were, near midnight, in their glad rags, heading to the Christmas Hotel, ready to meet the impending climax head-on. Hurray for us! Brenda thought.

They struggled up the clifftop path on what was proving to be a stormy night; the stiff salty wind off the North Sea blowing Effie's new hairdo all to hell. Both of them were queasy from too many fairy cakes.

Up ahead there was music coming from Mrs Claus's hotel. Even more raucous and festive than before. They entered through the grand main doors at the front and were greeted by the clinking of glasses and the amazing sight of what had to be the event of the season.

There they all were. All the masked superheroes and crime-fighters that Great Britain had ever known. Hundreds of them, all togged up in their skintight outfits again. Mrs Claus had invited them in order

97

to pay tribute to their efforts at keeping the populace safe, but that was a laugh, Brenda thought. If they'd but known, they were here at the behest of one of the biggest supervillainesses Britain had ever known.

Effie dragged Brenda straight to the drinks. 'Here's a glass of something scrumptious.' She gazed speculatively at the party-goers. 'No one will ever hear a bad word against Mrs Claus, will they?'

'Cheers. What's in this cocktail?'

Effie shrugged. 'No idea. Come on. Let's mingle.'

Brenda wiggled her corselette straight and smoothed down her frock. It was a second outing for her black velvet number. 'You're right. Let's mingle like mad.'

Brenda would think, in retrospect, that perhaps she was somewhat overconfident that night. She thought she was safe as a result of Effie's protective spell in the form of golden sponge and icing sugar. Perhaps, she would later think, she had had far too much faith in Effie's magical gifts and her enchanted buns.

'I'll go this way,' Effie decided, peering into the colourful crowd. 'You take the east wing of the hotel. The drinks lounges and the buffet room. I'll head for the dance floor . . .'

Brenda stared at her friend in mild surprise. It was as if some spirit of devilment had seized Effie. She was eager for the off. She was just about hopping up and down with the fervent need to dance.

Before she knew it, Brenda was left alone in the crowd. She took a deep breath and prepared to mingle bravely. With her foaming green cocktail held aloft, and feeling reasonably invincible with her best frock on and her wig set in a rock-hard beehive, she nudged her way through the glamorous mêlée. She drew quite a few stares. Not least from those gossipers who had heard her reviled on Whitby FM, or who had heard she was the one who found the tinsel-trimmed corpse of Mrs Midnight in the hotel lavs.

But Brenda ignored those curious stares. She put on a big brassy grin and shrugged off their accusing looks. She was impervious in a private shell of quiet calm until she bumped into . . .

'Robert!'

'Brenda!' He grabbed her for a swift hug. 'I'm here with Sheila Manchu . . .' He was wearing a superhero outfit of his own, hired for the occasion. It was a perfect replica of the Nightmare Man, a now-deceased horror from the fifties.

Sheila Manchu had come dressed as no one but herself. She was in one of her revealing gowns, all bosom and ostrich feathers. She fluttered and flapped at Brenda and cooed over her frock. 'Oooooh, Brenda. I don't believe a word of it. The rumours about you being evil and demented.'

'Cheers, lovey.' Brenda grinned queasily, and finished off her strange cocktail.

Robert lowered his voice. 'I've seen that horrible Mr Timperley, done up in his cat outfit. He's up to something. Slinking about on the edges.'

Brenda drew herself up to her full height and gazed over their heads, as if scoping out the crowd. 'Well, I'm ready for him. Honestly, I could give him such a pasting. Him and Mrs Claus, and Mr Danby. The things they've put me through, these past few days.'

Sheila started patting her again, which always irritated Brenda. But you couldn't tell Sheila Manchu that because it would hurt her feelings. Sheila was saying, 'Don't you worry yourself, Brenda. I know what it's like to have tongues wagging at my back. But the people of Whitby won't really turn against you. You belong here with us.'

'Thanks, Sheila. That's good to hear.'

Robert gathered up their empty glasses and offered to fetch them some more drinks. 'Might as well.' Sheila nodded. 'While Mrs Claus is paying for it all. Have you seen her, by any chance, Brenda? Have you clapped eyes on that evil old bag?'

Come Dance with Me

Effie was across the other side of the Christmas Hotel, gyrating – as she herself would describe it – like billyo on the dance floor. All in the cause of her investigations, of course.

With a few judicious jabs of her bony old elbows, she had cleared a nice space in the middle of the floor and was busily strutting her stuff. Later on she would come to wonder whether she hadn't been overdoing it a bit. Later she would marvel at her lack of self-consciousness in dancing by herself, bang in the middle of that crowd. She would come to think that perhaps she had got the quantities wrong in the fairy cakes, and had experienced some funny side effects. It was just as she was swinging her two-piece jacket around her head that she came abruptly to her senses . . . and it was at precisely that moment that *someone* tapped heavily on her shoulder.

Effie froze. 'What . . .?'

She whirled to see who had interrupted her dance.

An extremely tall man was staring down at her. He was very still and self-possessed. She held her breath as he smiled at her. 'May I interrupt this dance?'

Effie felt a shudder run deep through her whole body. She couldn't stop staring up into his great, gloweringly handsome face. The disco lights gleamed on his glossy black hair, tingeing his complexion sea-green, though he was no less attractive for that.

He said it again, in that deep, rumbling voice. All the marrow in her ancient bones gave a lovely shiver at the sound of it. 'Will you dance with me, Effryggia Jacobs?'

He must, she decided afterwards, have been standing about eight feet tall. Broad as a double-decker tram. The dancing crowd around her drew back at the sight of him. They cleared a larger space for the two of them and . . . ooh, it was like being in a gerontophile *Saturday Night Fever*. He took Effie in his great manly arms and the music swelled, right on cue, into something waltzy, suitably romantic, and yet still Christmassy.

He told her: 'I haven't danced with a beautiful woman in a very long time.'

'Y-you're very good at it.'

'Frank hasn't lost his touch.'

His curious use of his own name led Effie to wonder aloud how he had known hers. For one dizzy moment she thought that he was perhaps a fan of hers. He had tuned into *The Night Owls* on Whitby FM and heard her talking on there. She was, of course, getting something of a name for herself with her guest appearances on that show. But when she asked him how he knew her name, he didn't answer. He simply swept her up in his big, brawny arms, and she was like a rag doll, devoid of volition for several dangerously smoochy songs.

It was while they were dancing to a more up-tempo cha-cha-cha number that she was able to draw back slightly and get a better look at him. He was in a tux. Very smart. The strobing lights made his deep, dark eyes flash with passionate intensity, gleaming and glinting off . . . the *bolts* in his neck.

Effie went rigid in the middle of the cha-cha-cha.

'What? What is it, Effryggia?' Frank demanded. 'What's wrong? Why are you backing away like that?'

Effie was turning hysterical. She could feel it rising up inside of her as she struggled to escape his grasp. 'Get away from me! It's you, isn't it? It's really YOU!'

He pursued her, playing dumb. 'What?'

'Don't come the innocent with me, Sonny Jim,' she spat. 'I know who you are, and why you're here! You're HIM, aren't you?'

He chuckled. He was right on her tail, weaving with her through the dancers. His low voice raised her hackles in a furious, but still sort of sexy way. 'I'm Frank. That's who I am. Pleased to meet you, Effie.' He grabbed her arm none too gently in his cold, meaty fist and turned her to face him. Effie let out a whimper of alarm. He shoved his face close to hers. 'Now, where's this woman of mine? Where's Brenda?'

Hostage Situation

Brenda's head jerked up. Those screams sound familiar, she thought.

She was talking in an obscure corner amongst the potted palms with Captain Crisis from Stoke-on-Trent. He was, she had to admit, a bit of a disappointment. She touched his arm. 'Excuse me, dear, would you? That sounds rather like a friend of mine, doing all the screaming.'

Then she was barging her way through the chock-a-block function rooms, raising complaints as she shoved and jostled. Why was no one else responding to the screams? Couldn't they hear? Did they think it was normal, to hear an old woman shrieking for mercy like that at a party?

'Brenda! You're here!' came a familiar voice. Mrs Claus was blocking her path across the main reception in her motorised chair. 'I knew you would come!'

Brenda was curt. 'Mrs Claus. Good evening. Of course I'm here.'

The festive hag's eyes ruched up nastily. 'You're brave, I'll give you that.'

The screeches were louder now, rising in ululating panic above the disco music.

'Look,' Brenda snapped. 'Get your motorised scooter out of my way, will you? That's Effie screaming her lungs out through there . . .'

Mrs Claus shrugged. 'Is it? You two are always getting overexcited about something or other.'

Then Brenda could hear Effie shouting, 'Brenda! Brenda, where are you?' This was followed by a wave of raised voices; one huge cry of dismay emanating from the ornate ballroom.

'Mrs Claus, I'm warning you,' Brenda growled. 'You've got in my way once too often recently. If you don't let me pass, I'll knock your head off your shoulders.'

The owner of the Christmas Hotel was enjoying this. 'You'd attack a woman in a motorised scooter, would you?'

'You know I would.'

Mrs Claus's eyes were twinkling like currants in a bun. They darted about, checking that her staff were in place to protect her. 'My elves would bring you down in a flash.'

'You wouldn't dare have a fracas like that in your precious hotel.'

'Just you try it, lady.'

Effie's voice came again; desperate, ghastly, closer now. 'Brenda! Run away from here! Get away!'

Now others were sounding as panicked as she was. The crowd were getting wind of something terrible going on. They tensed and started to move. Panic went zig-zagging through the rooms.

'What's happening?' Brenda asked.

Mrs Claus grabbed at guests as they went scattering and pushing past, looking for the exit. 'What's all that hullabaloo?'

The air was rife with shrieks now, drowning out the music almost completely.

Then Effie was in the room. Her voice was much clearer. She could see Brenda now, and was yelling directly at her: 'Brenda! Brenda – you must get away!'

'Ah,' Mrs Claus murmured. She smiled to herself. 'I see.'

Brenda saw what she was looking at. 'Oh. Oh dear.'

Frank was standing in the entrance to the main ballroom. He raised his voice commandingly: 'Silence! Everyone shut it! Stop screaming!'

Silence fell. Even in the other reception rooms, there was a gradual dampening down of the party atmosphere as Frank made his presence known.

'Stop that stupid music! Everyone listen to me! Listen to Frank!'

Brenda couldn't take her eyes off him. 'F-Frank!'

His squareish head swivelled to face her. He glared at her with great solemnity. 'There you are. At last. I'm here with you.'

Brenda kept very still. She paused and managed to keep her calm. She said, 'Frank . . . put her down.'

But Frank was still gazing in raptures at the object of his desire. 'My missus. My fiancée. My bride.'

Brenda had other concerns just then. She tried again in a very steady voice. 'Frank . . . I'm telling you . . . put Effie down at once.'

Frank was holding Effie high above his head: one hand round both her skinny ankles and the other clamped around her throat, almost constricting her vital passages. He held his hostage aloft, straight above his head like a living football scarf, and it was this bizarre sight that had set the party panicking. Effie managed to squawk to her friend: 'I'm choking, Brenda! I can't breathe!'

Frank snarled, and gave Effie a thorough shaking. Gasps of horror ran about the room. 'Who? This old bag? Ha! We've been having a little dance, haven't we, old woman, eh? I think she even thought I was interested in her for a second. Ha! Old hag.'

Effie tried bravely to retain her dignity. 'Let me down . . . at once!'

Brenda's mind raced. She knew that it was down to her. Only she could put a stop to this situation. He could kill Effie here and now. She knew he was capable of it. He could rip the old woman apart. Burst her like a Christmas cracker. Brenda had to step in quickly, and she had to do it now. She should have done it already, but she was transfixed by him. She couldn't believe she was staring at him. That he was here, in front of her. She swallowed her stampeding fears and bellowed at her fiancé: 'I'm telling you, Frank. I'll . . . talk to you. I'll step outside with you. If you let Effie go. Just . . . don't hurt her.'

Effie's voice was now a beleaguered squeak. 'Brenda, don't bargain with him. He's a monster. Just get out of here. Save yourself.'

'Don't try to be heroic, Effie. Let me deal with this.' A curious thought struck her. 'Your magic fairy cakes weren't much cop, were they?'

Mrs Claus whirled her motorised chair around and she gnashed her teeth and screamed at Frank: 'Kill them both, you fool! They've been thorns in my side for long enough! Kill the both of them! Strangle them! Stomp on their brittle old bones!'

There were, it had to be said, some murmurs and cries from the party-goers at this. It wasn't the kind of request people expected their convivial hostess to make.

Mrs Claus realised this and put on a fake laugh, furious with herself. 'I was joking! Only joking!'

Then Robert came fighting his way through the crowd, gleaming with sweat in his cumbersome Nightmare Man outfit. 'Brenda! I'm here! Can I help?'

He was startled by the grimly determined set of Brenda's jaw. 'I don't think so, sweetheart. This is something I'm going to have to face all by myself.'

Sheila was at Robert's heels, all of a flap. She wailed, 'Who is that? That terrible man?'

Robert gasped. 'Is that who I think it is?'

'It most certainly is, lovey,' Brenda told him. Then she raised her voice again, in a way that her Whitby friends had never heard before. It was a voice that brooked no refusals. 'Frank! I'm giving myself up. For the sake of Effie, I'm giving myself up to you. Now . . . let her go. Put the poor old biddy *down.*'

The crowd was holding its breath as Frank glared at Brenda. There was a beat of silence as thoughts criss-crossed his face. Would he give up his hostage? Effie was just about passing out with tension, vertigo and pain as he held her there. Some superheroes, she thought wildly. Look at them all! Staring up at me! Who's come to my rescue, eh? Not bloody one of them! Only Brenda! Only Brenda's brave enough to speak up on my behalf.

Then the darkness came swirling in as Frank made up his mind and dropped her, without warning, through the air. It felt like she was falling about twenty storeys as the monogrammed hotel carpet rushed up to meet her. She hit it with a thump and a clatter and decided she'd best just lie there for a bit. The dark circles encroached on her vision and she passed out, prostrate in the grand entrance.

The gathered crowd sighed as Robert dashed to her. 'It's okay! I think she's all right!'

Brenda was still grim-faced. 'Thank you, Frank.'

He dusted his palms and took a step closer to her. 'Now you must come with me, Brenda. You must keep your word to Frank.'

She nodded. 'We can talk. I'll come outside with you. We'll talk. That's all.'

Now there was an urgent gleam in his black eyes. 'You must come with me. You must, you must.'

He was too close. She couldn't stand it. 'Calm down, Frank.'

'Give me your hand. Come! Come!' He ignored all the spectators as he grabbed at her and seized her fingers. There were mutters of speculation around them as they turned towards the exit. Brenda, too, pretended that the crowd wasn't there.

Robert cried after her: 'Brenda! You don't have to go! Don't trust him!'

She gave a bleak smile. 'It's okay. It's fine. I just have to give him a few minutes.'

Woozily Effie stirred in Robert's arms. She looked around to see what was happening. What had she missed? 'Brenda . . .?'

'I'll see you in a few minutes.'

Brenda lowered her head and followed her erstwhile fiancé through the double doors, and out on to the freezing promenade. The doors crashed grandly behind them.

Effie's confused voice rang out in the quiet hotel: 'Where's he taking her? What's he going to say to her?'

Together

'You look just the same,' Frank told her.

Brenda tossed her head. 'Rubbish.'

They had wandered along the dark front and on to the grass. They had passed under the huge jawbones of the whaling monument, which Frank gazed at for a few moments. Awkwardly they walked along together, with all this silence brewing between them. The wind was stronger now, and though the rain had abated, it was still a horrible evening to be out and about. Brenda shivered and hugged herself, and wondered how long Frank was going to detain her.

As their feet swished through damp, unkempt grass, the sounds of the sea grew louder, and that was consoling somehow. The sea reminded her of where she was, and the life she belonged in. But then she would look at Frank's handsome and brutish face and she would remember the life that had been intended for her.

Eventually they came to a standstill, staring at each other. He persisted with his compliments. 'You look even better than ever, Brenda. You look wonderful.'

'Flatterer. You look different, by the way.'

He shrugged. 'Frank has had a rough life.'

'It wasn't much of a picnic for me either, you know,' Brenda snapped.

Now he was off in some kind of reverie, his expression softening. 'I must have last seen you before the war, I think. Long time ago.'

'I'd forgotten about that. The last time I remember was way before that.'

He smiled at her indulgently. 'Your memory was always patchy.'

She took a step backwards, away from him, and hardened her tone. 'What's this about, Frank? Why have you come chasing after me? Drawing attention to ourselves like this? These are dangerous games you're playing.'

'You sound so cold. So distant from me.'

'Of course I do!' she cried. Did he know nothing about her life? Didn't he realise how careful she'd had to be? How hard it was to keep inconspicuous? Here he came, wading in with his colossal feet, ruining everything she had achieved. Destroying her whole life here in Whitby. Her voice broke as she threw at him: 'You're nothing to me! Nothing!'

Frank looked down at the ground. 'Harsh.'

'It's true!' Brenda yelled. 'I've worked so hard to make myself into a normal person. An ordinary, obscure, unremarkable woman.'

Frank shook his head earnestly. 'You'll never be that. Not to me.'

'But it's what I want to be! That's all I've ever wanted. To be human.' He couldn't see the point, she thought. He really couldn't see the point in anything she wanted.

'But we *aren't* human, Brenda,' he said. 'That's just what we're not.'

Brenda was becoming angrier by the second. She flung out her arms and tried to stop herself lashing out at him. 'I could brain you! You've jeopardised my whole life here. I love it here. I even fit in. At last I've found somewhere where I fit in . . .'

'Lucky you,' he said.

111

'But you've ruined it.' Brenda forced herself to calm down. She needed some answers from him, she remembered. 'What are you doing hanging about with that Timperley bloke anyway? And with that she-beast Mrs Claus?'

He gave a massive shrug. 'I don't know. I would have thrown in my lot with anyone just to get back to you.'

'Don't go pretending you think anything of me.'

'Frank loves you! I've loved you for more than two hundred years!' Brenda snorted. 'Rubbish.'

But he was speaking the truth. He lowered his voice and looked straight into her eyes. 'Ever since I watched you first open your eyes. Ever since our father looked down at you, with horror etched on his face. And ever since he tried to put a stop to you, even before you had taken your first step . . . even then, I was already in love with you.'

She felt like choking. She felt her gorge rise. She backed away from him yet again. 'You don't know me. You know nothing about me.'

Now there was a horrible tender relish in his voice as he advanced on her. 'I know more about you than anyone does. Don't you see? Frank watched you being spliced together, bit by beautiful bit, all through that winter. I watched our father, Herr Doktor Frankenstein, working busily and stitching you together with such patience and skill and carefulness. I watched you grow . . . I watched you taking shape . . .' There was a ghoulish, lascivious glee about him that had Brenda just about mesmerised to the spot.

'Stop . . .' she gasped. 'I can't bear this.'

The man-monster was merciless, however. 'I loved you before you even knew yourself. Before you drew your first breath.'

She covered her ears with her palms and shook her head, shouting, 'Frank! Stop! Leave me alone!'

There was no holding him back now. Centuries of pent-up desire were being given vent. 'I was the one who begged Herr Doktor to create you. I inspired your creation. You only exist because of me! And your only purpose is to belong to me!'

Brenda felt herself go very cold and still. 'No!' she moaned. She twisted and whirled herself around. Her velvet frock was dampened by the rising sea mist. It clung to her like clammy hands as she struggled to flee across the clifftop. Her feet pounded on the grass and she hardly knew where she was running. All she could hear was that pleading, needy voice in her head, rising above even the boom of the sea and the gathering storm.

Frank was calling after her: 'Brenda, come back! You can't run. Not any more!'

She screeched at him, and the wind tore at her words. 'Go away! You horrible, seedy old man! I want nothing more to do with you! Go away!'

He ran after her. A chill went through him. She was getting away again. He had to pick up his pace. 'Come back here. Come to Frank!' He plunged into the thickening darkness with his loping stride. 'BRENDA!'

Brenda was right by the cliff edge now. The wind howled about her, trapping her in a vortex of white noise and confusion. 'Get back! Leave me alone!'

He was near her once again. He had caught up with her flight, almost effortlessly. 'Give me your hand, Brenda. You were made for me.'

Brenda screeched as his face loomed above her. 'No, Frank. I'd rather . . .'

'What? What would you rather? Stop playing games with me,

woman!' His huge meaty hands reached out and grasped her wrists.

'I'd rather not exist at all.'

'No. Get back from the edge. Stop it, Brenda. Don't . . .'

Her hands broke free of his grip. She heaved forward and shoved at him, using every ounce of her strength to push him away from her. At the same time she was propelling herself backwards. Her arms windmilled madly and Frank seized at her once more. Then they were lashing and tearing at each other, blows landing thick and fast.

'That's it!' Brenda bellowed, right into his horrified face. 'I've had enough of you!'

And she wasn't sure if it was him, or her, or the chilling wind that thrashed about them, but there was a sudden wrench and the wet grassy earth slipped out from beneath them. Both Brenda and Frank shrieked and clung to each other for the briefest of seconds as they shot over the edge and tumbled into the wild tumult below.

Pursuit

There were faces pressed to the glass all along the front of the Christmas Hotel's sea front conservatory. The weather was so filthy, however, no one could tell what was going on outside.

'I can't see! It's too dark . . .'

'They're too far away . . .'

'She ran over the grass and he went after her, I think . . .'

'Leave them to it, I say.' This was Mrs Claus's hectoring voice, keen to get the party started again.

'Shut it, you, you old bag,' muttered Effie.

Robert came to a decision, 'I'm going out there after them.'

'I'm coming with you,' said Effie, and they started shoving their way through the murmuring crowd towards the main entrance.

The voice of Mrs Claus rang out: 'Forget them! Just a silly domestic. Get the music back on. This is Christmas Eve! It's Christmas Eve again!' One of her elves restarted the music, and James Last's Christmas album came blasting out of the speakers. 'Dance, you fools!' the proprietress boomed at her costumed guests.

Meanwhile, Robert and Effie were running full pelt into the rising storm.

'Brenda! Brenda!'

'Brenda, where are you? Where've you gone?'

They were on the dark grass. They tottered into the blackness beyond, not knowing how safe the ground was up ahead. How close was the cliff edge? The sea seemed very loud and imminent. But there was no sign of Brenda. No voices, raised or otherwise, from the domestic spat.

Effie was chilled to the marrow in a second. Suddenly Robert grabbed her arm and cried out: 'Oh my God. They aren't here any more, are they?'

Cop Shop Vigil

Effie couldn't stand plastic chairs. She sighed and changed position slightly, cursing her aching joints. 'What good are we doing here? Sat here waiting all night?'

Robert was reading the noticeboards for the fifteenth time. 'They know what they're doing.'

'Who, the police?' she barked. 'Do you think so?'

Robert turned to her. He looked very grey-faced and quite ridiculous in his cardboard Nightmare Man outfit. 'They'll have men down there . . . on the cliff. And down on the beach.'

'But we could be out there! We could be out there searching too.'

'I know.'

Effie lowered her voice, suddenly conscious that the desk sergeant might be earwigging. 'If anything's happened to her . . . We should never have let her go out there with him.'

'There's no use saying that now,' said Robert stiffly.

'I know how . . . strong he is. How powerful. When he was dancing with me, he had those huge arms of his all the way round me. I felt like he could just snuff the life out of me at any moment. And then he had me up in the air, like a doll, like something made of paper . . .'

'But Brenda is strong as well. You know how strong she is.' Robert came to sit beside her, his superhero costume squeaking on the seat.

Effie wasn't convinced by his blandishments. 'Hmmm.' She stood and wandered about the spartan room for a while. 'Why won't they let us go and help?' she muttered crossly. 'Down on the beach we could . . . I don't know . . .'

Robert's expression was very dark. 'The tide will still be in.'

'Oh.' She could picture it suddenly. The vastness of the purple dark. The freezing, endless, depthless water. The heaving churn of it. The deathly cold. The creamy violence of the North Sea's rollers crashing in remorselessly against toothy, savage rock. And somewhere in all of that, Brenda. She gulped. 'Oh, of course. I hadn't thought.' She darted a look at Robert. 'If she really did fall into that, do you think she stands more of a chance . . . or less of a chance of surviving than if the tide were out?'

'We still don't know what happened to them both, Effie,' he said bleakly. 'We have to hope.'

There was an embarrassed cough then. The desk sergeant was trying to gain their attention. He was a sheepish-looking man with a dent in his forehead and a sloppy mouth.

'Yes?' Effie snapped. 'Is there news?'

'Nothing yet. Our boys are still out there. They haven't turned anything up yet. Our best chance is first light. It's still a few hours away.'

'Just as I thought,' Effie said harshly. 'You've done nothing, have you? You don't care about Brenda. She's nothing to you.'

'Now, Ms Jacobs. That's just not true. I suggest you go home.' He motioned briefly to Robert, who noticed that the desk sergeant only had two fingers, one on each hand. Robert's attention fixed on those

118

lonely wagging digits for a weird, lucid moment as the policeman instructed him: 'You, lad, you'll accompany her home, won't you? And we'll let you know what happens as soon as we have any news.'

Robert blinked and said briskly, 'Okay. Come on, Effie. You're doing no one any good, staying here and upsetting yourself . . .'

Effie surprised herself – and the two men – by letting out an abrupt snarl. 'Brenda was right! The whole police force here . . . Aickmann and the rest of them . . . they're all inside Mrs Claus's handbag. She's got them right where she wants them. They aren't bothered about finding Brenda alive. They all want her out of here. They all want rid.'

The desk sergeant looked worried. 'She's raving now. I suggest you get her home, son. Ring in the morning.'

Robert stepped forward warily to look after Effie. 'Okay,' he said. She turned to him and he watched the fight die in her eyes. 'Come on, Effie,' he said gently.

Dark Before Dawn

They walked in silence through the deserted streets for some time. The night air was freezing in their lungs and there was a definite tinge of winter on the way. Effie reluctantly took Robert's arm as they approached some of the slippier narrow streets. At last she said to him, 'You'll think I'm a fool for shouting and carrying on like that.'

'Hardly,' he said. Now they were taking very tiny steps on the frost-streaked paving stones. The night all around them was at its inkiest and most sinister. Robert went on, 'I feel like we should both have made even more of a fuss. They were hardly bothered. They treated it like it was a normal, everyday occurrence – an old lady being dragged over the cliff edge by her estranged husband . . .'

He felt Effie shiver inside her winter coat. 'Don't!'

'I'm still in shock,' Robert said. 'I can't believe she's not here with us now. I just expect her to suddenly pop up, with that lopsided grin, holding out her arms and going, "Surprise!"'

'Yes, I feel that too.'

They emerged from the warren of dark streets and the harbour opened up before them, bathed in pale light. 'All that time, waiting in that terrible room, I was expecting her to come galumphing in, you know, like she does.' Robert laughed a little. 'She'd be mortified that we had alerted the police . . . that we had started a manhunt for her. "Why are you making such a big thing of it?" she'd say. "You should have known a little thing like dropping off the West Cliff wouldn't hurt me. I'm invincible! I'm indestructible! Of course I'm safe and sound, you daft ha' p'orths."'

Effie barked with amusement. 'That's just how she tries to use Yorkshire phrases, you're right. That's exactly what I'd have expected too. But she didn't, did she? It's hours now, and she's not turned up.'

'No.' They paused to examine the faint streaks of daylight above the headland. They were pink as streaky bacon, edged with a distant yolky gold.

'Oh, Robert. I'm sorry. I've only just realised. You've been through this before, haven't you? Something like it. Last spring. With your Aunt Jessie.'

'Yeah,' he said softly. 'Exactly the same thing. She went over the cliff too, during a formal do at the Christmas Hotel.'

Effie's tone was hard. 'One of these days, something will have to be done about Mrs Claus. She gets away with too much.'

'Jessie never came back. But that was because she was shot, Effie. She was shot before she plummeted down the cliff. Assassinated by Henry Cleavis, remember?'

'Do I remember? It was the same bullet that grazed my temple, en route to your poor Aunt Jessie. It knocked me into a coma for nigh on a week.' Effie patted his arm and led him away from the view, back on their way. 'I'll not forget that episode in a hurry. I don't think I've been quite right since that coma, to be honest.' She startled herself by saying this, all of a sudden. But it was true. The thought had come out of nowhere, but it felt utterly right. She tried to chase it up, adding: 'Weird feeling of . . . I don't know . . . dislocation and . . .'

'And?'

'Power,' she said. That was it. That was how it felt. A rippling and a surging, just out of view. Under the surface. 'Yes, power. Somehow. A burgeoning of my . . . powers. Hmm.'

Robert looked surprised. He had heard certain things about Effie from Brenda during the past year or so. He knew more about her than he was supposed to. He said, 'Your . . . inheritance?'

Her manner turned brisk. 'Let's not go into that. Listen, I am sorry about your Aunt Jessie. You know I never condoned Professor Cleavis's gung-ho tactics. All that shoot-the-monster-in-the-head business.'

He shrugged. 'All I was saying is that . . . it was a very different case. Jessie I can accept is dead and gone for good. But Brenda . . . Even if she fell all the way into the sea . . . well, we don't know what special reserves of strength she has, do we? I don't even know if she can swim.' Robert plunged his hands deep into his sheepskin pockets, thinking hard. 'She isn't like us, though, Effie. Because we are her friends, we collude in the happy illusion that she is just another old lady. A human being. But she's more than that. Much more. If anyone could survive a fall like that . . . even if that is what actually happened to her tonight . . . then surely it's Brenda.'

Effie turned to him with a smile he'd never seen before. She looked enthused and . . . hopeful, even. 'You're right. I know you're right.'

'We have to hope.' He smiled. He had delivered Effie to the doorway of her antiques emporium, right next to the dark windows of Brenda's empty guest house.

'Good night then, Robert.' Effie, of course, didn't need squiring all the way home, even in the middle of the night, but, she reflected, it was indeed quite pleasant to be treated like a lady once in a while. Especially after a nasty shock.

'I'll be back in the morning, Effie,' he told her, as she grappled with all her front door locks. She gave him a friendly wave as he set off up the hill to the Hotel Miramar. He was a nice, dependable lad, after all, she thought. Maybe she had been wrong about him. Now she was glad she had company in her worried vigil over Brenda. This was something that would be horrible to face alone.

Effie turned back to watch the sky lightening by degrees over the bay and the stark remnants of the abbey. Oh, where are you, ducky? she muttered fiercely. Where the devil have you got to now?

Effie at Home

Effie stared at the portraits of her aunties on the walls of her home. They looked twitchier, gloomier, more insinuating than ever before. She knew that they were telling her, of course, that they could have seen this coming. They always said things like that. They always told Effie that she had been a fool. An idiot girl, letting herself in for trouble. She could never, ever do anything right.

And what was more, her aunts had never liked the look of that Brenda. Too much badness in her. Too much . . . too much of something they didn't like to even think about.

And that had made Effie furious. It had made her scorn her own aunties. Even dear Aunt Maud, who had tried to put her off her new friend. Saying that Brenda would undoubtedly come to a bad end. That she would take Effie with her, to whatever heinous destiny she would ultimately have to face.

Of course, Effie had never told Brenda any of this. Oh dear, no. She'd have been horrified. Though Effie always felt that Brenda could sense the aunts' disapproval. Whenever she had come round Effie's house, they were twitching on the walls. Frowning and sending her the evil eye . . .

They all thought that Effie should protect herself better. That was what they had all always thought. Unlike her dead aunts, Effie couldn't do magic. She couldn't hex herself up and protect herself, like they all once upon a time and even now still could, in the life beyond. Effie was leaving herself open, vulnerable, to the world and its nasty doings, and her aunties on the wall were in continual despair over this.

And in these early hours after the night into which Brenda had vanished, Effie was feeling more alone and unprotected than ever before . . .

Whitby FM

'Welcome once again, my lovely, lovely listeners. Welcome once more to *The Night Owls*. With me, your genial host, Mr Danby.

'Now, after all the kerfuffle and evil upheavals here in Whitby just lately, I thought it would be nice if we kept things rather gentle on tonight's show. Let's have a calming and relaxing night, eh, listeners? So, no heavy debates or arguments or recriminations. Let's all try to get along in peace and harmony.

'Ah. Line two. It's Effie, isn't it?'

'That's right, Mr Danby.'

'And how's our wonderful Effie this evening?'

'It's your fault. All of it.'

'I'm sorry, my dear. I'm afraid I don't understand.'

'She was . . . is the most wonderful woman. And you tried to ruin her. You tried to turn everyone against her and blacken her name.'

'I assure you, my dear, I didn't do anything of the sort. Who are you talking about anyway?'

'You know who. And you know what you did, too. You were dead against her. You did everything you could to . . . to . . .'

'I think our Effie's been on the cooking sherry again, listeners.'

'She's gone!'

'Who's gone?'

'Brenda! That's what you wanted, wasn't it? You wanted her out of town.'

'I'm sorry, but I really don't . . .'

'You'd have organised a pack of marauding peasants if you could, all brandishing flaming torches and setting light to her bed and breakfast.'

'I assure you, Mrs Jacobs, all I had was public safety and interest at heart . . .'

'Oh, shut up. She's gone now. You can't hurt her any more.'

'When you say gone, do you mean she's left Whitby?'

'I don't know.'

'Or do you mean . . . passed away?'

'I don't know. We just don't know.'

'I heard rumours of some of the events at the Christmas Hotel last night. Some said they had seen a monster on the dance floor . . .'

'I was there. I saw most of what happened.'

'But you don't know what happened to Brenda?'

'All I know is that when we went outside to find her, right on the cliff edge, she was gone. And so was her old man.'

'They'd gone over the top?'

'Perhaps we'll never know. But there was no trace of her.'

'Oh, really?'

'I don't even know if we'll ever see her again . . .'

81 Whitby

By the morning, the police had cordoned off the cliff edge and the beach below, to prevent ghoulish rubberneckers from getting too close. Wrapped up against the battering wind and sleet, Robert and Effie went to inspect the scene.

'I'm glad they're doing it properly,' Robert said, as they gazed down at the policemen moving about slowly on the damp sands below. 'They've got loads of men out.'

'That's good,' said Effie, trying to sound positive.

'I want to find Mr Timperley,' Robert said suddenly. 'He was the one who brought Frank here. He's to blame for this.'

'You're right. That worm of a man.' Effie hadn't slept a wink in those remaining hours of the night. She had sat in her front room and shivered. Ringing *The Night Owls* hadn't helped one bit. Her thoughts had become bleaker and bleaker, until Robert had knocked at her door again to bring her down here, where the police were conducting this (as it seemed to her) token manhunt.

They went back to watching policemen poke about in rock pools and kick at humps of sludgy muck.

'They're not going to find anything, are they?' said Effie.

'Don't say that.'

'I've just got this feeling. She's gone for good. We've had her in our lives for a while. And that's it. She's gone. That's our lot.'

'Like an angel,' Robert said.

Effie cast him a glance, unsure of how ironic he was being. 'Don't push it,' she said.

He gave a weary smile. 'She'll turn up,' he said. 'You'll see. She'll come back to us.'

'Someone else went over these cliffs, earlier this year. Brenda and I stood here watching the police like this. The body was smashed there, down on the rocks. Rosie Twist, the journalist.'

'Oh God, yes.'

'That was Mrs Claus's work too.'

'At least . . .' Robert said. 'At least this isn't like that.'

'But, you know, if there was a body, we'd know something. And Brenda's body . . . well, you know.'

He looked at her. He wasn't sure where this was going. 'What?'

Effie fixed him with a strange, hard gleam in her eye. 'If it was lying down there, damaged . . . Well, she's got various options, hasn't she?'

'Eh?' He went very still.

'Did she never tell you?' demanded Effie.

'Uh . . .' Robert wasn't at all sure what she was on about.

'We could always block out what Brenda really is . . . was . . . because she always made such a valiant effort at blending in and seeming normal. But she did have these secrets, Robert. She had this other life. Lots of other lives. She really was over two hundred years old. She really was . . .' Effie took a deep breath before finishing her sentence, 'made of dead things.'

'Please don't say that, Effie. She was . . . is Brenda. Our friend.'

Effie went on. 'All I'm saying is . . . Oh, I don't know what I'm saying. Something she tried to tell me on a few occasions, about the laws of nature. She never fitted in with nature, you see. She was supernatural, her and Frank both. They weren't supposed to exist. That's what made them so unique.' She smiled. 'That's why she loved nature so much, I think. Sunsets over the bay, wildflowers up on the hills, even the daft squirrels in that back garden of hers. She delighted in all of it. Because I think she felt so separate from it. She envied and adored the natural world. She was like a tourist there. Here. But I think she thought nature hated her. And wanted her dead.'

'Surely not? That's . . . irrational. Mad.'

Effie tutted and shook her head. She looked at her companion as if he had missed the point all along. 'She *was* irrational, Robert! That's what Brenda was!'

'I wish you wouldn't use the past tense about her.'

'I'm dead on my feet,' she said apologetically. She could see that Robert was feeling a bit wobbly this morning. She had to go gentler on him. 'I'm gabbling. I hardly know what I'm saying.'

But one of her utterances had stuck with him. It ran through his mind as they turned away from the activity at the crime scene and strode back to town and the workaday world. 'Nature wanted her dead . . .' he repeated.

Effie patted his arm. She thought about trying to jolly him along. But you shouldn't shield people from the truth, she thought. No matter how uncomfortable it might be. She left him in the town centre, before nipping off to fetch her few groceries. As she sent him off to his work, she told him, 'Brenda might have been best friend to both of us, Robert, but she had a curious destiny. A mysterious destiny. Something the likes of us just can't understand. Yes, nature wanted her dead. You see, to the natural world, Brenda was an abomination.'

An Unsatisfactory Interview

They sleepwalked through the rest of the day, with no official word forthcoming from the police or anyone else. About halfway through that desolate day, Effie was brought up short by the realisation that one of the things that might make searching for Brenda rather difficult was her lack of papers.

She was fortifying herself with a cup of strong tea with a dash of whisky as this thought came to her. Abruptly she put down the soggy fairy cake she'd been toying with and sat down heavily. No papers. No official self.

So Brenda didn't exist in the real world. Not in any proper sense. No birth certificate, of course, for the only woman on earth not of woman born. No passport, for the woman who slipped through boundaries in the dead of night with all her belongings in one carpet bag. No driving licence necessary for the woman with no car; who sat patiently at the very back of the bus. Nothing on paper. Nothing to show for herself.

Brenda had always carefully avoided any official probing into her circumstances and her background. Even now Effie didn't understand how she could have owned a house and run a business and conducted herself in the everyday world. What weird magic must she have been employing? What strange kind of deflection spell had she used on bureaucratic eyes?

Effie was quite conscious that she had never quizzed her friend further than she wanted to be quizzed about little things like that. Brenda had her ways and means, and she liked her little secrets.

But now, on that terrible, slow afternoon, the police were asking awkward questions. Questions that came straight to Effie's door. She was visited in her shop that afternoon.

'She was your friend, you say. You must know.' Aickmann could smell the whisky that laced Effie's tea. He looked at her and she seemed exhausted. She was swaying as she sat there, rigid-backed and glaring at him. He persisted, gently. 'You must know more about her background, her details, than anyone else.'

Effie rolled her eyes at the policeman. She had never liked him. A gangly, officious type. She thought she detected an edge of viciousness in him. Something about him disturbed her. She didn't know what it was, but ever since he had come here to Whitby, less than five years ago, she had always thought it'd be best not to get on the wrong side of DCI Aickmann. Now here he was. Drinking tea in her shop and probing at her with these quiet questions. They went on and on. Gentle and endless. This was how he'd get to the truth of anything. Wearing his victims away. Eroding their defences. Effie had willpower, though. Even depleted as she was, she could put up a good fight. She told Aickmann once more: 'You don't understand what a private person she was. She told me hardly anything.'

'But surely . . . family, friends, her last place of employment. I mean, where did she live before she came here to Whitby?'

'I'm not sure.' Effie blinked, and realised that this was quite true. She had no need to be evasive, or lie protectively on her friend's behalf. She found that Brenda had divulged very little about her past lives. 'She always said she had lived all over the place. Many different towns and cities over the years. She always gave the impression of not really wanting to talk about it. She had walked away from those places and that was all there was to it . . .'

Aickmann pulled a sceptical face. 'Very convenient. When did she come here? When did you first meet her?'

Now Effie let her impatience wash over her in a great, caustic wave. She snapped, 'I fail to see what relevance all this has.'

'I am building up a picture, Mrs Jacobs.'

'*Ms*, please.'

Aickmann tried to soften his tone again. 'If she has simply run away, then she might have gone to one of her of her previous places of residence.'

'Now you're making her sound . . . flaky somehow. Like she was never really part of this place. Look, she hasn't just wandered off in the night. She hasn't run away. We saw her! She was having a row, a violent row, with this old fiancé of hers . . . this nasty man she hadn't seen for years.'

Aickmann was pleased. Now she was talking. 'So you say,' he said.

'He had threatened violence already . . . he had manhandled me rather roughly inside the Christmas Hotel, and in front of witnesses. Brenda took him outside so he wouldn't be a bother to anyone else. He was out of control . . .'

Aickmann gave his notebook a rapid flick. 'Other witnesses we've spoken to this morning didn't mention the threat of violence. They said Brenda went out to talk to a man, but—'

'Who was this?' Effie said sharply. 'Who have you talked to?'

'Ah, I can't disclose that, can I?'

'Mrs Claus, I bet. That Timperley, too. Can't you see? They've been out to get Brenda. They've been trying to besmirch her name.'

'Ah yes. Now you've mentioned this before. Some kind of smear campaign.'

Effie took a deep breath. 'Mr Danby, the radio DJ on Whitby FM. His late-night show, *The Night Owls*, has been running what amounts to a campaign of hatred against my friend.'

'Aren't you putting that rather strongly?'

'No, I don't believe I am.'

The detective leaned forward and pushed his bony face too close to hers. 'Do you think Brenda has been perhaps discouraged by this bad publicity of late? Perhaps she has felt less welcome in her adopted town.'

Effie swallowed. She felt the whisky fumes cloying like mist inside her head. 'Yes, I, er, I don't know. She wouldn't cave in to what a man like that said about her. I told her she should sue. But she couldn't be bothered. Too much fuss, she said. Brenda wanted a quiet life, you see. No bother.' She felt tears creeping up on her. This was all too much. 'That's all she ever wanted.'

'I see,' said Aickmann, looking disgusted at her emotional wobble. 'Well, if you've really no ideas about where she might have family or ties or any kind of links with other places . . .?'

'I'm afraid I don't.'

Aickmann grunted, and hopped off his stool. 'Well, that's as much as I need to ask you for now, Mrs Jacobs. Thank you very much. We will keep you posted, as and when there are developments in this.'

And that was it. Effie showed him out on to the street, out of the front of her shop. She slammed the door, locked it. Made sure the 'Closed' sign was showing itself to the public world. She couldn't afford not to open the shop. But she couldn't sit there in her antiques emporium, trying to keep a brave face, as a succession of nosy Whitby denizens came trooping through to have a look and see how she was taking recent events. She sat in her back kitchen amongst the propped canvases and bric-a-brac and she sobbed like a baby. She drank more tea with whisky in it and found that she got a little drunk.

As the afternoon advanced and teatime came and went, Effie was on the brink of a miserable stupor. She started thinking back over that very unsatisfactory interview with DCI Aickmann, and how curt and unfriendly he had been. His suspicions had been plain on his square face. Brenda was no good. She was a dodgy character. She hadn't even told Effie, her best friend, where she belonged. Effie couldn't even say where she had lived last.

But . . . Brenda belonged here. That's what I should have said, thought Effie unhappily. She had found her place at last, amongst good friends, and everything that had come before hardly mattered any more. But in the face of Aickmann's authority and bland disinterest, she had crumbled and mumbled and got it all wrong.

The phone gave a quaintly piercing ttrriii-iii-nnggg, and Effie snatched it up.

'Effie? Listen, I've been thinking,' said Robert, and she felt oddly reassured to hear his voice again. 'I've got the evening off. You've got a key to Brenda's place, haven't you?'

'Oh my God,' she said, as the thought hit her. 'Does she have any guests staying?'

'Timperley has moved out. He was her only one this week, luckily.'

Effie nodded, glad to hear it. She went to her secret drawer in the cash desk and poked about. 'I've got my key. We should go round there.'

'Clues,' Robert said. 'There must be something. Something in there that can tell us . . . something.'

'You're right.' She had stood up too quickly, she realised. The room was swirling about a bit. 'When can you come down?'

'Now,' Robert told her.

Home Safe

With a clatter and a jangle of keys, they entered Brenda's home as if they were burglars. No, thought Effie. Worse than that. We're creeping into her home and up the steep side stairs as if we were entering a haunted house.

Oh, get a grip on yourself, girl. Set a good example for Robert. Aloud she said to him, 'I don't like the idea of going hunting through her private things.'

'Me neither,' he said. 'But needs must, Effie.'

As they reached the upper levels of the house, it was stuffier. The rooms hadn't been aired all day. There were still the lingering traces of the last meal Brenda had cooked in her beloved kitchen. The top landing light was on, a dusky welcoming pink.

'I have this fantasy,' Effie said. 'I think I dozed off this afternoon, so maybe I dreamed it . . . but it's where we go up into her attic rooms and there's music playing. One of her crackly jazz LPs. And there's that familiar aroma of spicy tea and the lights are on, all warm. And when we open the door to her sitting room, there she is, in her favourite armchair, looking at us like we're crackers. "What are you doing creeping about? Why do you look like that? Weren't you expecting to see me? But this is my place. Of course I'm here." '

'Hmm,' said Robert, as he joined her at the top of the stairs. 'I've had similar thoughts. That she just somehow landed softly on the rocks and got up and toddled back home, without a fuss.'

'It'd be lovely, wouldn't it? Her just sitting there, in the room at the top of the house.'

They were both looking at the closed door to her sitting room, and both, she knew, were putting off the moment when they would open it.

'But can't you feel it?' Robert asked. 'The house might be warm, still, with a few lights on. But there is a feeling here of absence. Like something has gone from the heart of it.'

'Yes, I can feel that.'

But Brenda's house wasn't silent. Effie wondered if Robert had heard them too, those noises, as they had advanced oh so carefully up the stairs. Effie could hear tiny scratchy-scratchy noises from the attic. *Tappity-tap. Tap tap tap.* They were feeble, she thought: they were flagging. But if Robert had heard them too, he didn't say a word.

Effie steeled herself and marched across to the sky-blue door that led to Brenda's living room. She threw it open.

'There,' she said, thrusting her head into the room and sounding more gung-ho than she meant to. 'Nothing there. No one home.'

Robert followed her into the room where they had both spent so many pleasant hours. Here they had whiled away cosy evenings with Brenda playing hostess and plying them with her home cooking and booze. And here they had sat up late, on several occasions, caught in the midst of one of their investigations. Racking their brains and piecing together clues. Gossiping and fathoming out bizarre mysteries. But now the room was desolate. Even though cushions still bore the imprint of their owner, and tea things had been left out on the breakfast bar, and several newspapers and books were strewn on the coffee table and chair arms, there was an awful feeling of abandonment about the once-welcoming room. Dust had started to settle, and as both her friends knew, that was a rarity in Brenda's place.

Effie went to sit in the bobbly green armchair. Robert clicked on a lamp or two, and tried to make the place a little more hospitable. Effie was saying, 'The thing is, with Brenda, there was so much that was mysterious. Even to me. She would mention various people and places that she had had connections with over the years . . . but you'd only hear half the story.'

'You heard more than I did, probably.'

'It was as if she didn't want the disparate strands of her life ever to touch or to mingle . . . Which makes it a hopeless task, when it comes time, like now, to contact people, to inform them . . .'

Robert could see that Effie was worn out. It was as if she was fading away. He would have to be the proactive one. He would have to take the lead in this search through Brenda's stuff. 'Quite,' he said, glancing about at the shelves of her wall unit. 'I don't suppose there's an address book, or a computer . . .'

'No computer, no.' Effie heaved herself reluctantly to her feet. 'Come on. I'm not being much use just sat there, am I?'

They spent a fruitless hour going through drawers and cupboards, working side by side, examining things and turning them over, and trying to lay them away again as carefully as possible. But most of what they found related only to the day-to-day running of Brenda's guest house. Immaculate linens, folded just so. Cupboards crammed with tins of polish and bottles of cleaning fluid. Heaps of freshly laundered dusters and cleaning cloths. It seemed that Brenda had a mania for cleanliness. But what got to Effie was that there was nothing personal there. Nothing that would yield up any kind of clue.

Robert said, 'I'll go through the books on the shelves, in case there's anything slipped inside . . .'

'She never had many books,' Effie said, coming to see.

On the wall unit there were volumes of Milton, Shelley and Blake, and some mystery novels from the 1960s. Soon Robert and Effie were looking at each other, exasperated. But what were they even searching for? Some kind of message from their missing friend? A message telling them she was all right, after all?

Perhaps they were looking for evidence that she had even existed at all. That thought brought Effie up short. As they moved about quietly, almost furtively, she voiced this silly idea to Robert, and he treated it with the snappishness it deserved.

'You're letting your imagination get the better of you. Of course she was real! She was someone we saw nearly every day for the best part of two years!'

'But it makes you think, doesn't it? I mean, I don't think I've got any snaps of Brenda. I'm not very handy with a camera and I don't care to have my own picture taken . . . but if you remember, when she and I took that trip on the coach to the Lake District, to Grasmere . . . all the snaps I took . . . Brenda came out somewhat hazy and blurred. She said she must have been moving every time, but it was strange. There was more to it. It was as if the camera film and the chemicals, whatever they use, were rejecting her.'

'Now you really are talking rubbish,' Robert told her.

That was when Effie had a breakthrough. A blinding flash of inspiration. 'Her safe! Robert, her wall safe!'

'What?'

'Do you remember? During all that fuss to do with the possessed garden furniture in the beer garden of Sheila Manchu, Brenda was fetching things out of her safe.' Effie was gabbling at him triumphantly. 'I remember her saying something to watchacallim, Professor Cleavis, her shady paramour. Anyway, she's got this safe, in this very room, and it's filled with all her special stuff. Secret stuff.'

They set about hunting for the safe at once, quickly deciding between them that it quite obviously had to be behind one of the pictures. There were a couple of dodgy local watercolours of Whitby scenes; an oil of Robin Hood's Bay, and then a number of murky reproductions of great big swirly scenes by John Martin and Turner. Effie went running her shaking fingers along the plaster-and-gilt frames, rapping and pressing as if she did this kind of thing all the time. And at last her patience was rewarded. One of the frames – the Turner – budged a little under the slightest pressure of her hand. She prised it away from the wall and found it was hinged like a door. And behind it was another door. A safe door, clunky and impregnable, and neither she nor Robert had an idea as to how to get it open.

'That's pretty frustrating,' Robert sighed. 'If only we knew a safe-cracker or a real burglar or someone. I bet everything we need to know is inside there. The whole lot.'

'I could kick myself. This is precisely the kind of thing I should be able to do. It should be a doddle to me.'

Robert glanced at her. 'You mean, magically?'

She looked abashed. 'I've never been that proficient with the skills my aunts before me took such pride in.'

'Hmm. You couldn't give it a try anyway, could you? Just give it a little whizz?'

'You don't understand magic.' Effie gave him a fearsome frown. 'If you go dabbling willy-nilly, you can make things ten times worse.'

'I suppose so. But I thought you were our local witch. I thought you did magic stuff all the time . . .'

'It's something I've shied away from all my life.'

'I see.'

They both stared at the dull, implacable safe door. They both knew that it must surely hold every one of Brenda's secrets. Everything would lie inside there. They would be able to find out just where she was, and how to get to her, if only they could open that blasted door.

'I daresay I could have a look in the old books back at home. Sometimes I can rustle up a spell or two if I have the instructions, the recipe, so to speak . . .'

'Hang on! I've got it!' Robert suddenly cried out. 'I know who can do this!'

'Who?'

'Who do we know with criminal connections?'

Effie pulled a face. 'Lots of people.'

'Fair point. But who is really famed for being married to a crime boss? Who do we know who's bound to have the necessary skills to crack a safe like this?'

'Ah.' Effie beamed. 'You mean Sheila Manchu.'

'The delectable Sheila.' Robert nodded fiercely. 'It'll be a breeze to her.'

In Reception

Robert was working at the reception desk at the Hotel Miramar, while Sheila Manchu hovered voluptuously behind him. It was a busy day, since all of the spillover superhero guests appeared to be leaving town at once.

'Of course, Robert,' Sheila told him. 'Anything I can do to help. Dear Brenda. She was such a boon to me. When there was all that to-do with the poison-pen letters, and then that wicked garden furniture . . . and then Goomba, the bamboo god from the dawn of time . . . Well, let's just say I owe Brenda one.'

Robert was relieved. 'I finish this shift at six, don't I? Will you come down to the B and B with me then?'

Sheila nodded firmly. 'And there's still no word at all from the police, or anyone?'

He pulled a face. 'As far as they're concerned, Brenda was dashed to bits on the rocks below the cliff and washed away to sea. Or she simply wandered off, along the clifftop, and subsequently left town. Either way, never to be seen again. And good riddance, apparently. They don't seem too fussed.'

'Poor Brenda.'

In the Grotto

Meanwhile Mrs Claus was glaring up at Effie. 'I agreed to see you as a courtesy, Effryggia. I don't have to consent to being quizzed by you like this.'

Effie refused to be intimidated by the woman, even here in her own baroque sitting room at the Christmas Hotel. She kept steadfastly to her point. 'Have the police spoken to you?'

Mrs Claus tossed her head, so that her bauble earrings clattered and chimed. 'What on earth about? Brenda's demise? Why would they need to speak with me?'

'Because it happened slap bang outside your hotel,' said Effie in a steely tone guaranteed to make any but Mrs Claus tremble. 'Because you, my dear, are *involved*.'

'Hardly. In case you hadn't noticed, I was busy hostessing a masked ball. I had quite enough going on, thank you. I wasn't outside, pushing women off cliffs.'

'You might as well have been. You invited that . . . brute to stay here. To jump out of the shadows and give Brenda a shock.'

'Who, Frank?' Mrs Claus shook her head pityingly at her inquisitor. 'He was her fiancé. He had a perfect right to know where she was, and to see her.'

'You had no right to interfere.'

'I didn't bring Frank here,' Mrs Claus protested. 'That was Harry the Cat, Mr Timperley. It was his doing. I just put Frank up, for a day or two. And I found him a charming companion. A little rough around the edges maybe, but he's had a hard life. And now, I suppose, he's dead too. What a waste. Ah well.' She glanced surreptitiously at the clock on the mantel. It was almost time for calling the bingo. She raised an eyebrow at Effie. 'Anything else?'

'You're a very cold and ruthless woman, Mrs Claus.'

She smirked, horribly. 'Am I indeed, Effryggia?'

'But you are too complacent. You think you can get away with absolutely anything. But one day you'll go too far.'

'Will I?'

'You'll trip yourself up. You won't be all-powerful for ever.' Effie found herself bending right over the Yuletide hag in the chair, grinding out her threats between her teeth, and only just restraining herself from slapping the woman.

'All-powerful, indeed,' chuckled Mrs Claus. 'My dear, I think this disappearance of Brenda's is turning you doolally. Have you been fortifying yourself with the old cooking sherry again, Effie?'

Effie's control snapped at last and her hand flew up to smack her enemy in the mouth. In an instant she felt herself held, very firmly, and led backwards, away from Mrs Claus. The elves had stepped in – seemingly out of nowhere – just in time. Effie grunted in frustration. Her palms were tingling with violent intent.

'Ah-ah,' Mrs Claus simpered. 'Now, you know I won't have any nastiness. Not on my premises.'

'One day,' Effie swore, still wriggling in the elves' grasp, 'I'll get you.'

'Oh! I think that was a threat.'

'I'd curse you if I could.'

Mrs Claus wiggled her stockinged toes with glee. 'With your witchy powers, hmm? Never mind. Look, I'll forgive you your hot-headedness today. But only because you've suffered a loss. Let her go, elves. Show her to the front door.'

'I've asked everything I want to ask anyway,' said Effie, struggling to regain her dignity.

Mrs Claus called out to her as she was led towards the sitting room door: 'Consider this, Effie. Brenda has just walked away. She's left you behind. Abandoned this life of hers in Whitby. Surely you must know that she has a long, long history of such behaviour. Why, that was what drove Frank so mad. She wandered away from him and kept running away. Now she's done the same here, and abandoned all her lovely, loyal friends.'

'No . . . that's not true.' But wasn't there a wriggling, niggling doubt in Effie's mind? Hadn't Mrs Claus articulated exactly the thing that Effie was fearing?

Mrs Claus shrugged, like it was the least important topic in the world. With a wave she dismissed her servants, and commanded them to escort Effie from the premises. 'That's my explanation. But I couldn't care less. I couldn't stand the ghastly bloody woman.' She gave a mocking regal wave. 'Goodbye!'

Effie's Hopes

The people Effie saw in town kept giving her their condolences. They were shuffling up and telling her they were sorry for her loss. Like Brenda even belonged to her. Everyone seemed to know they were best friends. They used to parade about the town together with linked arms sometimes. Effie had never had a friend like that before.

She had felt like a girl. A girl let out of school. Did that sound silly? she wondered. Her life had been rather lonely. Especially since the last of her aunts left the physical realm, in 1968. Brenda had become a big part of her life all of a sudden, so many years later. Her presence made quite a big dent in Effie's solitude.

Effie could feel her hackles go up when people told her they were sorry for her loss. She would think, How do you know she's dead? How dare you presume?

She'd be getting her groceries, going about town, doing normal things. Veins thumping crossly in her temples as she lowered her head, and mumbled her thanks to them. Those fools, those interfering idiots. As if a tumble over the cliff edge could have harmed Brenda. As if the wild sea could have drowned her. What did they know?

Brenda was resilient and strong. She had survived so much. But

Effie had to remind herself that these people, they were strangers, and they didn't know anything much about Brenda.

Effie was keeping her hopes up. Brenda hadn't been smashed to smithereens on the ragged rocks below. She just knew it.

Stashed in the Attic

They were back in Brenda's rooms and the place was feeling less abandoned and bleak. Robert and Effie were accompanied by Sheila Manchu, who was all flustered and breathy as usual, whirling about with a canvas bag. 'I've brought all the tools I think I'll need,' she told them. 'I'm no expert, mind.'

Robert told her, 'I'm sure you'll do your best.' He believed it, too. Sheila might be a bit flighty, and she might have a very dubious past, but he knew that she was a harmless soul.

Effie took command, deciding that they had best get on with things. 'It's behind that Turner oil sketch.' She marched over and peered at the murky picture closely. 'Do you know, I've the oddest feeling this isn't a reproduction. It's the real thing.' She sniffed it thoughtfully.

'What's an oil sketch?' Sheila frowned, fussing with the array of clunky tools in her swag bag.

'Never mind,' Effie sighed, and swung back the painting. 'Here's the safe. Can you do anything with it?'

Sheila came to peer at the hefty door. 'Hmm. It's quite an old-fashioned one. I'll see what I can do.' Then, with a degree of concentration Effie would scarcely have thought her capable of, she set to work safe-cracking. There came a series of very focused clicking and whirring noises as her manicured fingers whirled the dial and she pressed her ear to the door to listen.

Robert was relieved by this evident expertise. 'Sheila will do it. Shall I make some spicy tea?'

Effie was off in a reverie. 'She might have run off with him,' she said. 'What?'

Effie shook her head rather glumly. 'He was her fiancé after all. He might have convinced her to go with him. We don't know what he might have been saying to her, up on that clifftop . . .'

Robert, dismayed to hear Effie going on like this, tried to bustle past to the kitchen. 'Oh, I don't think so, Effie.'

She pursued him. 'We both know how soft Brenda was. Is. Heart made out of caramel, easy to melt. And if he'd been giving her the old sob story, about how terrible his life had been without her, how he'd let himself go to pieces . . .'

'It's true, from the bit I heard, that his life sounded pretty wretched,' Robert conceded. 'Depressing. He hadn't made a proper go of it, like Brenda did hers. But he had no right to simply demand that she abandon her life and go with him . . .'

Effie watched Robert fuss around with tea things. He knew where everything was, as well as Brenda herself did. Effie said abstractedly, 'Maybe she did actually have some feelings for him. Who can say? The ways of love and desire . . . they're all mysterious.' Especially to me, she thought unhappily. What do I know about anything?

The kettle was boiling now and she watched Robert assemble the tea pot and cups on a tray.

Effie sighed, catching her breath in the gurgling steam. 'I feel out of my depth in all of this.'

Robert boggled at her. 'Do you really think Brenda would just steal away in the night with her . . . man-monster? Without a word to any of us?'

'Oh, crumbs. Maybe she would.'

Then they heard Sheila's quavering, excited voice calling from the front room: 'I think I'm making progress! I think I can actually do it! Oh, Mu-mu, you've trained your girl well!'

Hefting the tray of tea things, Robert shouted back, 'Brilliant, Sheila!' He glanced at Effie. 'I hope we find something useful in there . . .'

They hurried through and crowded round Sheila just as the safe gave its final clunk and whirr of surrender, and its heavy door swung submissively open. Everyone applauded.

'Let me see . . .' said Effie, shoving her beaky nose in first. 'There're all sorts of things in here . . .'

'Look at this! A tiara! Jewellery . . .'

'There's some right old tat, too,' observed Effie, turning items over in her hands and examining them with her expert antique dealer's eye. 'What are these things? Mementos? Looks like a ginger jar filled with ashes. Papers . . . papers! Let's see those.'

'Some stuff in funny languages,' said Robert.

'Does anything look useful?' asked Sheila, secretly feeling that the attention had turned rather quickly away from her triumphant fiddling of the lock.

'I feel a bit guilty,' Robert admitted, 'poking about in her holy of holies.'

'Too late, saying that now,' said Sheila, 'After I cracked her safe and all.'

Effie took charge once again. 'Look, let's get everything out and lay it out on the coffee table and go through it systematically. I'll get on with that, and Robert, you pour the spicy tea.'

Robert knew that at certain times, it was best just to give in to Effie's plans. 'Okay.'

They sipped tea and worked intently for some time, examining Brenda's prized knick-knacks and souvenirs from her long, long life. It was like some weird version of *Cash in the Attic*. Except that, apart from Effie, they were no kind of experts. They were turning these funny old things over and over and trying to guess their significance, rather than their value. In some instances they were at a loss as to what the curious objects even *were* . . .

'Any idea what this is?'

'You've got me there . . .'

Sheila gave a sudden scream. 'Ugh, look!'

Effie peered over her glasses at the shrivelled thing Sheila was dangling at them. 'Monkey's paw. Oh dear.'

'I thought it was *human*.' Sheila shuddered, and dropped it back on to the coffee table.

Robert was frowning, roving his eyes over the collection of rolled manuscripts, electronic gadgets, sparkling gimcrackery and souvenirs from a hundred adventures. 'If this stuff was precious to her, and it must have been, she wouldn't have just left it behind, would she?'

Tappity-tap, as if in response, from the attic space above them. Robert blinked. Had the others heard that? *Tap tap*.

Effie gave no sign that she had. She pursed her lips and said, 'I don't know. This guest house was precious to her as well, wasn't it?'

Directly above them, through the ceiling, came a dreadful scratching noise.

Robert was almost relieved to see Sheila stiffen and exclaim: 'Listen! What's that?'

Effie glanced up and said, matter-of-factly, 'Noises from the attic space above this.'

'What?' cried Sheila. 'Could she . . . could she be up there?'

'I don't think so, dear.' Effie smiled sadly. 'But something is.'

'How do you know? She could be hiding up there, for all we know . . .'

Robert set about making himself feel brave. 'We'd . . . we'd better go and look.' He stared at the painted Artex of the ceiling. 'What if it's Brenda? What if it's her?'

'How do we get up?' asked Sheila.

'Hatchway on the landing,' Effie said. 'Come on. But it's not her.'

'How can you be so sure?' gasped Sheila.

'Effie, you know something that we don't,' Robert said. 'What is it?'

Effie took a deep breath. 'Look, the two of you had better brace yourselves.'

Then she turned all businesslike, leading them out of the sitting room, into the hallway. There, she pulled the rope that opened the attic hatchway. The three of them stared into the oblong of darkness above.

Now the *tappity-tap* noises were very loud.

Tap tap tap.

Effie glanced at her companions, then set foot on the metal ladder. Robert felt awkward. Should he really let an old lady go first, into possible danger? But Effie seemed very sure of what they would find up there in the dark. He went next, and Sheila brought up the rear. All the while, the agitated scritchings and tappings were becoming more intense.

'Ooh, I'm no good with ladders,' Sheila said.

'What is it we're going to see?' asked Robert, feeling slightly shaky now.

Effie said, 'I wouldn't bring you up here unless things were desperate.'

'Tell us! What's making all that noise! It's getting worse!'

'They know we're coming,' Effie hissed. Now she was clambering into the dark hole at the top. She turned to whisper, 'They can hear us. Sense us.'

'Who can?' said Sheila. 'Did she keep pigeons up here? Bats?'

'Not quite,' Effie said, standing aside as her fellows joined her, breathless and quivering with nerves in the cramped attic space. All three of them were hunched over and clutching each other as Effie fumbled for the light switch. 'Look.'

Click.

The noises stilled for a moment as harsh white light doused half the room. There was enough light for the three investigators to see what the room contained, however.

On a series of neat shelves and purpose-built wooden racks, Brenda's spare limbs and organs were hanging in tidy profusion. They twitched and thrummed with vital life. They even seemed to stir as if they could see their visitors and were attempting to give a nervous wave in welcome.

They were terribly naked, was Robert's first thought. He felt like he was intruding, just by being here, and staring at that selection of pale pink, coffee-coloured, and blue-black legs and arms, or that jar crammed with eyeballs, sticky as humbugs in their preservative juice. The organs were the most disturbing sight, he thought. The glossy purple-greenness of them; the vats and bottles of them, neatly labelled. Hearts and spleens and everything in between, jostling cosily in their little cardigans of yellow fat and gossamer tissue.

'Oh my God,' said Sheila.

Robert was just as dumbstruck. 'It's . . . it's . . .'

'It's pretty hard to get used to at first, I know,' sighed Effie, remembering her own first encounter with Brenda's disembodied parts. 'But don't be scared. There's nothing frightening here. Nothing that can do you any harm.'

Sheila's voice came out in a squawk. 'But . . . it's all bits! Bits of bodies . . . and stuff.'

'Brenda's spare parts, yes.' Effie frowned.

'That's horrible.' Sheila looked away, itching to be back down the metal ladder.

'No, no, it's not horrible,' said Robert. 'I can see now. It's how she's lived so long.'

Effie smiled at him. He was a bright boy. She elucidated as best she could: 'She rotates them, you see. I'm not sure of all the ins and outs of it, but she keeps herself young and fresh by swapping things about a bit.'

Suddenly Robert's eyes gleamed. 'Are there enough parts here . . . for a whole one?'

Sheila sounded disgusted. 'What?'

'Is that why we're here?' asked Robert.

Effie stared at him. She had a new respect for his quick thinking. 'Goodness, I hadn't even thought of that! I don't know if it would work. Do you mean . . . put our own, new Brenda together from all these bits?'

He clucked his tongue. 'Oh, but the brain. We wouldn't have the brain. There's only one of those.'

Effie mused for a moment. 'I suppose it depends where we believe the actual *essence* of Brenda resides . . . whether that's in the brain or the heart or . . .'

Sheila had heard quite enough of this nonsense. 'Look, maybe you two are happy philosophising in this . . . charnel house. But I'm going back downstairs. I feel sick as a parrot, I do.'

Robert shook his head at her. 'It isn't a charnel house, Sheila. These pieces of Brenda aren't dead. They're all alive. They are still linked to her.'

'Yes, I feel that too.' Effie smiled at him. 'I'm glad you say that, Robert.'

'They're moving and twitching and just . . . seething with energy. They are a part of her!'

'Yes, you're right.' Effie was grinning.

Sheila stared at the faces of her two friends, lit eerily from the landing light below, and looking ghastly in their new enthusiasm for all those twitching body parts. She felt nauseated, but she knew she had to keep her feelings to herself at this point.

'That's what they're trying to tell us,' Robert said. 'All that tapping and scratching. They are trying to draw our attention . . .'

'To the fact that . . .'

'She's alive still!' Robert shouted. 'Yes, she's alive!'

Sheila – who was paying more attention to the horrible sight before them – gave another sharp scream. 'That one's coming closer! Look!'

They all turned to stare. One of the raggy-ended hands had let itself down carefully from its perch, and now it was crawling, crabwise, over the wooden rafters towards them. It made a horrible slithering noise as it came, trailing shiny purple tendons behind it.

'I can't look at it.' Sheila gulped.

Effie frowned at her. 'There's nothing to be scared of, Sheila. It's just one of her hands. Just her hand.'

Now, as it paused right before them, the hand made an impatient tapping noise.

Effie bent forward. 'Yes, dear? What is it?'

'It wants something,' said Robert.

Sheila turned away. 'This is just ghoulish . . .'

Now the hand was tapping its fingers much harder in a staccato pattern. Then the fingers were flexing themselves and bunching up and stroking the ground. To Robert's eyes they seemed to be doing a kind of mime.

'Got it!' he cried. 'I know what it wants. Paper, a pencil . . . Have we got something?'

'She wants to tell us something!' Effie said.

Robert had fetched out a pencil stub and a flier for some kind of club that he found in his back pocket. 'Here, I've got this.'

Effie watched proudly as Robert crouched to pass the writing materials to the impatient hand. 'Oh, Brenda! You're in the land of the living still! I just know you are!'

The hand flattened the scrap of paper to the raw boards of the attic and hefted the pencil up very carefully, pausing and then plunging its point swiftly into the page. 'There, it's doing it,' said Robert, as the moving hand started to write and the hollow noise of the lead filled their ears.

Brenda's friends tried to read upside down in the dusty gloom. 'What's she saying?' asked Effie. 'Her handwriting was always so poor . . .'

Robert was closest. He leaned in to see. The hand was struggling with the paper, trying to hold it still as it scratched out the words. At last it seemed to be finishing. 'Hang on,' Robert said. 'She's saying . . .' He blinked in surprise and stared again. 'Oh.'

Effie tried to bustle forward, into the glaring lamplight. 'What? I can't make it out . . .'

But Sheila could. She had turned around now and she could see exactly what the horrid hand thing had written on the paper. She said it aloud, so that Robert and Effie could be in no doubt.

' "*I AM IN HELL*",' she read.

Stepping In

It was very good of him, Effie thought. Brenda's business might have gone under without his help. She had fifteen guests booked in for that following week. They were arriving in droves and they all had to be fed and looked after. So what Robert did was take some time off from Sheila's Hotel Miramar and move into Brenda's home, where he rolled up his sleeves and got on with it. Effie was rather pleased. She was in the habit of thinking that the younger generation was very inconsiderate. But now she could see there was more to Robert, and she was starting to understand what Brenda had seen in him.

One morning he was working his socks off in the dining room, wielding plates of Full English Breakfasts, when there came a sudden knocking on the downstairs door. At first he ignored it, but whoever it was became insistent and Robert had no choice but to hurry down and see who it was making such a fuss.

It was a very smart and trim little man with a gleaming bald pate, which he revealed when he whipped off his hat and gave an ironic bow. 'Good morning. I am Mr Danby. You are . . .?'

'Yes, I know who you are. You're the radio DJ who locked us in that room and tried to gas us. And then you set all of those primitive apewomen on us.' Robert shivered and watched his breath emerge in

160

a bright plume of smoke. It was the coldest morning yet this autumn and he had better things to do, he thought, than cross swords with this insinuating gimp.

'Oh yes, of course. You must be Robert. How are you?'

'Bit frazzled.' Robert frowned. 'Look, what are you doing here?'

'I saw that there was light and life in Brenda's home again.' He spread his small hands and beamed. 'I saw that she had guests. I wondered if that meant she had returned home safely once more.'

Robert's mouth fell open. 'What would you care about that? You were one of the ones trying to run her out of the place!'

'Not true, my friend,' sighed Mr Danby, tutting and shaking his head. 'And all I am doing now is showing some simple human compassion, and interest in my fellow human being.'

Later that morning, when Robert was round Effie's telling her what Danby had said, she rolled her eyes and let out a bleak cackle. 'Is that what he said? Human compassion? Ha!'

'He's a foul little man,' Robert said. 'For a second you'd believe him, and then you see this malicious glint in his eyes and realise that he's sort of mocking you, the whole time he's talking to you.'

'That's right. Did I ever tell you about the time Brenda kicked his arse in The Deadly Boutique?'

Robert nodded quickly, keener to continue with his own story rather than listen to one he'd heard before. 'Anyway, the thing is, he was standing there with a couple of small suitcases, and it turns out he's after a room for a couple of nights!'

'What?' cried Effie. She stood frozen in the act of popping some furry-looking biscuits on to an antique tea plate.

'There's something the matter with his present place. I couldn't work out what he was on about . . .'

Effie couldn't believe what she was hearing. 'You didn't let him have a room in Brenda's house?'

'Well,' said Robert. 'I thought it was wise, you know, to keep your enemy close to you. Isn't that what they say? So you can keep an eye on them?'

She stared at him, perched there in his blue denim shirt and his jeans, going on like he knew it all. Letting some funny, evil man into Brenda's home! She treated the young man to one of her hardest stares. 'No. It's a very foolish idea. He could be doing all sorts round there!'

Robert was determined not to quail under Effie's disapprobation. 'And I also thought, well, money is money, and we have to keep Brenda's business afloat.'

Effie pursed her lips. 'He hypnotised you, didn't he?'

'No, he didn't!'

'He does his mesmerism on everyone,' Effie said heavily.

Now Robert wasn't so sure of himself. Suddenly he could picture Mr Danby standing in Brenda's side passage with his luggage, and the smarmy man was saying, 'And you really don't mind if I stay as long as I like?' And Robert was nodding quickly, eagerly, and telling him: 'Of course not, Mr Danby. I will give you Mr Timperley's room. It's at the front, with a lovely view of the harbour . . .' And he was turning to show him to his room. Oh my God! Robert thought. Effie's dead right! The slimy get hypnotised me!

He was jerked back to the present and felt abashed. Effie was saying, 'I think it was his expert mesmerism that made him such a good talk-DJ. He had people saying all kinds of things they never meant to.'

'I know,' said Robert. He felt less bad knowing that it wasn't just him who was easily put into a trance. 'Do you still listen to his programme?'

'Not since I realised what was going on,' Effie said. 'What with him demonising our poor Brenda.'

Robert stirred the rather strong lukewarm tea Effie had made him. 'He'll be out most nights anyway, broadcasting, won't he? He'll probably sleep during the day.'

Effie shivered. 'I once had a man-friend who slept through the day. It can be quite inconvenient.'

'Do you mean Alucard?'

Effie flinched at the mention of the name. But it suddenly opened her floodgates and she gave a little sob. 'Oh, I wish he was here. He'd help us sort things out. And get Brenda back.' She struggled to regain control. No need to make a fool of herself in front of this young man. She straightened up in her chair and sipped her tea quickly, then added, 'Oh. Remember. Cod Almighty tonight for our meeting. Friends of Brenda.'

Robert nodded briskly and put down his stewed tea. 'Righty-ho. I'd best get back to the ranch.'

'Ranch?'

'I mean the B and B,' he said. 'Work to do. See you tonight!'

Creeping About

When all of the holidayers were out and about, seeing the town, Robert was creeping about indoors. He crept up the side stairs and wondered if Mr Danby was, in fact, still in.

His new room was directly underneath Brenda's living rooms. Robert would pass his door on his way up and down, many times each day. When he paused on that landing, craning over the banister, he saw that Danby was occupied in the bathroom down the hall. He was running a bath, Robert could hear the rumbling gurgles of the old pipes, and see steam curling across the ceiling. Mr Danby had left his room door open.

Robert made the decision before he even knew it. While Danby was locked in the bathroom, Robert was going to check out his room and his stuff. He didn't know what he thought he was going to find. But it seemed like a way of getting an advantage over his enemy.

Robert tiptoed across the landing. Floorboards groaned. He darted into Danby's doorway. Peeked inside. Danby had drawn the bright orange curtains on the clear day outside so that an opaque light filled the room. It was like stepping into a room filled with jelly.

Danby had unpacked only a few things. Some notebooks, micro-cassettes and sheaves of notes were strewn rather messily on the armoire and the table by the window. He had hung up a number of rather small, wrinkled shirts on the padded coat hangers in the wardrobe.

Robert thought he heard something then and froze. But it was coming through the wall. The bath was in the next room. Mr Danby was singing in there. 'Stormy Weather'. The thump had been him knocking the wall with his elbow, perhaps, as he scrubbed his back with a loofah or somesuch.

The two battered suitcases were on the bed. One had its straps undone. It would be easy to just . . . flip it open.

Nothing unusual. Folded underwear, vests. Robert dug around gingerly, in case anything sinister was concealed underneath, but there was nothing. Robert decided he was being foolish. He had been holding his breath for a full minute. Slowly he let it out, and breathed again, and let the suitcase lid quietly drop back down.

The other, smaller case still had its straps and buckles in place. Well. He might as well have a quick look, just in case there was anything untoward. The straps jingled and he cursed them. As he wrestled with the antiquated thing, the ancient bedsprings jounced and he braced myself for discovery. But Mr Danby carried on singing 'Stormy Weather'.

Robert threw open the lid of the second suitcase.

And the tiny, wrinkled woman lying inside opened her eyes in astonishment. Then she looked furious. She balled up her fists and opened her mouth, and screamed at the top of her voice.

Fish Supper

Some hours later, a rather calmer Robert was in a newly pressed silk shirt and telling his tale to the Friends of Brenda in a corner booth in Cod Almighty.

'I was out of there before you could say "evil homunculus".'

Sheila Manchu had crumpled the menu in her dainty hands. 'What was it? *Who* was it?'

Robert took a deep breath and went on: 'The scream was so piercing I could hear it at my back as I ran away, all the way up the top flight of stairs. There came all this splashing from the bathroom as Mr Danby leapt into action and out of his bath. I could hear the doors clashing and him shouting, "What's wrong? What's wrong?"'

Sheila's eyes were popping out of her head. 'But what was it?'

Effie looked rather sanguine about Robert's story. She nodded grimly. 'I know who it was.'

Robert looked at her searchingly. 'You've seen her before, haven't you?'

'She was wearing white robes, wasn't she?' asked Effie. 'Like a tiny habit?'

Robert nodded firmly. 'Yes. It was the abbess, wasn't it?'

Sheila was none the wiser. 'Who?'

'From the abbey,' explained Effie, very quietly. 'She's thousands of years old. Mr Danby says he's her son, but I can't see how that can be. Anyway, he protects her and carries her about in a suitcase.'

'That's horrible,' gasped Sheila.

'When he had that Deadly Boutique of his, it was the abbess who was being fed all the life essences he collected.' Effie looked grim, recalling this, and remembering how close she herself had come to being reduced to a form of macrobiotic sludge. 'They were draining all this stuff out of their customers using a deadly machine, and she was meanwhile sitting upstairs, drinking in all of the life force!'

'Hideous!' cried Sheila. 'No wonder you felt compelled to put a spanner in the works.'

A rare expression of pride flitted over Effie's hawklike features. 'That was one of the first cases that Brenda and I worked on together.' She focused again on the present matter. 'Now, what on earth is the tiny midget doing having herself installed in Brenda's B and B?'

Robert winced. 'I should have refused to let him have the room, shouldn't I?'

'There's no helping that now,' Effie told him.

'It's like vampires, isn't it?' mused Robert. 'Once you invite them in, you've got them for good.'

Sheila put in, 'That's true of lots of people.' Suddenly she perked up. 'Oh, here's our order.'

The three Friends of Brenda sat very quietly as the waitress delivered their steaming, delicious plates. Robert was particularly looking forward to the mushy peas, which were a speciality here.

'No Brenda this evening?' asked the overly friendly waitress. 'That's unusual.'

Effie told her, 'She's gone away for a while, I'm afraid.'

The waitress put her hands on her hips and frowned heavily. 'She didn't pay no heed to what that DJ was saying on the radio, did she?'

'No, of course not.' Effie clearly wanted the waitress to drop the subject and just go away. She stabbed at her chips with her fork.

'Dunno what he had against her,' the waitress went on heedlessly. 'Nice old sort, I always thought. Well, she shouldn't let gossip chase her away.'

Effie rolled her eyes. 'I'll be sure to tell her that.'

'My best customers, you are, you and her.'

'Thank you,' said Effie stiffly, and watched her with daggers as the waitress turned and lumbered away.

Sheila lavished vinegar on her fish supper and blinked tearfully. 'Brenda needs to know that, that's she's got friends in town.'

'Getting messages to her – that'd be tricky,' Effie commented, frowning and fiddling with a sachet of tartar sauce.

'Okay,' Robert said, in a more official-type tone. 'If we're talking about the . . . situation now . . .?'

'Yes.' Effie nodded. 'The meeting is open.'

Robert happily took charge. 'Okay. Do you really think that was a true message? What the hand wrote?'

Effie was glad to divulge what she had been thinking in the days following that strange scene in Brenda's haunted attic. 'Those body parts of hers are very sensitive, she told me once. They are attuned to minute vibrations in the ether. They can tune in to any unconscious or conscious thoughts floating by . . . and articulate them. I suppose it's because they're waiting, twitching, for brain signals. So they pick up on messages floating past. And so, if Brenda is somehow sending us messages . . .'

'So she's telepathic now?' asked Robert.

'I don't know!' shrugged Effie, taking a very small forkful of crispy batter. 'But it makes sense, doesn't it? Her getting her disembodied hand to tell us where she is . . .'

Now Sheila broke in. Her tone was despondent and incredulous. 'Hell? You really think she might be in *hell*?'

Effie nodded very slowly. The atmosphere in their little corner of Cod Almighty seemed to gather darkly, chillingly about them. Even the sixties music from the jukebox faded away as the shadows drew in and the temperature dropped. Effie told the others, 'Yes, I do indeed think she might be in hell. Brenda always used to say she'd end up down there. She'd joke sometimes, but she was in deadly earnest. No soul, you see. Not of woman born. Her . . . father dabbled in necromancy, sorcery. Doomed her before she was even alive.'

'That's so unfair,' said Robert.

Sheila sighed, and went on tackling her jumbo-sized cod. 'I bet half the people who belong in hell don't end up there. I bet it's all unfair and mixed up. Such is life, isn't it?'

'So . . . Effie,' Robert asked earnestly. 'Do you think Brenda really was killed by her fall from the cliff?'

'It looks that way,' nodded Effie. 'If she's sending messages from . . . down there.'

Sheila looked up quizzically. 'You said her handwriting was quite bad, didn't you?'

'Shocking,' said Effie. 'She would pop notes through my door and I'd be squinting at them for ages.'

'Well . . . I've been thinking.' Sheila's face went into contortions. It was as if she was having doubts about sharing her thoughts with her friends. As if they might think her a fool. She took a deep breath and decided that she had to at least voice her thoughts. There might be something in them after all. She said, 'Could it be possible . . . Don't laugh at this . . . But might that note that the hand wrote . . . might it have just said, "I AM IN HULL"?'

Effie blinked at her. 'What?'

'Hear me out,' said Sheila quickly. 'I've been thinking this over. What if she landed safely in the sea, but got swept a little way out and couldn't swim back to us? What if she was dragged down the coastline for several miles and . . .'

'Ended up in Hull?' asked Robert.

Sheila banged her open palms on the tablecloth in exasperation. 'Surely it's more feasible than . . . the other option?'

Effie sighed heavily. Her expression was full of disgust as she regarded the owner of the Hotel Miramar. She said, 'If Brenda was in Hull, she could have just phoned us from a public call box. Or jumped on a bus. Or even hitch-hiked. It's not that far away.'

'Oh,' said Sheila, gutted to hear her idea shot down. 'I hadn't thought about that. I suppose you're right.'

Effie shook her head woefully. 'Hull indeed.'

Robert felt that Effie was being too scathing. 'Sheila's just trying to figure it out, Effie.'

'There's nothing *to* figure out,' Effie snapped. 'Brenda has told us herself. She is dead and she has gone to hell.'

'That's a bit cut and dried, isn't it?' Robert asked.

'Hmm?'

'I didn't think you'd ever just . . . give up on her like that. "Oh, she's dead. Never mind, then."'

Effie looked at him and was surprised to see him looking so upset. 'That's not what I'm saying, young man.'

Sheila was on the brink of tears. 'I can't believe she's dead. I felt sure she was still alive . . .'

Robert was staring intently at the inscrutable Effie. 'So what exactly *are* you saying?'

Effie pushed away her barely touched plate and dabbed her lips with a napkin. 'I'm saying that going to hell isn't necessarily the end of the story.'

'What?'

'Sounds pretty final to me,' Sheila said.

Effie gave a wry smile. 'If we lived anywhere else but Whitby, that might be true.'

Robert had a curious sensation. A small surge of fear. 'I don't understand. What are you on about?'

Effie paused and laid her crabbed hands flat on the tabletop. She considered them for a moment and then looked up to stare her two companions dead in the eye. 'We're going in after her,' she said. 'That's what. We are going to hell and we are going to bring her back.'

Open and Shut Case

It was late, and they were in Brenda's rooms, playing some of her old jazz LPs.

'To be fair,' Robert said, clinking his sherry glass to Effie's, 'she does have a hotel to run.'

'I've never seen Sheila Manchu scarper so quickly.' Effie rolled her eyes. 'The way she skedaddled up that hill.'

'Disconcerted, I shouldn't wonder.'

Effie looked gloomy, slumped there in the bobbly chair. 'Hmm. I don't suppose we can count on her help in this mission. What about you, Robert?'

He was instantly alert. He looked prepared to dash off right this minute into the unknown. 'Oh, I'm with you. Whatever needs doing. If you think there's any chance of rescuing Brenda.'

Effie stiffened and straightened up. 'I think we should do whatever it takes.'

'Cheers, then,' said Robert, and knocked back his nightcap.

Then Effie was on her feet, as if struck by a sudden thought, and was fiddling with Brenda's tranny. There was a shriek of static as she muttered, 'I want to check something. Ah, yes . . .'

The liquid tones of Mr Danby reverberated through the cosy

sitting room. '. . . And so the question I'm asking tonight is whether any of my listeners actually do really believe in the presence of supernatural beings . . .'

'*The Night Owls,*' sighed Robert. He whistled under his breath. 'His voice gives me the creeps. I don't know how I ever listened to it before.'

'Quite,' murmured Effie. But she was busy thinking, and tapping a long, thin finger against her nose. She wasn't really listening to what Danby was saying at all, Robert noticed. 'So, if he's broadcasting this live – as he must be, given that it's a phone-in show . . .'

In a flash Robert saw what she was getting at. He sat bolt upright. 'Then he isn't downstairs in his room, guarding his old mama!'

'Exactly!' Effie cried.

'Hang on,' Robert frowned. 'What do you want with her?'

She was already halfway across the room. 'You'll see. Come on. Finish your sherry.'

He already had. He got up quickly to follow. 'You're going to wake her up?'

Effie paused dramatically in the doorway, a faraway look in her eyes. 'I want a word with the old abbess.'

And so Robert found himself creeping down the stairs and into Danby's room after Effie. She had the door open easy as anything with one of Brenda's spare keys. They made only the slightest, tenderest of sounds as they eased past the half-open door and took tiny footsteps across the worn carpet.

Effie warned her companion, 'You don't want the other guests knowing we're sneaking about . . .'

'You're right. But there are only a couple, two right at the bottom of the house. They won't hear us.' Robert was disconcerted, though. The quality of darkness down here in the awful Danby's bedroom was different to that anywhere else in the house. It was as if the man's evil had seeped out of him and tainted the atmosphere. It was soupy and noxious, the dark down here, and Robert couldn't wait to be out of it.

'Where's his case?' hissed Effie briskly.

'Up there, on the wardrobe.' Robert flicked on the bedside light, revealing a half-rumpled bed and a room strewn with belongings. None of them seemed particularly strange or mysterious. Only the battered leather case on the wardrobe emanated a weird feeling of foreboding.

'Help me.' Effie was up on her toes, reaching to manhandle the case. They scuffled and scrabbled, but at last they wrestled the cumbersome object on to the bed.

Effie paused momentously. 'Here goes.'

She reached forward unflinchingly and untied the buckles. Then, with a swift glance at Robert, she flipped the lid.

Robert peered down at the tiny, wrinkled face of the abbess. Her eyes were like two dark pickled walnuts. She was swaddled in immaculate bindings, but there was about her still the slightly mildewy and earthy scent of the tomb. 'Ugh,' as Robert put it succinctly.

Effie studied the dozing midget with care. 'She's deeply asleep again. But yes, it's her. The same one.'

'How many could there be?'

Effie was deep in thought. She whispered, 'I wonder what the best way is to . . .'

Robert stared at her, deferring to the old woman's greater

knowledge of these supernatural affairs. He wondered what she was about to do. Some kind of incantation, perhaps. A curious arcane spell, accompanied by potions and powders . . .

Effie reached forward and gave the tiny abbess a smart slap round the face.

Robert gasped. 'Don't hit her too hard! You'll knock her block off.'

Effie tutted at him. 'I think,' she said with some authority, 'that this abbess is made of sterner stuff than that.' With that, she slapped the slumbering homunculus once more.

'I think she's stirring,' Robert said, backing away without even realising it. A horrible sensation of dread was making its way through his entire body.

He seemed to lose all sensation for a second as the abbess came to, all in a rush, and let out a huge shriek of alarm.

'Shut her up!' Robert gasped, staring appalled at that open mouth with its tiny pearly, pointed teeth. 'Stop her!'

'Abbess, stop!' shouted Effie, and next thing, the screams were muffled and blocked as Effie quickly shoved a pillow over her little face and pressed down.

'Don't suffocate her!' cried Robert.

'STOP! BE QUIET!'

Robert suggested, 'Hit her again!'

Effie whipped away the pillow and slapped the screaming face. Abruptly the abbess fell still and quiet in shock.

'She's all right,' announced Effie.

The abbess's voice emerged as a frightened croak. She stared wildly up at her persecutors, but could seem to make little sense of who they were, or what was going on. 'What are you doing to me? Who are you people? Frederick . . . where are you?'

'Your son isn't here,' Effie said. 'He's at work.'

Robert wondered at how terrifying he and Effie must look to the diminutive woman. The lamplight was behind them, making them silhouettes looming menacingly over the suitcase.

Though scared, the abbess fought to put some authority into her voice. 'What are you doing to me? Put me away! Put me back where you found me!' Her face was screwed up like an ancient and furious baby.

'Sssh, it's all right,' Robert told her. 'We don't mean you any harm.'

'Yes you do! You must do! You've got me out in order to kill me!'

Effie said, 'That's not true. We've come to you because—'

But the abbess screeched and interrupted her. As Effie had dropped her guard and softened her voice, the tiny person had recognised her. 'You! Effryggia!'

Effie leaned closer. 'Yes, it's me.'

'I know you,' seethed the abbess, spittle all down her miniature robes. 'I saw you up at the abbey. The night we sent Alucard spinning down into hell. We opened up the Bitch's Maw and sent him to his doom, didn't we?'

'Yes,' said Effie, with some misgivings.

'You were there with that friend of yours,' mused the abbess. 'The beast-woman. The unnatural one.'

'If you mean Brenda, yes.'

Now the abbess's expression turned crafty and even more gleeful. 'And she is gone, isn't she? Gone for ever.'

'No!' Effie cried.

'Gone for the moment, then. However you want to put it.'

Effie tried to take control of the situation, telling the abbess, 'Your son, he was trying to send her away . . .'

She frowned heavily. 'Now why would he do that? He knows that I want Brenda here along with you. He knows that I commissioned both of you to do a job together. He was there when I commanded you . . .'

'Yes, he was,' said Effie, thinking about the oleaginous Danby. He had been lurking in the shadows. Standing at a safe distance. Watching and studying, and not really involved. He had been his mother's carer. Her caddy, waiting with the special suitcase. All the time he had been observing, and drawing up his own secret plans.

Robert was puzzled by this mention of a job that the abbess had commissioned Brenda and Effie to do. 'What job was this?'

The abbess stiffened, glaring up at him. 'Who is this boy anyway?'

'A friend,' Effie told her, and turned to him impatiently. 'We were told, Brenda and me, to keep an eye on the Bitch's Maw, the gateway into hell, which is concealed beneath the ruined stones of the abbey . . .'

He nodded. 'Brenda mentioned something of the sort once.'

The abbess spoke up again, her voice rising in strength and brimming with the authority of centuries of experience. 'It's hardly a secret. This town is visited by creatures and demons coughed up by the overflowing underworld. We need the likes of Effie and Brenda to keep a careful watch on who goes in and out.'

Robert's ears pricked up at this. 'So the way in to hell is a two-way street? People can come *and* go . . .?'

Effie nodded darkly. 'And they do so with alarming regularity.'

He grinned, seizing her arm and making her wince. 'Effie, you were right then. If Brenda is down there, we can get to her. Bring her out again!'

'Hmmm,' said Effie cautiously. She shoved her nose even closer to the small, supine nun. 'Abbess, would you please tell us if you happen to know whether our Brenda is in hell right now. We received a message, you see—'

The abbess interrupted. 'I don't know.' She appeared to be listening to some inner voice. Something faraway and subtle. For a second her lined face brightened, but then she frowned heavily and shook her head. 'It used to be easy to tell, once upon a time, who was where and which way was up.' She sighed very deeply and, even lying down, seemed to slump her shoulders resignedly. 'Not so any more. The world is much more complicated. Involved. Treacherous.' Her pickled walnut eyes glimmered at them dangerously.

Effie drew herself up to her full height and announced bravely, 'We want to go and fetch her.'

The abbess's eyes widened slightly, and then, to her visitors' surprise and alarm, she gave a mad kind of giggle. 'Fetch her from hell? Fetch. Fetch. Fetch. She is a *fetch*, isn't she? That's precisely what old Brenda is. A fetch caught in the Bitch's Maw.' The abbess curled her tiny toes in pleasure.

Effie was determined to stick to the point. 'Can we do it? Can we go there in safety?'

The abbess scowled up at her. 'There's nothing safe about it. You start out on such a journey and you have already given yourselves up to misery and death. You have gambled with the remainder of your lives. There are no guarantees of anything.'

'Nevertheless . . .' said Effie stiffly.

The abbess seemed to turn gentle. A note of concern, even, crept into her voice. 'You want to go there because she is your friend. But, Effryggia, you leave the gateway untended. And unguarded. If you go down there, Whitby is open to untold dangers. We are all terribly, terribly vulnerable, as a result of your pursuing this madcap quest.'

Effie blinked at the flattery. 'Do you really think Brenda and I were that good at our job?'

The nun shrugged. 'You were reasonably effective. You saw off Goomba the bamboo god.'

'That's true . . .'

Robert joined in with the appreciation. He clapped Effie on her bony shoulder. 'You put yourself down too much. You've faced all kinds of weird things in recent months.'

'Yes, we have.' She grunted with embarrassment and returned to her main point. 'But . . . will you help us, Abbess? Even if it means leaving the gateway unguarded for a little while?'

'Face it,' said the abbess. 'You have no idea when, or even if, you would ever return from hell.'

'Perhaps,' Effie sighed. 'But I also know that this place isn't safe without Brenda. I can't carry on doing that job alone. I'm not strong enough without her. I haven't got the heart for it, like she has.'

'You're right,' the abbess told her with a slight nod.

'We must save her,' Robert said grimly, quite determined not to be left out.

'And you, young man? You are prepared to enter into hell for your friend also?' The abbess peered at him from her makeshift cot with hauteur.

'I bet I've been worse places.'

'We shall see.'

'You'll help?' Effie asked hopefully.

'I will,' the abbess assented. 'Now, you must fasten me back into this case and carry me out across the town e'er this night is through . . .' Her voice rumbled on in a musical chant of instructions, which Effie and Robert listened to very carefully. All the while they were trying to be brave and not to think: We're going to hell. We're actually going to hell. Tonight! This very night!

We're Going to Hell and – Hopefully – Back

She was heavier than she looked, so Robert did most of the carrying. Effie followed him as he lugged the case containing the ancient abbess across town, over the wide mouth of the bay, accompanied by the lashing wind and sleet and the mocking chorus of gulls. The streets of Whitby were curiously empty, late though it was. As if the people knew that uncanny things were going on, and it was probably for the best if they were already abed that night . . .

'I hope we know what we're doing,' Robert muttered.

Effie snorted. 'Of course we don't.'

'We're going to hell!'

'For a friend' she reminded him, hushing her voice as they turned into the narrow confines of Church Street. 'For our best friend.'

'It's still hell.'

They passed a few dark shop windows. Effie froze outside the bookshop. 'Sssh. I think . . . we're being followed.'

Robert nodded grimly and hugged the precious case to his chest. 'Yes, I thought I heard something as we came over the bridge. Couldn't see anyone . . .'

Just then there came the unmistakable slap of feet on the cobbles behind them.

'There!' Effie jerked her head. 'It's like someone flat-footed . . . or someone wearing slippers.'

'Here, hide on this corner.' Robert drew her into a narrow alleyway. 'We'll get them as they—'

Just in time they ducked aside as the slapping footsteps resumed, quicker now, more desperate-sounding, tapping along the street leading up the hill. As the steps passed their hiding place, Robert let out a horrible cry and barrelled out into the lane.

Sheila Manchu screamed blue murder. She was in one of her floaty negligees and ululating like crazy. 'Get off me!'

'Sheila!' Robert gasped. 'What are you . . .?'

She stared wildly at the two of them, relieved but still heaving with the effects of her scare. 'I felt guilty,' she panted. 'I left you in the lurch. So . . . I followed you. I want to help.'

'Ha!' cawed Effie, sounding not unlike one of the gulls wheeling over the harbour. 'You won't be as keen when we find out what it is we're doing.'

Sheila was steadfast. 'I don't care. I owe Brenda my help.'

'Tell her, Robert,' commanded Effie. 'Then see what she says.'

For a second Robert was caught wondering why his voluptuous employer could never manage to wrap up warm, even on a freezing night like this. He stared at her and then he announced: 'We're going up to the abbey to find the Bitch's Maw. And then we're descending into the underworld. To bring Brenda back from hell.' He smiled in what he hoped was a reassuring manner. 'That's our plan.'

Sheila's mouth hung open. 'Oh!'

Effie regarded her with gleeful scepticism. 'Still as keen?'

'Er, well. Oh . . .'

'Why don't you just toddle off back to the Hotel Miramar?' Effie said impatiently. 'Running about in your night things indeed. You'll catch your death.'

But Sheila had made up her mind. She folded her dimpled arms and set her mouth determinedly. 'No. I don't care where it is you're going. I'm coming with you.'

Robert glanced at Effie and hefted the heavy case. 'She looks pretty resolute to me, Effie.'

Effie studied her, still not very convinced. 'Hmm. You won't hold us up, will you? Being all girlie and shrieky and having hysterics all over the place?'

Sheila was stung by this. 'No, I won't!'

'Very well then. You can help Robert carry the case. We've got to get it up the hundred and ninety-nine steps. Now come on! Quickly! And keep it quiet!'

Sheila stepped forward to shoulder her share of the burden. 'What's in the case?'

'You'd never believe us . . .' Robert whispered, and the three resumed their journey through the old part of town, where the elderly houses inclined towards each other across the narrow pathways and the whole lot was steeped in purple dark as the moon was suddenly vanquished and lost to sight.

Take Me Home

Some time later, having struggled breathlessly up the steep curve of the hundred and ninety-nine steps, Effie, Robert and Sheila were stumbling in the long grass towards the ruins of the abbey, high above the town. They dragged the case with them, lashed on every side by the freezing rain. Here they were exposed to the elements, at least until they could scuttle behind the roofless and crumbling walls of the abbey. Robert found himself glancing backwards at the warm lights of the town and the distant facades of the comfortable hotels, and he couldn't help wishing that he was home tonight, instead of attempting this. Instead of going where they were hoping to go this evening.

Effie barked out suddenly, 'Be careful with her. Don't bang her about.' She was concerned about the abbess, and how she must have felt every one of the hundred and ninety-nine steps. Her tiny vampire's teeth must be rattling in their sockets.

'We're trying our best,' gasped Sheila Manchu, trying not to sound too exasperated.

Effie was studying the lie of the land. She squinted into the wind, and at the grand, imposing edifice before them. 'Now, it's a little while ago . . . but I think it was over that way, the far corner. It's more overgrown now, of course . . .'

Sheila frowned at her. 'Are you saying you've really got a tiny old woman in that case?'

'Hmm,' Effie said absently. 'She was the abbess here. A thousand years ago. According to legends and the texts in my collection, she ruled this place with a rod of iron. A cruel, wicked person. But then, by all accounts, she had to be. The gateway was under here the whole time. They had some very strange adventures . . .' As she recounted this, Effie was marching ahead through the overgrown grass. It lashed about their ankles, as if threatening to tangle them up and drag them back. The wind itself was batting them backwards; the sharp sleet stinging their faces. Sheila was one all-over mass of gooseflesh. But still the three of them ploughed onwards and into the plotted terraces and gnarled foundations.

'Can't we just let her out now?' Sheila said. Her arms were hurting quite badly by now. She longed to drop her end of the case. 'Perhaps then she can tell us where this . . . um, gateway thingy is.'

Effie turned to stare at her with some *froideur*. '"Thingy"?'

Robert interposed himself between the two ladies. 'Good idea,' he told Sheila, and lowered his end of the case to the frozen grass.

Effie sighed and relented, but made sure that they didn't open the catches and buckles until they had the case in the shelter of a tall and moss-encrusted abbey wall. They flapped open the lip and drew back the wrappings very cautiously.

'Mother Abbess . . .' Robert murmured gently, his voice only just audible over the wind that shook the headland.

He was answered by a petulant snarl. 'What's this?'

'She's awake,' Robert nodded. Sheila made a slight grab for his arm and managed to contain the shriek that had risen unbidden with her gorge.

'Where am I?' gnashed the old lady, thrusting her head out of the case. 'Where have you brought me?'

'The abbey. Like we said.'

'Where is Frederick?' The abbess was starting to thrash about in her swaddling bands, and her voice was rising in awful panic. 'Where is my son? Oh, I'm weak . . . I can hardly . . . WHERE IS MY SON?'

Effie tried to calm her. 'He isn't here, he—'

'But I never go anywhere without him! How can you take me out into the world without Frederick? What have you done?'

'But . . .' said Effie, 'I thought . . .'

'Take me back! Take me back at once to where Frederick is! I am not safe here!'

Robert didn't know what to do. 'She's having a hissy fit . . .'

'Jesus,' Sheila said. 'Shove the lid back on her.'

'Abbess, we don't have time to fetch Danby now,' Effie told her crossly. 'We brought you here so you could show us how to open the gateway. The Bitch's Maw. You did it last time. Do it again.'

The abbess kicked her tiny legs and shook her clenched fists in the air. 'But I thought you would bring my son! Who will look after me when you are gone? When you have descended into the Awful Deeps, who will I have then? I will be stranded here, and helpless . . .'

Robert had a sudden thought. 'Sheila, maybe you could stay here and look after her . . .'

'Uh-uh. No way. I don't like the look of her. Awful little thing. I'm coming with you lot. I'd rather go to hell than be stuck here with her.'

The abbess threw back her head and screeched: 'Where is my son?'

'This is just great.' Effie groaned. 'Why didn't we think?'

'Take me home at once!'

Robert clicked his fingers. 'I've got it. Abbess, if we could let your son know where you are, would you be okay with that? Would you still send us through the gateway? If we could guarantee he would come and get you?'

She stared up at him, her dark eyes swarming with mistrust. 'I would still be alone here for some time. Vulnerable in the night.'

'But not for long,' Robert pointed out. 'He would come straight away for you, I am sure . . .'

'How will you bring him here?' the nun snapped.

Effie was losing her nerve. 'It's all going wrong,' she moaned. 'Before we've even done anything, it's all gone completely wrong.'

Sheila elbowed her. 'Ssh, Effie. Robert's obviously got an idea of some kind.'

Robert was already getting on with it. He had his mobile out and was jabbing musically at the buttons. 'I'm going to ring him.'

'Ring him?' The abbess didn't know what he was talking about.

'It's a phone-in show, isn't it? I'm going to ring in and tell them: you'd better put me straight through. It's a matter of the gravest importance. And I'll tell him we've got his mother.'

Phoning In

'I'm sorry, caller, but who on earth are you? What do you mean, you've got my mother?'

'You know who we are. You know that we are desperate.'

'Err, I'm not sure I believe you, actually. And what do you think you're doing, phoning in and saying awful things like that? What are you after, money?'

'We need your help, Frederick Danby. We need you to come at once.'

'It may have escaped your notice, young man, but I'm hosting a radio talk show just now . . .'

'If you don't come, we will simply have to take your old mother with us where we're going. And I don't think you'd like that.'

'Look, how do I know you aren't lying to me? How do I know you've really got my mother?'

'I'll put her on the line. Hold on.'

'Hullo? Are you still there, caller?'

'Frederick? What are you playing at?'

'M-Mother?'

'Come at once! He's telling the truth, Frederick. They've got me captive. They've dragged me all the way across town to the gateway, and they are desperate. They'll leave me out here . . . or worse, take me with them . . . Frederick, you have to come!'

'It really is you, Mother! The gateway, you say? Mother . . .?'

'Effie Jacobs here, Mr Danby. Now, you know me. You know I don't mess about. We've got her here and she's going to help us sort out this mess with Brenda. Now you'd better get over here . . .'

'All right, all right . . . I believe you . . .'

Là-Bas

Sheila stared at them. 'Now you've gone and told all of Whitby where we are!'

'Doesn't matter,' Effie snapped. She tossed Robert's mobile back to him. 'We'll be gone soon, won't we?' She returned her attention to the occupant of the leather suitcase. 'Now, Mother Abbess, we need to find this thing again . . .'

With an almost inaudible grumble, the tiny woman agreed to help with the final stages of their descent into the underworld. They had to spend some minutes hacking and yanking at the tangled bushes and matted grass that stood around the base of the ruins, until at last a ruined doorway was revealed. To the unsuspecting eye it was hardly a doorway. Just a dark patch. A ragged aperture. No one in their right mind would think to clamber into it, surely, and explore the dank abscess beneath the abbey stones.

'Is this how you remember it, Effie?' Robert asked, peering into the narrow gap. It was rimed with frost, and as he touched it, the stone felt sticky under his fingers.

'Just about.' Effie frowned. She was wearing her expert face, just as she did whenever she was called upon to talk about antiques and nick-knacks. 'That time, of course, we had Alucard with us. He'd pulled a fast one on us. Well, on me, at any rate. Brenda never trusted the old devil. He was pretending to be all lovey-dovey with me, but all he was after really were the old books in my back parlour, one of which revealed the location of this gateway . . .'

'I remember. Brenda told me the whole thing,' Robert said. 'Mind, it's not that hard to find, is it? Just a few old bushes in front.'

Effie looked for a moment as if she was having second thoughts as she stared at the dark patch in the wall. 'I never thought we'd all be looking for it again, and jumping into the Maw ourselves . . .'

The abbess gave a small cough and pointed out to them, 'You know, I cannot help you, once you are down there.'

'That's all right,' said Effie brusquely. 'I didn't think you would. We can look after ourselves.'

'You're very brave, Effie.' Sheila was short of breath and on the verge, she thought wildly, of having a funny turn. 'We don't know what to expect, do we?'

Effie pulled a face. 'Brave indeed. Foolhardy. I don't know what's become of me. I used to be so sensible.' She sighed deeply. 'Ah, well. Time we were off to meet our destiny. Through the hole in the wall. Come on. Robert, have you got a lighter?'

'Better than that. Pen torch. I like to come prepared for these dos nowadays . . .'

Effie flashed him a rare, encouraging smile. 'Excellent, dear.'

Robert went first. He trained the slim beam of his torch into the hole and led the way very cautiously. For a second he fretted about Sheila's chances of squeezing her voluptuous form through the gap, but soon he saw that the tunnel beyond was wider than it seemed. Once past the obscure opening, the cavity in the abbey wall slipped beneath ground level and became altogether more roomy.

The hidden passage was still a nasty, slimy, rather forbidding place, however. Their party crouched and slithered and clung together as they advanced underground, and they could feel their flesh creep with every step as the cloying cold took hold of them and began to seep into their still living, trembling bones.

On our way to hell, Robert thought. And buried alive. The ground is reaching out for us. Sucking us down to the underworld. He pictured goblins, ghouls. The roasting pits and pyres of hell. Demons and . . .

'I'm sure it wasn't too far along.' Effie suddenly spoke up. Her tone was reassuringly normal.

The abbess was sitting up in Sheila's arms, looking perky and still rather vexed. 'We should have waited for my son.'

'He knows where to come,' Robert said. 'He will find you, don't worry.'

'He might have been of assistance,' said the abbess peevishly.

Effie snorted with laughter. 'Him? Of assistance? He's caused more bother in the past couple of years than anyone!' Then her tone became more intent as she demanded, 'Tell me, Abbess, why was he so keen on getting rid of Brenda?'

'I'm sorry . . .?'

'All his recent efforts,' Effie said, her voice hollow in the low tunnel. 'Setting people against her. Spreading stories about her. Saying on the radio that she's a demon-possessed monster, and so on. Colluding with Mrs Claus to—'

'I don't know what you're talking about,' the abbess snapped. 'What my son Frederick gets up to is his own business. He is a grown man. I don't know what he does.'

'Well, then, let me tell you. He's made poor Brenda's life a proper misery in recent weeks. He's been bad-mouthing her all round town. And really, if you think about it, the reason she's ended up in this ghastly situation is down to him in the end!'

'I don't believe you.'

'Ask him.' Effie was glad to get some of this off her chest. Perhaps the abbess could do something to sort out her wayward, horrible son. 'When he comes up here, you can ask him what he's got against Brenda.'

'But he knows that Brenda is vital. She is the one we need here, standing guard over the Bitch's Maw. He knows that . . .'

Robert said, 'Well, he obviously disagrees, the way he's been carrying on.'

The abbess's face crumpled in dismay. 'I don't understand. Frederick wouldn't disobey me. He would never do anything that went against my plans and wishes . . .'

'I think you'll find that's precisely what he's been up to,' Effie warned.

Now the abbess looked as if she was going to start wailing and gnashing her teeth again. 'Oh, it's so hard to know everything that's going on. I spend so much of my time in that suitcase, hardly knowing one day from an other. I can't keep track of things. And I'm so old now . . . my energies are so low . . . I am too dependent on Frederick . . . I can feel my control slipping . . .'

Sheila patted her on the head. 'Never mind, dear. We'll get Brenda back, you'll see.'

The abbess was struck dumb with fury. Never, in a whole millennium, had anyone patted her on the head like Sheila Manchu had just done.

Suddenly Effie was spreadeagled against the far wall, pressing her ear to it, listening intently. 'This looks like the place. This smoother wall. Yes . . .'

Then they could all hear the curious hum that she had picked up. A deep vibration. An ancient source of power. Something that seemed to go down into the heart of the black earth below, a sound that reached right into the heart of them all.

'Feel it,' said Effie, in a strangely excitable tone. 'It's alive with some form of demonic energy.'

The abbess was distracted from her mortification at being patted on the head. She nodded solemnly and told them, 'Yes. We are here. Stand back.' She slapped at Sheila's ample arms and told her to put her down. Then she set out, hobbling slightly, towards the wall, mumbling and muttering under her breath.

Secret words, Effie thought. Yes, and they were things that Alucard took from my books, too. That was why my library was of such importance to him. Not just the location; it was the words and the spells as well. They are what is needed to open up this Maw . . .

The wall ahead was glowing now. It was as if the rock was turning molten. It pulsated with scarlet, orange, black and a piercing gold. It ran in hot rivulets and bulged and seeped and wept joyfully: all the colours swimming into one as the wall swirled into a vortex. A whirlpool was opening up before them. A wormhole. A spiral that hypnotised them and filled them, head to toe, with the desire to go to hell. Alucard was drawn in, Effie remembered. She could see now how he had stood on the brink and gone unresisting as the abbess had consigned him to hell. He had been flung, twisting and turning through the hot flaming air into the world below. Her beloved, gone for good.

'Wow,' said Robert, so prosaically that it jolted Effie out of her reverie. 'That's impressive.'

'Oooh!' gasped Sheila.

Effie deliberately turned away from the coruscating Maw. She needed to concentrate, and the tumbling colours were distracting her. 'What worries me slightly is that when we were here last time . . . when you tricked Alucard, Abbess . . . he was pulled into that swirling wind. He was flung through the open skies, and it looked rather uncomfortable. At least he could fly. But I'm an old woman! I can't go flinging myself about, and doing acrobatics . . .'

'No, of course not.' The abbess nodded.

Both Robert and Sheila were still peering into the misty morass of the vortex. He was trying to see what lay beyond; where the spiral terminated, and where it would land them. 'I think I can make stuff out . . . shapes . . .'

Sheila was holding on to him, on tiptoes, 'We're above a landscape of some kind. Is that it? Is that hell?'

'That's it. You just have to step through the rock wall, now that it's fully melted away . . .'

'What about coming back?' said Effie sharply. 'How do we get back into our world?'

The abbess gave a small, nonchalant shrug. 'As you know, the Bitch's Maw is open to those in the know. You will find it again if you are meant to, and you will travel back to your own world.'

This didn't reassure Effie much. 'How can you be so sure?'

'Because you have to!' seethed the abbess. 'You simply have to succeed in this mission, Effryggia. If you do not, then you leave Whitby and the whole world unguarded. Hell will be able to disgorge itself willy-nilly on the earth.' Suddenly she sagged. Her face looked even more haggard in the hectic light. 'Now go. Leave me here for my traitorous son to find me. And take my blessings with you.'

'We will.' Effie nodded. She was mollified by the fact that the abbess clearly thought rescuing Brenda was a serious mission.

'What do we do?' asked Robert. 'Jump? Throw ourselves into that thing?'

All around them the rising noise of the Bitch's Maw seemed to chime off every particle in the air. It was a golden, trumpeting, heraldic noise. It was hard to concentrate on anything at all as the colours rushed and the notes from hell grew clearer, and more profound.

Effie was shouting. 'I don't know! Step through together . . . the three of us . . . hold hands . . . we'll go together.'

Sheila held out her hands, but she was quivering with suppressed hysteria. 'Will it be flames? Like they used to say in church? The priest used to tell us there'd be fires and . . .'

'It doesn't feel like that . . .'

'Come on! Together!' Effie urged wildly.

Then the abbess was struck by a rather useful thought. 'Take the escalator! There's an escalator right in front of you! Step out on to the escalator!'

At first Effie couldn't believe her ears. Then she looked down at her feet. Straight ahead of them was the sliding steel grille of the first step of an escalator. It slid effortlessly away from her and then plunged calmly into the chaos below. There was even a banister rail on either side to cling on to. Effie screeched with relief that she wouldn't have to go flinging herself anywhere. 'She's right! There's an escalator! Come on! This way!'

Sheila and Robert hopped on to the moving stairway with her, and the transition, their odyssey, felt smooth and painless. 'We're going! We're really doing it!'

The noise around them whipped up even more keenly, like a

tempest of music and light. Their high, triumphant voices were drowned out as they descended, clutching the shining banisters.

'Goodbye, Abbess!' cried Sheila Manchu, to the diminishing and vanishing figure at the top.

'We'll be back!' promised Effie.

The abbess's voice still reached them. 'You must succeed! Be brave, my friends! You must be braver than you've ever been before!'

The noise of the gateway reached an ear-popping climax in the stuffy confines of the tunnel. Then abruptly it cut off, and the abbess nodded with satisfaction. The Maw had closed once more. The melting wall before her became just bare rock again.

'There,' said the abbess, her body thrumming with the infernal energies it had absorbed, even from that tiny glimpse of the world below. 'Gone. Gone to hell.'

She had barely a second to recover when there came the clattering, stumbling noise of someone coming up the tunnel behind her. She turned, scowling, to see that it was who she expected it to be.

'Mother? Are you there? Mother!'

'I am here, Frederick.'

He came to a stop before her, staring at her worriedly. 'I came as quickly as I could. I abandoned my show. I ran to the East Cliff . . .'

'Good,' she said, without much enthusiasm. 'I am glad you are here.'

Mr Danby peered around, blinking into the darkness. To his mother he looked blind, useless, molelike. 'Where are they? The ones who had you captive. Oh, they're a ruthless lot . . .'

'They did what they had to do,' she told him.

'Did you . . . send them away?'

'I did what I had to do.'

'You sent them down to hell.' He gave a wet grin. He could barely contain his triumphant glee. 'Well done. Best place for them, I'd have thought. But . . . they went willingly?'

'Oh yes, quite willingly.'

'Strange . . .' Now Danby was keen to go home. This fetid, wormy place wasn't the kind of joint he hung around in. He and his mother deserved better than this foul hole. He remembered: he had all of Brenda's house to himself now. Her home was his. And Effie's, too. And everything both homes contained. Surely all of that fell to him now. Danby was shaking in his patent leather shoes with pleasure at the very thought of this.

The abbess gestured regally at her suitcase. 'Come, you must carry me home again. I am worn ragged by the evening's exertions. Hurry, Frederick.'

Danby stared in horror as the abbess tottered and staggered drunkenly. 'Mother!'

She clutched at her wattled throat as if she could hardly draw air. 'I . . . I . . .!'

Danby hurried to support her. He felt clumsy and useless. 'What is it?'

'It's too much. I . . . The effort of opening up the gateway tonight . . . I'm not strong enough . . .'

She struggled briefly in his arms, then gave a sharp and terrible cry. Danby stood impotent. He didn't know what he could do to help her. She groaned suddenly.

And then the old abbess was dead.

'Mother!' he cried, disbelieving at first. 'Mother! You can't . . .!' Come back to me! Mother!'

As he clutched her almost weightless body to him, he thought wildly: Now we're all stuck . . .

Brenda

It must have been her third or fourth morning in that place. She was losing track of the days. She didn't know where she was. They hadn't let her out of the room. It was about six feet by four. Hardly room to turn around. A horrible little bunk, stale-smelling. There was a window, high up. Raggy bit of pale curtain hanging down. That was the one smear of light during the short daylight hours.

Where was she? Who had brought her here?

She spent quite a lot of time each day banging on the heavy wooden door, which refused to budge.

'Let me out! Let me out, you bastards!' She sank down on the nasty bunk in torpor. I'm turning feral, she thought. I'm hitting things and swearing at people I can't even see.

Her strength was depleted. She felt like a bag of bones. In her prime she could have smashed that door apart. She could have smashed the whole place apart. No one could ever keep her prisoner, not for long. Except now, perhaps, she thought miserably. She had been defeated. She could feel the hopelessness welling up in her, threatening to take her over at last.

Then the guard came in with a tray of not very tempting tea.

'Wait! You have to tell me—'

'We don't have to tell you anything. Eat this.'

'I'm not eating any more of that muck.'

'Then you'll starve.' He turned to go. She squinted at him, trying to make out his features, his uniform.

'Tell me where I am!'

'Obvious, isn't it?'

'I . . . I thought I knew.'

The guard smiled at her nastily. 'Usually it's the most obvious answer that's the right one. That's what I find. The first thing that comes into your head.'

'In that case . . .'

'You know in your bones where you are. You know, don't you?'

'Someone must have rescued me. I remember . . . coming to the very edge of the cliff. I remember being at the brink . . . and the world swaying wildly about me. I didn't know which way was up or down. I was about to fall. To plummet to my death. Someone must have . . .'

The guard chuckled. 'Saved you in the nick of time?'

'They must have. Or maybe . . . I fell . . . Yes, I remember falling. I do remember that. Did I somehow survive the fall? I wasn't dashed to bits on the rocks below? Did they find me alive? Did they . . .?'

'What do you think? What do you think your chances were?'

'I don't know.' Brenda pressed her hands to her face, as if feeling for damage. 'I know I am strong. I am hard to kill.'

'Yes, that's true. That's very true.'

'But the clifftop was very high. The sea was so violent that night. And him! What about him? We were fighting, hand to hand. We were like crazy people. Like animals. Tearing at each other. Biting each other. Clinging together . . . Did he fall, too?'

'Yes,' said the guard. 'He fell.'

'And . . . is he dead?'

'He is as alive as you are.'

'Oh. I see. But that hardly answers my question. Where am I? Where have you brought me? And is he here too? Are you keeping him prisoner as well?'

'No. He is not a prisoner. Just you.'

'Why?' She was startled by the rising panic in her own voice. 'What do you want with me?'

'You'll have to see.'

'People have tried to hold me captive before, you know. There are those who have tried to prise away my secrets for profit. They want to know how I tick. Those who were ghoulishly fascinated by me. Is that why I'm here?'

The guard was wryly amused by this. 'Not exactly.'

'Then WHY? Why can't I just go home?'

'Your home's a long way away now. You're not going back there.'

She felt a sob lodge in her throat. 'What?' Suddenly the darkness about her seemed absolute. She looked at her guard and couldn't even pick out his sneering features any more.

'Don't upset yourself,' he told her. 'Don't get yourself worked up. Cheer up, Brenda. You've got big, exciting things coming your way.'

She hardly dared to ask him: 'What things?'

The guard turned to leave. But before he slammed and bolted the door again he jeered at her, saying: 'You're getting married in the morning . . .'

Strange Arrival

Snow was whirling down over the headland. It settled and drifted in the remains of the abbey, smoothing its crevices and tattered edges. The sky over Whitby raged and heaved, as if in protest at some cataclysmic breach; some curious forbidden thing going on behind the scenes.

The townspeople were deaf to the storm lashing their headland and the wet black cliffs. Tonight they were celebrating and thronging the narrow streets in full festival garb. Even the howling, thrashing sea in the harbour, setting the moored boats bobbing and threatening to tip, hardly caught their attention as they swanned about the town under the glowing lamps.

It was like this every night here. The party never ended from one day to the next. There was never any respite from the howling storms or the manic gaiety of the crowd. And the snow swept in from the north, softening the harshness of the rock and the crumbling ruins on the East Cliff.

Anyone straying in that direction this evening would have seen a very strange sight indeed. Seemingly out of nowhere and unprovoked, a small gap of clear blue sky opened up above the abbey. The storm clouds swept around it and were sucked into a brief swirling vortex that made the snow fall upwards for a minute or two, and the winds blow backwards. And then a gleaming silver escalator descended from the sky, very efficiently and neatly, bearing the forms of three rather startled-looking passengers.

'There's the ground! We've almost made it! Hold on, ladies!' one of them was shouting.

'Snowing! It's snowing!' cried another, clasping herself to the clunky banister.

The mechanical steps eased themselves gently to the frosty ground and sizzled there where they met the snow. The escalator shunted and whirred and delivered its two older ladies and one young man safely at their destination. They swayed there uncertainly for a second or two, as the snow pelted down around them. The three gazed up at the turbulent sky and the familiar ruins and tried hard to get their bearings.

'It's not really what you expect, is it?' said Effie at last.

They turned as one as a weird noise erupted behind them, and watched the escalator retreating into the sky. Its work now was finished and it shrank back up into the vortex, which gave a final lurid flourish and was gone.

'We did it! We're here!' gasped Effie, shivering violently.

'But . . .' said Sheila. 'But it's . . .'

Robert frowned. 'It's freezing, I know that much.'

Sheila wouldn't be deterred from explaining what she had noticed upon first stepping down into this new world. 'But . . . look! The stones . . . the abbey ruins. The lights over there, over the harbour. Don't you see?'

Effie wrinkled her nose. 'Hmmm. How strange.'

Sheila cried out with frustration and disappointment. 'We're still here! We're still at home! We haven't moved at all! We're right back where we started from!'

'No, I don't think so,' Robert said, quite calmly.

'But look! That's Whitby down there. Still! There's the West Cliff and . . . what's this? It's a ruddy great big abbey!' She threw out her arms wildly.

'It's different,' Robert insisted. He could sense it. He could feel something altered about the air, about the wind that lashed around them. 'We are in a different place, Sheila.'

'It's a swizz!' Sheila shouted above the storm. 'It's a rotten swizz! We haven't gone anywhere at all!'

Effie shook her head briskly. 'On the contrary. I think we have made a considerable journey.'

'What?'

The older woman tutted with impatience. 'Look at the abbey. It's different, isn't it? There's more of it, for one thing.'

'God, you're right,' said Robert, peering through the hectic darkness.

'Maybe,' Sheila conceded.

Effie started stumping off through the thick, crusted snow. She led the way to the brow of the tall hill, to where they could observe the rooftops of the town. 'No indeed,' she murmured. 'I think this is where we are supposed to be.'

'In hell?' warbled Sheila in a frightened voice, plodging heavily to keep up. 'This is hell?'

'I think so.'

Sheila gulped. 'And it looks just like home?'

Effie smiled bleakly. 'Who'd have thought it?'

'Look, ladies.' Robert announced his willingness to take charge of their expedition. 'We're going to freeze to death up here. The storm's getting worse.'

Effie turned to him. 'What do you suggest?'

'Well,' he said, thinking fast. 'At least if this *is* hell, we know our way around already. Let's find a place where we can have a sit and get warm, and think . . .'

Sheila's eyes bulged slightly. 'Our homes! Are our homes here in hell, do you think?' Her long white hair and her flimsy outfit were billowing around uselessly, making her look even more helpless and alarmed than ever.

Their homes? Robert wondered. 'I don't know,' he said.

'So, are we dead then? Are we dead now?' Sheila had a catch of panic in her voice, which both her companions noticed.

'I really don't know,' Effie said stiffly, and continued to walk through the frosty grass.

'There's so much to think about,' Sheila moaned to herself. Suddenly she felt very alone in this new yet familiar place. The wind was howling at their backs as they wandered away from the abbey, towards St Mary's Church and the top of the hundred and ninety-nine steps. They would be tricky to negotiate in this storm. Sheila was saying, 'Maybe we should have thought about it all a bit more before we came here.'

'It's too late now,' Effie pointed out.

Robert, who was a little way ahead by now, striding along on his younger, stronger legs, suddenly called out: 'Look! Come and see!'

He was standing on the top step. All of Whitby was laid out before them, rather grandly, on both sides of the harbour. 'What is it?' Effie asked, hurrying forward.

'All of Whitby,' he said. 'All lit up like it's Christmas.'

'Perhaps it *is* Christmas here,' she said. 'Perhaps it's Christmas every day in hell.'

Sheila said, 'It looks familiar, but . . .'

'But strange,' Effie finished for her. She gathered herself up and prepared to descend the perilously frosty steps. 'Come on, you two, we've got to find somewhere to get warm, at least.'

Elf Imprisonment

There came the sudden clanking of chains, unbolting of locks, and squealing of the cell door.

Brenda cried out into the swarming darkness: 'I'm not going anywhere until you tell me where I am.'

Her guard was brusque. 'You've got no choice. You've got to come with me.'

'Where? Where are you taking me?' She was forced along, with shuffling steps, out of her cell and into some kind of dimly lit corridor. She trembled inside her heavy chains. 'At least take all this gubbins off me.'

'No chance.'

'They're hurting me. Could you loosen them, please?'

'And have you turn violent on me?' The guard gave a sour laugh. 'I've been warned about you.'

'Warned about me?'

He nodded, and gave her a shove. 'How you can turn nasty. Violent. You're stronger than you look.'

She felt tears boiling up. Frustration, more than anything. Despair hard on its heels. 'Not right now, I'm not strong. Not after being cooped up in there.'

'C'mon. Get a shift on. The mistress wants to see you.'

Instantly Brenda's attention was piqued. 'The mistress, eh? And who might that be?'

He smirked. 'You'll see.'

They turned a corner and emerged into a corridor of scarlet flock wallpaper and fluttering gas-fired wall lamps. At first Brenda thought she was imagining things, but she could hear music. Was that right? Some kind of tinkly, shimmering, distant music. She turned to her captor in the guttering flame-light and studied his jowly, expressionless face. He was younger than she'd imagined. And familiar.

'I couldn't see you properly before. Now I can.'

'So?'

'You're an elf. You're dressed as an elf . . .'

And now the music insinuating itself into Brenda's head was quite obviously Christmas music. Sleigh bells and delicate, shivery chimes. Her gaoler was in a green and scarlet elf outfit, felty and smirched with muck. He scowled at her. And now she knew exactly where she was.

A Horrible Epiphany

As they negotiated the – in places – treacherous steps into the old town, they would look up now and then at sparkling Whitby. The snow still swirled about them, and the noise of celebration pushed at them, drawing them in, down from the hill.

'It really is home,' Sheila said, clinging to the wooden balustrade.

'I've lived in this town a very long time. All my life,' Effie said, and her voice was full of foreboding and gloom. 'My family has been here for hundreds of years. And this isn't quite the same place. Not really.'

Robert said, 'But it looks like it . . . and smells like it, and feels like it . . .'

'Curiouser and curiouser.' Effie smiled wryly at him. 'Yes. In some ways it feels and looks and smells more like the place than even the real place does . . .'

Robert pointed over the rooftops. 'Down in the harbour, look.' He could hardly believe what he was seeing. A strange, denuded forest of masts, clustered at the docks. 'Tall fishing vessels . . . whaling ships . . .'

Effie gave a sort of thoughtful growl, pulling her coat lapels tighter and shivering. 'And the abbey partially restored back there. It's like a jumbled-up version of the place . . .'

'Still bleeding cold, though,' Sheila pointed out pragmatically. 'That wind's whipping up a bit. Can we find somewhere warmer to sit and take stock?'

So they made their way down the remainder of the sweeping curve of the steps to stand on the downward-sloping cobbled streets of the East Cliff. Here the houses leaned in close and all the warrenlike passageways emerged into the cobbled thoroughfare. They saw people out and about, late at night . . . Was there some festival going on? Was this fancy dress? There was such a strange mixture of ancient and modern dress – Victorian bustles and wing collars and the rough weave of ancient peasant garb. They even spied a few hairy, horned Vikings striding about through the festive crowd.

It was a strange historical jamboree that thronged the streets that night. People were laughing and singing and cramming their faces with sweets and hot fried delicacies from the stalls in the marketplace. It made their own town seem rather sedate by comparison.

'The Walrus and the Carpenter,' Robert pointed out happily. The bay windows had been given a fresh coat of orange and pink, it seemed, and the glass panes glowed welcomingly. 'It's open, look. Even this late in the evening.'

Inside it was as busy and noisy as it was on any of its heaviest days. Only one table was free. Luckily it was Effie's favourite one, by the window. She squeezed ahead, and sat down with some relief.

'Oh, thank God,' Sheila said. 'I feel like we've been travelling for hours.'

'All we've done really,' said Robert, 'is go up the hill and back down . . .'

Effie's eyes were piercing as she turned her bright gaze on him. 'It's considerably further than that, young man.' Her whole face seemed lit up and excited, as she drank in the details of their new environment.

'It's so busy!' Sheila smiled. 'Do you think it's like this every night in hell? It seems so jolly!' A shadow of doubt passed across her face. 'What have they got to celebrate?'

Robert had gone rigid in his seat. He was staring past the tables, into the furthest recesses of the café, by the kitchen door. 'No . . . it can't be . . .'

Effie was alarmed by his expression. 'What is it, Robert?'

'The waitress,' he said in a strangled voice. 'She's just come in from the kitchen, look. *Look who it is!*'

Sheila – whose eyesight had never been very good – was getting up out of her seat and squinting. 'Who is it? What's going on?'

Suddenly Effie could see the reason for Robert's agitation. 'Oh!'

He had gone white. 'It's her! It's my Aunt Jessie!' With that, he jumped to his feet and wriggled past their table, knocking over his chair as he went.

As he hurried to the rear of the room, there was something of a stir amongst the other patrons of the café (more Victorian bustles, more peasant garb and Viking helmets laid aside). Robert was pushing and shoving and causing a kerfuffle in a way he wasn't used to. But he had to see if he was right. Was he hallucinating, even?

He took hold of the waitress's arms. 'Jessie, Jessie . . . it's me!'

The woman turned, startled, to stare up into his face. She shook her head in confusion. 'R-Robert?'

He yelled out in delighted relief. 'You're alive! You're here, I mean . . . and you're back to normal! Back to your old self!'

Then their gabbling voices were muffled as aunt and nephew embraced clumsily, while the whole café watched on.

'But Robert . . .' she said at last, her pleasure turning to dismay. 'You can't be here . . . How are you here?'

He couldn't believe how amazing she looked. She was like his old Aunt Jessie. Young again, vital. Nothing in the slightest wrong with her. Her skin was unlined and glowing with health. Her hair was sleek and auburn and only on her head. Her limbs were straight, untwisted. Her hands were dainty and not equipped with razor-sharp claws. 'Look at you!' he gasped. 'You survived! You returned to your proper form!'

She looked astonished at this. 'My proper form?'

'Don't you remember?' he asked. 'When you were . . . transformed?'

'Was I?'

He was starting to feel self-conscious and confused. He struggled to explain. 'After that business at The Deadly Boutique, you were changed . . . You went back and became a womanzee!'

'A what?' She looked mortified for a second, and shook her head to clear it of the terrible images his words were beginning to conjure. 'It's all a bit vague in my mind, to be honest . . . how I came to finish my life on earth and end up here. I don't remember much at all. It was a bit confusing.' Now she looked tearful, and Robert felt his heart go out to her. 'I just know I didn't get a proper chance to say goodbye to you . . .'

He grinned. 'Now we're here! Me and Effie and Sheila Manchu . . . Look, they're at the window table over there!'

Jessie looked, but didn't react how he expected. She didn't look in the slightest bit glad. Her face fell abruptly. 'Oh, but that's terrible . . .'

'What? Why terrible?'

Aunt Jessie's face had gone white. Her voice had turned hollow.

She looked up at him as if she was caught in the middle of a horrible epiphany. 'But . . . if you're here, then you're all dead. You're as dead as I am, if you're here now . . .'

The Grotto

Suddenly Brenda said, 'I know who you are now. I remember your face.'

Her guard smirked like he couldn't care less. 'Is that a fact?'

'Martin,' she said. 'Martin the elf. I saw you die, Martin. I saw you killed, out on the sands. You were torn to pieces by Jessie the womanzee, right before my eyes, when she was running about on a rampage.' Brenda still had nightmares about that night, back in the spring. And yet here he was, acting all tough and nonchalant about it.

'Dunno what you're on about, Brenda.' He carried on loping down the endless corridor. Brenda had no choice but to go with him, and as they went along, the music was getting louder.

'Oh, I think you do know, Martin. You used to be a friend of Robert's. And it was you who was saying that all the elves at the Christmas Hotel were enslaved and kept that way because of the drugs Mrs Claus fed you in the cocoa, keeping you all passive and obedient. And you were doing terrible things for her . . . Don't you remember? You met with me, on the pier, and you confessed to murdering for your mistress. You killed Rosie Twist the journalist, the editor of *The Willing Spirit* . . .'

'I don't remember anything about that.'

'How are you still up and about, Martin? What are you doing here?' She shook her head. Was she in a terrible trance? Had she gone mad? 'I saw you ripped to shreds . . . torn limb from limb . . .'

He tossed his head arrogantly. 'That's hardly possible, is it?'

Brenda narrowed her eyes. 'That depends.'

He came to a halt. 'Hush now. We're here.' They were standing before an ornately carved door, painted white and gold. Before Brenda could say anything, Martin rapped on it smartly and a voice from within called out to them.

'Enter!'

The door squealed open and they were admitted into what Brenda could only describe as a grotto. This was the source of the Christmas music they had been hearing, and in the tinsel-strewn heart of it sat a partially familiar figure.

'I've brought her as requested, mistress. Bound in chains, like you said.'

Mrs Claus bowed her head in a regal fashion. 'Very good, Martin.' She beamed. Then she got up out of her golden chair and swept across the room towards them, trailing her emerald skirts behind her in a most becoming fashion. She studied her new guest carefully, enjoying the prisoner's startled reaction. 'We don't want to be taking any chances with Brenda. We don't want her on the loose. She packs a hefty wallop. Good evening, Brenda.'

Brenda squawked: 'Mrs Claus!'

The young woman smiled warmly. 'You seem very surprised, dear.'

Brenda was frozen to the spot, her eyes just about on stalks. 'You're walking about! You're young and slim . . .'

Mrs Claus looked down at herself, almost absent-mindedly. She examined her own svelte form, and put one unlined hand up to her cheek, where it briefly touched the eggshell smoothness of her face. 'Ah yes, you're right. I'm quite different from the Mrs Claus you know on earth, aren't I? I rather prefer this aspect of me. Shall I give you a twirl?' She did so, flaring out her velvet dress.

'"This aspect" . . .?' Brenda asked haltingly.

Mrs Claus came to a standstill and laughed at her confusion. 'This is how I look in hell, Brenda. This is the hellish version of me.' She shrugged, as if it should all be obvious.

'What . . .?' Brenda gasped. All she could think was that it just wasn't fair. Here was another aspect of her enemy, and it was gorgeous. Typical.

'Oh, I'm extremely lucky, dear. I get to live in more than one world at once. That happens to very few souls. Hardly any, in fact. Isn't it a riot? I get to queen it over the Christmas Hotel on earth and in hell. And here it's all so much nicer. So much more festive.'

Brenda's shoulders slumped. She gazed down at the distressed remains of her own party frock and the rusted chains that still bound her. 'I'm really in hell, then. That's where I've ended up.'

'Oh yes indeed, my dear.' Mrs Claus nodded enthusiastically. She went back to her throne, flung herself down, and started to jab a wooden fork into a box of Turkish Delight. 'After that fall from the cliff there was no chance you were ever going to survive. You're quite, quite dead. And here you are! Isn't it wonderful?'

Brenda narrowed her eyes. 'What was Martin talking about earlier? About getting married in the morning?'

'He was always a dreadful blabbermouth.' Mrs Claus rolled her eyes.

'What did he mean?'

Mrs Claus patted the chair next to her. She tried to put on a friendly, compassionate face, but failed dismally. 'Come and have a sit. Sherry and Turkish Delight. Clank your chains over here . . .'

'Tell me what he meant!'

Mrs Claus paused for a beat. It was no good. The woman was going to be difficult, and demanding. She would simply have to be told the truth. She smiled again and said, 'Frank is here too, dear. He brought you here. It's him you're going to marry, of course. At last! At last! And he can hardly wait!'

His Strangely Recovered Aunt

Jessie had completed her shift at The Walrus and the Carpenter and, though tired, she was bursting with enthusiasm at the thought of accompanying her friends across town. There was so much to show off to them. She wanted them to see it all, and appreciate the place like she did.

Out in the street, in amongst the festive crowds in all their finery, the three friends looked a bit cowed and worried by it all. Jessie tried her best to seem reassuring as she led them down the hill, through the winding streets towards the harbour.

'Don't you like it more than the town you've left behind?' she asked. 'Don't you just love it here? Hasn't it got more life and pizzazz than the actual place we used to know?'

Robert frowned. It was actually quite difficult, squeezing through the crowd and keeping together as a bunch. He had to keep excusing himself between witches, Roman centurions, druids and Vikings. Not everyone was all that polite. 'I don't know, Aunt Jessie. I suppose you're right . . .' For a moment he was reminded of a trip to Venice he had once taken with his favourite aunt several years ago. Then, as now, she had led him through a chaotic fancy dress procession, just like this. He wondered if she was reminded of that same trip. But

Jessie was pushing on ahead, grinning and completely at home in the crowd.

Effie had come over all grumpy. She was at Robert's elbow saying, 'It's still hell, isn't it? At the end of the day, it's still not the best place to be.'

Jessie heard this and whirled around. She stopped in the middle of the crowd and shouted at them: 'Oh, you don't know anything yet. You've only just got here. I've been here several months now and I'm proper settled in. I've made a new life for myself, new friends . . . A whole new start! And look at me – young again!' She was sounding a bit like a religious convert, Robert thought sadly. It was like when she got in with the Jehovah's Witnesses for that year all over again. She was prey to these passing fancies. She was a Muslim for a bit, too. And a Goth.

Effie was staring at Jessie narrowly. 'I remember what trouble it caused last time you got yourself rejuvenated, Jessie.' Robert reflected that no one could pour cold water on silly fads like Effie could.

Sheila Manchu could never bear for people to fall out and have rows. Especially in public. For such a wanton-looking woman, she had quite a low embarrassment threshold. 'Sssh, now. Don't bicker, everyone,' she exhorted them. Then she spread her arms wide to take in the heaving vista of the bay. 'Look! Look at the harbour! Look at the beautiful ships!'

Effie wasn't going to be distracted by a nice view. She pursed her lips. 'Yes, it's very nice, Sheila. But I prefer my own Whitby, thank you very much. In the real world above.'

'Hm,' said Jessie, cross because Effie had done her best to squash her fabulous mood. 'Well, I think there are a few surprises in store for you, Effie Jacobs.'

Effie glared at her. 'And what do you mean by that?' She wasn't sure she liked this hellish version of Jessie that had been restored to them. It was like talking to someone gone silly on drugs.

'Oh,' Jessie said airily, 'pleasant surprises is what I mean. Look, I'm rather tired after my shift in the café. Why don't I head home and Sheila can come with me? I've a place just by her Hotel Miramar, so we can walk together. Robert, will you come along?'

Robert found himself instinctively drawing away from Jessie. Why was that? he wondered. But he trusted his intuition. He always did. And something was warning him away from this aunt of his, delighted though he still was to see her back alive. He frowned at his own reactions and struggled to think up a worthy excuse.

Effie helped him out. She announced, 'I'm going to see if my house is there. My shop. Is it . . . is it all the same?'

Jessie was making her irritation at Effie all too apparent. She shrugged. 'More or less.'

'And Brenda's B and B,' Effie went on. 'Is that there?'

Jessie looked bored by all these questions. 'Most places are the same. It's some of the occupants who are changed about, as I'm sure you can appreciate.' She flashed her eyes at Effie.

Robert stepped in. 'And is *she* here, Aunt Jessie? Is Brenda down here?'

Jessie tossed her shining auburn hair. 'Brenda? Why would she be here?'

Robert told her, lowering his voice, 'We got a message, after she . . . died . . .'

This brought Jessie up short. 'Brenda died?'

Sheila nodded sadly. 'She plummeted to her presumed death off of the West Cliff.'

'Just like you did, Jessie,' Effie added tactlessly.

'I see . . .' Jessie mused. 'And you had a message saying she was here?'

'A reliable message,' Effie said, 'passed on by one of her spare hands.'

'She had spare hands?'

Robert decided there wasn't time to start explaining about Brenda's spare parts. 'So you've never seen her down here?'

Jessie's expression darkened. 'I know quite a lot of what goes on here. I see most new arrivals. I've never seen Brenda. I'd have looked out for her. You know I was fond of her, in my earthly life.'

They knew she was sincere. She looked shocked at the idea of Brenda following her to hell. If Brenda was here, surely Jessie would be aware of it. A horrible feeling of uselessness stole over Robert. 'Oh no. Have we come here for nothing?'

This hurt Jessie's feelings. 'Not for nothing, I hope.'

He could have kicked himself. 'No, of course not. I'm cock-a-hoop to see you again, Auntie.' His heart twinged at her disappointed face. He went on, however: 'But you see, we came here thinking we'd find Brenda.'

This was something that Jessie just couldn't get her head round. 'What? You went and *killed* yourselves, just to see your friend again?' And she couldn't keep that note of envy out of her voice. No one killed themselves for me, she was thinking – Robert just knew it.

'No,' Effie sighed heavily, impatiently. 'We took the escalator. Right through the gateway to hell. The Bitch's Maw. You don't have to do anything as drastic as dying in order to get to hell, you know.' Effie was keen to show off her greater sophistication, just as she always had with Jessie.

'Is that a fact?' Jessie mused. 'Very interesting . . .'

Robert spoke up decisively, 'Auntie Jessie, I'm going with Effie to check out Brenda's B and B. She might just be there. That'd be amazing! She might have kept a low profile . . .'

They could all see that Jessie was miffed her nephew didn't want to stick with her. As usual, Sheila stepped into the breach, keen to mollify any hurt feelings. 'I'll walk with Jessie up the hill to my hotel.' She brightened considerably and made a pantomime show of amazement. 'My hotel in hell! I can't wait to see what it's like!'

Effie glanced at her. 'Hmmm. Just the same, I'd imagine. Well, why don't we reconvene there this evening?'

'We'll have to synchronise watches, then,' Jessie said. 'Time does funny things here. It's dark almost all of the time. Days are extremely short, and not always in the right place.'

'Does it always snow?' asked Robert brightly.

'Most often,' Jessie said stiffly. She still felt betrayed by him. Why was he more bothered about the whereabouts of Brenda than he was about his auntie who had just about raised him? Underneath her pragmatic, cool exterior, Jessie was seething. She went on, 'All right, seven o'clock, in the saloon bar of Sheila's hotel.'

Robert watched his aunt and Sheila link arms and shuffle away across the footbridge and further into town. They were deep in gossip, and soon swallowed up in the crowd.

Robert jumped as Effie leaned over to whisper in his ear, 'I know she's your auntie and everything, Robert . . .'

He turned to look at her cunning face. 'But you just don't trust her? I know, Effie. I could tell. The looks you were giving her! Up and down, like you were highly sceptical of the whole performance.'

She studied him, realising what was under the surface. 'You too?'

He looked unhappy. 'Oh, she's my aunt all right. I'm sure she is. But she's different. Strangely confident and settled. The Jessie I knew was an anxious woman. She'd been flattened and wrung out by disappointment. I don't know if this is a new, improved version, or a fake . . . I just don't know.' He flapped his arms helplessly.

'We shouldn't take anything we find here at face value,' Effie said, narrowing her eyes and glancing about. She wore a hunted expression.

'You're right.'

'Maybe none of it is real . . .' she added, as they started walking again, towards the harbour, weaving through the carnival.

'Oh, it's real all right,' he said. 'I can feel it. It's as real as home. I suppose I shouldn't be surprised, after some of the weird things we've seen in the past year or so.' He paused to look at the dark waters and the crazy reflections from the lit-up boats. 'But what about that? Another Whitby.'

'I think I'm dreading what I'll find in my own home,' admitted Effie.

'I'll come with you,' he told her staunchly. 'And to Brenda's.'

She patted his arm briskly. 'You're brave.'

'Perhaps.' Robert severely doubted it. When he thought about where they were, and what it was they thought they were doing, he felt sick inside. He thought about what his strangely recovered aunt had said. They had killed themselves to come here. They had given up their lives for some wild goose chase. Was that right? Were they really dead and buried here, in this dream version of home?

Mincemeat

Brenda said, 'He's gone to some lengths to get me, I must say.'

Mrs Claus smiled. 'He's devoted.'

'Plunging us both into the underworld . . .'

'Some men just don't know when to stop.'

Brenda shook her head resolutely. 'But it's no good.' She toyed with the tiny silver fork on her side plate. She had been brought a festive snack: a mince pie lathered in cream. She was ravenous but had stopped after a few bites because the mincemeat tasted peculiar. She sighed and told Mrs Claus, 'I won't have him. I don't feel anything for him.'

Mrs Claus's tone was impassioned. Why was she so bothered about it? Brenda wondered, not for the first time. 'But you must do, Brenda. You were made for each other, literally. After everything he's done . . .'

Brenda shrugged uncomfortably in her chains. 'He's done nothing but think about his own selfish needs and desires. I had a nice little life in Whibty, and he's ruined it for ever.'

'Tush. Melodrama.'

But Brenda went on, in her stride now. 'When we were up on that cliff and we were talking, at last, after all this time, I even thought, wouldn't it be wonderful if I really did feel something for him?' She surprised herself by thinking this, and saying it to the woman who was holding her prisoner. What was making her so candid? Was there something in that tiny bite of mince pie she'd taken? She continued, her voice wobbling as she said, 'What if I went all weak and gushy and was overcome by emotion at the sheer sight of him? What if he really was my Mr Darcy, my Rochester, my Lord Byron?'

'So you really thought that?' Mrs Claus chuckled decorously. 'A romantic after all, Brenda.'

Brenda glowered at her. 'But I didn't feel anything for him. Not a sausage.'

Mrs Claus pursed her shiny red lips. 'He would be gutted to hear that.'

'I'm sure he would. And there's worse.' Brenda's voice filled with horror. 'I looked at him and I was repelled by him. Revolted. I could see the stitches in his flesh. Where the skin had puckered and buckled and worn smooth in patches like old, badly tanned animal hide. He was everything about myself I most despise. He was inhuman.'

'Yes, yes. He is that. But there's so much more to him.'

Her sudden tenderness made Brenda suspicious. 'What is it with you, Mrs Claus? Why are you so bothered about Frank? What's your investment? You harboured him in your hotel. You plotted and schemed to reunite us . . .'

'I did, yes,' admitted the chic proprietress. 'I'm a romantic at heart too, you see.'

'Rubbish,' Brenda scoffed. 'You're a troublemaker. You just want to cause bother . . . and horror. And you hate me. You hate me and Effie. But why?'

Mrs Claus delicately picked up a forkful of her own mince pie and chewed thoughtfully at the golden pastry and the glistening meat. 'Hate is a very strong word.'

'But it's true!'

'Yes, I do hate you. And Effie.' Mrs Claus sighed prettily. 'I loathe the pair of you. I'd have had you both wiped out ages ago, for getting in the way of my schemes, if I'd known that you'd wind up here, in hell, still getting in my way. If I could, I'd kill you again, and again, and so you'd descend layer after layer, through world after world . . .'

'There are more worlds beneath this one?' Brenda gasped.

'You really know nothing, do you? There are worlds and worlds, ever deeper, ever darker. It's easy to get lost in them, Brenda. Infinite Whitbys – just think about it – right under your great, clodhopping feet.' She waved her silver fork in the air as she described this vertiginous state of being, and then picked up a glass of ruby-red port.

'No . . .' Brenda was trying to picture it all. Her tired mind was swimming.

'Perhaps I shall do something truly wicked.' Mrs Claus grinned. 'I shall kill you and kill you and kill you . . . sending you down and down and down for ever more, quite lost in all the levels of hell . . .'

As Mrs Claus quaked with laughter, Brenda became aware of another sound in the room. There was a creak of floorboards. A whisper of movement behind the silk Chinese screen in the corner. Mrs Claus was becoming hysterical, and the person hiding in the corner of the room was stepping out of his cramped position to confront Brenda himself.

Brenda didn't breathe for a few moments as Frank emerged. He straightened up and strode, almost formally, across the room. 'No. Mrs Claus, stop taunting her.'

Mrs Claus wriggled with awful glee. 'Oh, but I'm enjoying it so much.'

Frank wasn't amused by these shenanigans. 'Leave her alone. You'll disorient her. You'll send her mad . . .'

Brenda stared at him. He seemed huge, standing in the centre of Mrs Claus's fancy boudoir. He was in his customary black, with a long, tattered coat and huge workmen's boots. Everything he wore seemed mouldy and grey. Everything looked as if it had been stolen from a grave. He was standing there in dead men's things, with a whiff of mildew on his breath. Brenda was shaking. 'Frank!' she said hoarsely. 'You've been in here the whole time.'

He nodded. 'Listening to every word of your interview, yes. Frank heard every word.'

She flushed with shame. He had heard her say some terrible things. She would never have wanted him to hear some of those things. How he repelled her. She swallowed hard. Her mouth felt thick with sugary cream and the strange tang of that mincemeat. She said, 'Get me out of here, Frank. Get me away from this woman.'

Frank looked at Mrs Claus. 'Let me unchain her.'

'She's dangerous.'

Frank's eyes burned like embers, furious and seductive. 'Yes, and so am I. You've gone too far. I'm setting Brenda free.'

'Free!' shrilled Mrs Claus, kicking off one of her shoes and taking a large swig of sticky port. She watched with a frozen, nasty expression on her face as Frank fiddled with the clunky chains, freeing Brenda. Two high red spots of pure pique appeared on Mrs Claus's delicate cheeks. She stuffed her face with another pie. 'Did you enjoy the mince pie, Brenda?' She grinned. 'Did you recognise the taste?'

Brenda shook her head. What was the woman on about? Then an awful thought struck her. 'What do you mean?'

'Maybe you should have one too, Frank. You knew him better than she did. Harry Timperley. Seriously. He's in the mincemeat, all ground up and spicy and delicious.'

'Balls,' Frank grunted, and yanked away the last of Brenda's chains.

Mrs Claus shrugged. 'Your friend Mr Timperley makes exceedingly good cakes.'

Brenda looked worriedly at her side plate, and then at the silent Frank.

Bleak House

Brenda's side passage was a lot less hospitable than her friends were used to. The wind howled along the streets of the old town, eddying and gusting in the ginnels, and bringing the snow to smother the narrow entrances.

Effie banged hard on Brenda's door, her knuckles chapped and freezing red.

'There's no answer,' Robert said, with his ear flat against the woodwork.

'Give her time.'

'I don't know,' he said, raising his voice above the wind, as it tried to snatch and whirl his words away. 'It just doesn't look inhabited, does it? Look at the colour of her net curtains, for example. Muck!'

'Hmmm. Oh, I felt sure we'd catch up with her here. Can you imagine?' Effie still tried to sound hopeful.

Robert shook his head. 'Too easy. It's never as easy as that.'

'I suppose. This whole place gives me the willies. Does it you?'

'Yeah. And I don't like the way that Sheila . . . and my Aunt Jessie are just so *into* it. It's like they want to *like* hell . . . like they can't see what it really is.' He shuddered.

'Maybe we're the weird ones,' Effie mused. 'Maybe we just

don't see its attraction. Maybe it *is* better than home, after all.'

'Shouldn't think so. I mean, it's hell, isn't it? There's bound to be some kind of catch . . .'

Effie suddenly gave up banging on the door. She was impatient, frozen to the bone. 'There're always catches, wherever you go. Look, Brenda's not at home. There's no one in there.'

Robert suddenly said, 'I've still got the key. Should work . . .'

And so, minutes later, the two of them were creeping once more into Brenda's empty rooms at the top of the house. This time there was something truly desolate about her home. The objects were the same. The furnishings and pictures were identical. But there was something terribly lonely and spiritless about the place.

'I hate seeing it all dusty and deserted like this. Brenda always has it spotless, and so welcoming . . .'

Robert was perplexed by the mirror-image aspect of the interior. 'How does that work?' he asked aloud.

Effie said, 'I wonder if her spare parts are the same in the attic. Her old treasures in the safe . . .'

'The wall safe's hanging open. Is that how we left it at home?' Robert moved over towards the metal door.

'I hope not. Look, all her precious knick-knacks hanging out . . .'

'Have robbers been in, do you think?'

'Don't know.' Effie busied herself with tidying Brenda's souvenirs, laying them very carefully back inside the safe. She picked up one desiccated article and dangled it before her. 'Here's the monkey's paw. Horrid thing.'

'Pop it in your bag,' Robert urged her, staring at the leathery fingers and their tiny blackened nails.

'What? Why? For a back-scratcher?'

'Might be useful. It was meant to grant wishes, wasn't it?'

'Oh, Robert.' Effie sighed. 'You do get carried away. It's just a nasty old relic.'

'Put it in your bag.'

'Oh, all right.'

Then Robert was fiddling with paper and pencil on the breakfast bar. 'I'll leave her a note on the kitchen counter. Just in case she turns up.'

Effie couldn't help thinking he was being far too optimistic. For herself, she couldn't imagine the Brenda she knew simply swanning back into this room and filling it with light and life. It felt too empty and lost.

And now, so did Effie.

A Bit Like Xanadu

The Hotel Miramar was lit up purple and gold at the top of the hill, past the museum and the tall Georgian houses. On the route out of town it glowed like a sultan's palace as Sheila and Jessie approached.

Sheila slowed her pace, astonished by the sight. 'Just look at that!'

'I think it looks wonderful,' Jessie said.

'Don't you think it's a bit vulgar?' asked Sheila worriedly.

'What's vulgar about it? It looks like an oriental palace from . . . I don't know, an old storybook. Something out of the *Arabian Nights* . . . Or "Kubla Khan". Xanadu. They made us memorise that, at school.'

Sheila stared at her home. 'But who's in charge? I mean, it's my hotel, but . . .'

'Come on,' said Jessie decisively, grasping Sheila's plump arm. 'I'll go in with you.'

'You needn't, Jessie.'

'It's okay. My curiosity's piqued now.'

Even the path was gravelled with chips of blue glass. Aromatic spices blended with the frosty air. The lashing winds died down as they moved warily towards the main entrance, as if the hotel was under some kind of glamorously protective dome. As they drew closer, a strange music came muffled from within.

Sheila was gabbling away to Jessie: 'Your Robert works for me, you know. At my own Hotel Miramar, in the real world.'

Jessie tossed her auburn tresses like someone in an advert for shampoo. '"Real" world, indeed! You'll soon learn to discard such old-fashioned distinctions.'

'He's a good lad.'

'I know he is.'

'He was heartbroken, you know, over your loss.' Sheila eyed her companion. She was testing her out somehow. She wasn't sure how or why. Like the others, she found something disturbing in Jessie's born-again insouciance. They paused under the luminous front of the Miramar as Jessie glared at Sheila.

'Aye, well, so he should have been heartbroken. I'm his Auntie Jessie, aren't I? I've looked after him most of his life. When his own family wanted nothing more to do with him. He's knocked around with me for a good long while. I've watched out for him over the years.'

Sheila gently probed, 'And he looked after you as well, didn't he? When you . . . turned womanzee.'

Jessie's expression hardened. 'I've told you. I don't have any memory of those days.'

'Strange . . .' Sheila shrugged.

Jessie changed the subject by abruptly turning to the reception doors and yanking them open. The curious music grew louder and Sheila stepped forward, ahead of her, as if she was being drawn home and compelled to set one dainty foot after the other into the Miramar's splendour.

'It smells exotic . . . it doesn't smell like home . . .'

At her back, Jessie was murmuring, 'Everywhere here . . . in this version of our town . . . everything is better, bolder. More exotic. You'll grow to love it, Sheila. Like I have done. It's a better place to be.'

Sheila wasn't sure about the gelid ambient lighting or the cloying music. She felt stifled suddenly, with Jessie going on in her ear like that. 'I don't know about this,' she said, in mild protest. 'I must say, I'll be glad to take that escalator back upstairs to the world above, once this little sojourn is over.'

Jessie gave a nasty laugh. 'Back upstairs? Oh, love. It's not as easy as that.'

'What do you mean by that?' Now it felt like they were floating in the heavily perfumed air. The carpets were so rich and thick, and patterned in such complicated arabesques, it was as if they were entering a labyrinth. Sheila couldn't quite see straight.

Jessie went on: 'Whatever Brenda and Effie say, about souls escaping from hell . . . it isn't as easy as that. It's not such a simple matter getting out of this place again . . .'

Sheila felt panic constricting her throat. She was warmer now. Beautifully warm. But she knew she shouldn't grow comfortable, or complacent. She knew somehow that this was wrong. This place was reaching out to her. Making her want to stay here. But she couldn't, could she? It felt all wrong. But it was dragging her under, into the softness of its interior. Sheila couldn't stop herself stepping further into the dark and towards the reception desk on the far side of the room.

A Drink with the Ex

They found a rather more muted corner of the ground floor of the Christmas Hotel: a window alcove overlooking the dark sea front. Brenda sipped a gin and tonic and stared at Frank in a kind of daze. She felt like she was sinking inside. Drowning and ebbing away as he stared back implacably. She noticed that his eyes were completely black, iris and pupil both. She had never noticed that before.

'I suppose I should thank you. Is that what you're expecting, Frank?'

He gave a rueful shrug. 'It's best not to expect anything. Not when it comes to you.' All the while he was wondering about Mrs Claus and Mr Timperley. Surely she was joking about the mince pies. Not even she would mince up one of her guests and allies, would she? Frank was confused. All he had to steady himself was the vision of Brenda before him in the tawdry hotel bar. Battered and bruised, she was still nevertheless the object of all his devotion.

She went on: 'I meant I should thank you for getting me away from Mrs Claus. Untying me.'

'Drink your drink.' He stared gloomily at his own bitter lemon. He was never a great conversationalist and inwardly he kicked himself. Brenda was a marvellous talker, he knew it. He would let her

235

down in this, in trying to express his muddled self, as in so many things. She would confirm her opinion of him as a worthless brute. What had she said to Mrs Claus? She was repelled by him. By his thick leathery hide. His ignorance.

Brenda was shaking her head and crunching an ice cube in an agitated manner. 'Just as well you got me away from her. I could give her a right thumping. Who does she think she is?'

He perked up, thinking hard, trying to impress her with the thoughts he'd had about Mrs Claus. 'Actually, I'm not too sure about that. She's obviously some weird supernatural being, isn't she? To exist here like she does, as well as up above. Powerful.'

'Well,' Brenda snapped. 'I'd still like to get my hands on her.'

'Calm yourself down.'

She gasped. 'Calm?'

'You're always over-reacting.' He cursed himself. Why did the things he wanted to say to her always come out so wrong?

'I like that!'

But then, she annoyed him so much. She said and did the wrong things too. When all he wanted to do was look after her, and cherish the silly bloody woman, why did she then have to go and be so difficult and twisty? He growled at her involuntarily across the bar table. 'Who was it started that fight on the cliff edge? Who was it that turned violent first?'

She looked abashed, turning away slightly in her seat. 'Well,' she said. He loved her looking slightly embarrassed like this. Girlish. Coy. All squashed into the overstuffed chair. Full of poise and elegance, his Brenda.

He beamed at her suddenly. 'It wasn't Frank who got punchy, was it?'

236

She frowned. 'Well, no. It was me. But that's because I felt cornered and frightened.'

He persisted, teasing her heavy-handedly. 'Really, it's your fault we went over the edge. It's down to you that we're here in the first place.'

Rage flared up in her like a pilot light. 'Blame the woman, then!'

Now Frank felt the words welling up in him. He was overcome with a rush of sudden articulacy. 'Over two hundred years Frank's had, wandering this earth! Most of them spent running after you, you daft old mare. And soon as I catch up with you again – it's crash, bang, bloody wallop! You smack him one in the gob, right on the edge of a sheer bleeding cliff. And then we both gets sent tumbling arse over tit down to hell! Well done, missus!'

Brenda looked downcast. She slurped the last of her gin. 'When you put it that way, it hardly seems fair.'

'It isn't. Frank has had a rough life, Brenda.'

She pulled her ruined evening wrap tighter. 'It hasn't been a bowl of cherries for me either, lovey.'

'But you have friends. A – a sense of purpose. A place you feel settled.' His brows knitted as he struggled to say exactly what he meant.

She sighed deeply, gazing around the Christmassy bar. 'I used to.'

'I've never had anything. I've never even had you.' Even Frank thought he was laying it on a bit thick by now. But he wanted to see how she would react. He'd say anything to get a reaction out of her.

'And you can stop that kind of talk,' she said curtly.

'You know what I mean.'

She switched topics, glancing about furtively. 'Am I a prisoner here?'

'In hell?'

She shook her head quickly. 'In the Christmas Hotel. Mrs Claus has given you charge of me. You took off my chains. Am I free to go?'

'I thought you were happy sitting here, having a drink and talking with me.'

'Well I am,' she said awkwardly. 'For a little bit. Having a natter. But I'd be even happier if I could leave. Orient myself. Get used to this place.'

'It's Whitby. It's the same as your home, just about.'

'Well . . .' Brenda tried to get her head round this, and what Mrs Claus had hinted, about worlds beneath worlds, and an infinite set of concertina'd layers. It made her feel a little bilious, on top of the slimline tonic. She said, 'I want to see it for myself. Will you let me walk out of those doors?'

He was downcast by her urgency to be off, but he said, 'I don't see why not.'

'Good.' She got up and hovered for a moment. She didn't know whether to shake his hand, or peck his cheek, or what. She was still inwardly furious that he had ended up dragging her down here, so she didn't bother with any of the social niceties. She simply said, 'I'll be going then.'

Frank stared up at her miserably, and told her, 'We'll be together soon enough. Bonded for ever.'

'What? Oh, you're still thinking we're going to get married.'

'You've no choice, Brenda,' he said, in a very level tone. His huge hands gripped the chair arms tightly. 'Frank loves you. Frank worships the ground you walk on. I always have.'

'Look, that's all very nice of you, Frank, but the feelings aren't – I'm afraid – reciprocated.' She waited for his hopeful face to fall. She waited for some kind of reaction. None came. He simply stared back at her. Trusting. Determined. Green about the gills. 'I don't want to hurt you,' she added.

Now he had a disconcerting deadness in his voice. 'That doesn't matter. You will marry me.'

She started to bustle away. 'Hard cheese, lovey. It isn't going to happen.'

'We will come and get you. When it's time.'

Brenda felt a shiver run right through her. She realised she had no idea what this man was capable of. 'We'll see,' she said, in a bogus carefree tone.

'The long-delayed nuptials, Brenda,' he called, as she put a rapid distance between them across the monogrammed carpet.

She tottered away, throwing back over her shoulder as she went: 'You'd be lucky. See you about.'

She stomped out of that hotel with huge relief, and yet her mind was still seething over the behaviour of Mrs Claus. Who did she think she was, taking prisoners all the time? And Brenda was still perturbed, of course, over the mince pies, and over Frank, who – believe it or not – was all of a sudden showing this more tender, thoughtful side to his nature. It took a few moments of stomping along the West Cliff, past all of the tall, elegant hotels, for Brenda to realise that Frank had been quite right. This was hardly a different world, this hell. In a strange way, she was already home.

She slowed her pace, entering the streets that took her into the heart of town. Past antique shops and bakeries, restaurants, gentlemen's outfitters. It was home but it was better than home. Busier, jollier. The atmosphere welcoming, unthreatening. Crowds were spilling out of every doorway and massing in the streets, ever thicker as she approached the centre of town. She tried to focus on them as she passed by, but it was confusing. There were so many types of dress and disguise, like Mardi Gras, or Goth weekend. There were bandaged mummies and Victorian ladies with their bustles and veils and their tiny, ineffectual umbrellas. There were cadaverous men, painted up like fanged zombies, as they did every Hallowe'en in Whitby. Here, of course, they looked just that bit more realistic, as did a werewolf, loping along by the gutter – Brenda glimpsed him clearly before he shot up an alleyway.

It was their profusion that was bewildering: the sheer number of souls on the street, but also the way they came from so many different eras. Medieval nuns swishing past, all devout in their crocodile line, eyes down. Chortling Regency fops, letting down their hair, crammed six deep at the bar in the tiny public houses. And no one took any notice of the tattered and bemused Brenda, limping along in ungainly fashion. She was used to drawing a few glances. A bit of attention always went her way, but that night there was nothing.

It was snowing. The air was silvery and shivery. There was a no-legged man outside Woolies playing carols on his accordion. A horrible, wheezing hurdy-gurdy noise that pursued her down the narrow lanes. Suddenly she was filled with a great desire to be back in her own home.

Reservations and Misgivings

The receptionist was a short, snooty woman Sheila had never seen before in her life. She flicked through a leatherette binder, running a silver pen down neatly printed lists. 'I am sorry, madam. But we have no record of your reservation.'

'I don't have a reservation.' Sheila was irritated as well as freaked out. She found herself whispering. This place was so much grander than home, with its marble floor and potted palms and swagged velvet drapes.

'Well, there you are then. The Hotel Miramar is booked solid for weeks. You won't get anywhere without a reservation.' The receptionist closed the book and smiled pityingly at the exasperated Sheila.

'I don't need a reservation!'

'I'm afraid you do. Everyone does.'

'Oh, this is hopeless,' Jessie broke in. She glared at the implacable woman behind the desk. She'd never had much time for people putting on airs. 'Look, mush. She doesn't need one because she owns this joint. It's her hotel.'

'I'm afraid that's quite impossible.' She was like a mannequin, unruffled by the growing agitation on the customers' side of the desk.

'It's different down here,' Sheila suddenly realised. 'Of course it is. The Miramar simply doesn't belong to me down here.'

'That's not fair!' Jessie cried. 'What are you supposed to do?'

Sheila flapped her gauzy sleeves. 'I don't know! I don't know how any of it works. We're not supposed to be here . . .'

For a moment the receptionist's frosty demeanour changed and she looked almost sympathetic. 'First day in hell, is it?'

'Yes, it is,' Sheila sniffed. 'And it's been awful.'

'It can be very confusing, I know,' she said. Then the phone on her desk gave a sharp ring. 'Excuse me,' she told them, and snatched up the receiver. There came a distorted mumbling from the other end. The receptionist frowned deeply as she listened. 'Oh. I see. Very well.'

Jessie turned to her new friend and told her, 'Sheila, this is useless. Why don't you just come to mine? You can freshen up there and we'll come back here for seven to meet the others . . .'

The receptionist jerked into action, waving her free hand in front of their faces. 'No – wait! You're wanted.'

'Wanted?' Jessie snapped. 'Who by?'

A curious sense of terror came over Sheila. Something clicked in her head as she realised something rather important. 'Oh my God . . .'

'Why,' smiled the receptionist, 'I mean, the actual owner wants you. The manager of the Miramar, here in this world.'

Sheila's voice had gone thick in her throat, like she had eaten a dozen Mars bars, one after the next. Her heart was walloping along behind her large chest, which was heaving as a result. 'He's here, isn't he?' she managed to ask.

The receptionist smiled and nodded encouragingly. 'He's in his sitting room. If you'll just go through, he'll see you now.' She set down the receiver on to its cradle.

'Who's she on about, Sheila?' Jessie growled.

Sheila turned to whisper to Jessie in a horror-struck voice. Underneath that, though, there was a tinge of thrilled pleasure. Of amazed delight. Jessie could hear it as Sheila hugged herself and said, 'It's my Mumu!'

Noises Off

'Wow,' said Robert, as they shuffled into Effie's shop. 'Just look at this place. It's gorgeous. And it's filled with . . .'

'Real antiques,' Effie huffed. 'Not like my place, you mean.'

'Well, you have to admit, Effie. It's pretty impressive.'

Grudgingly, she did so, as they crept around the room, examining the gleaming, polished wood of wardrobes and dressing tables, and peering into the depthless silver of flawless mirrors. Effie said, 'Something else that's better in hell than at home.'

Robert gazed at the glowing colours of the oils on the walls, the sheen of brasses and coloured glass. 'It's like it's here, all perfect, just waiting for you.'

'You mean, ready for when I drop dead?' she asked. 'Intriguing thought. Is that what happens, do you think?'

He frowned, feeling a bit philosophical as he ran his fingers along an armoire. Not a speck of dust in hell, it seemed. 'But then, that's like death is just a continuation, much the same thing as life.' He shrugged. 'Does that seem right to you?'

'Hmmm. I'm not sure about any of this,' she mused. 'Still, there's some nice stock here. Presumably all stuff that doesn't exist on earth.

Perhaps antiques that have been lost or destroyed over the years, that's the kind of stuff you get here.'

Robert balked at this. He examined the flaunting glass of the chandeliers. 'Come on, you're saying furniture goes to hell? Actual objects?'

'I'm a materialist. Maybe all matter goes to hell.'

All of a sudden he was on the alert. The room was warm, well lit and clean. Alarm bells rang in his tired mind. 'Wait, what if there's someone here?' He stared at her wildly. 'There must be! It looks so lived in. So warm and cosy . . .'

'More welcoming than my own place.' Effie nodded steadily. She steeled herself, straightening up for action. 'There's only one way to find out. Come on. Upstairs, into the living quarters.'

'Err, if you're sure.'

She elbowed him gently. 'Scared, are you?'

'Yep.'

'Come on,' she urged, taking the way through the side door and up the staircase, which in her own world was uncarpeted and noisy as anything. Here the stairs were silent with lush pile.

As Robert brought up the rear, he was starting to think that there was something almost eager about Effie's manner just then. Her face was rather flushed, just like when she'd had a little glass of sherry. She was excited. But why? What did she think she was going to find, in this house that was so much like hers?

Ahead of him Effie was muttering, 'The carpet, the flock wallpaper, none of the colours are faded. The lampshades aren't clogged with old cobwebs where I can't reach up to them. And it smells of rosemary, lilac, thyme. Garden herbs, just as it used to . . .'

'Used to?' Robert asked her gently.

'When I was a little girl.' She came to a standstill at the top of the staircase, her head cocked to one side. 'The house is just as it was then. Listen!'

At first Robert thought she had lost it. The shock of coming down to this weird place had robbed her of her senses, he thought. But then, there *was* something. He began to hear what she could. She looked down at him and her face was alight with pleasure. It seemed unlined in the golden light of the wall lamps. Her eyes were wide and shining. They both listened for some moments, poised there in the passageway, to the women's voices in the room ahead of them. Lots of women were in there, it seemed. They were talking, gabbling, laughing. Robert could separate out the strands of their different tones. He couldn't hear any actual words. The voices were coming as if from behind a heavy wooden door. There ahead. In the dining room. Effie was craning her neck now, straining towards the door on the landing. They were behind that door, these women. Their tinkling laughter, their more profound guffaws of shared amusement. It was the most welcoming noise Robert had ever heard.

Effie was trembling. She put one shaking hand over her mouth for a moment. 'Oh, listen, Robert! They're in there! My aunties!' She turned away from him, hastening along the corridor.

'Effie, wait!' he cried.

She was impatient. 'Don't you see? We're in the afterlife. They are here! Just as they were . . .'

'But—'

'But nothing!' she snarled. 'I must go to them. What will they say? They'll be amazed I'm here! They'll . . .'

He couldn't help feeling cautious. 'But we aren't supposed to be here, remember. We don't know how they'll react.' Now the voices from behind that door seemed even louder. It was a consoling buzz and hum of loud, carefree conversation, washing over the guests as they stood quibbling in the corridor.

Effie shook off his concerns. 'Oh, rubbish. They'll be delighted. Of course they will be. Come on!'

As Effie reached out to clutch the doorknob, it seemed to Robert that the chattering, festive sounds from beyond became louder. He could even begin to make out individual voices, rising and falling in friendly rivalry. He could almost hear the words they were saying now. He struggled to concentrate as Effie took a deep breath and prepared to twist the brass knob and go in.

'I never thought it,' she hissed. 'I never thought, even with all the magic in the world, that this could ever happen.'

Robert couldn't have stopped her going in even if he had wanted to. 'Just be careful, Effie.'

'I never thought I would see them again.' She beamed, quite transformed by the noise from the dining room. It grew almost unbearably loud in the split seconds as Effie tightened her grip on the doorknob, and it clicked and she suddenly thrust open the door.

On to abrupt silence.

Robert froze. Had the women all fallen quiet at once, all in the same instant? Had they been that shocked at the sudden appearance of Effie, their niece? He strained to see past the slight figure of the old woman, framed in the doorway. She was holding on to the door as if to life itself. Her body seemed to have been drained of all vitality in that tiny moment.

Now Robert could see why, as he stepped up right behind her.

The dining room was desolate. It was dusty and cold. The table was empty and the tablecloth was pure, untouched. There had been no fire in the grate, nor life in this place, for many years, it seemed.

Effie rocked on her heels, and her voice came out in a wordless moan: 'Nooooo . . .'

Robert shook his head. 'It can't be! How?' He hovered indecisively. Effie wasn't the kind of person you could hold or hug. She stood there, rigid with horrible disappointment, and there was nothing he could do to comfort her.

At last she rasped furiously, 'They've gone! They're not here!'

Lights Off and Somebody Home

At first Brenda was relieved, because it all seemed to be the same. Then, as she approached her beloved guest house, she started to notice the differences. There was no Leena and Raf's grocery underneath the B&B. The windows were dark and curtainless. But her B&B was there, apparently just the same, waiting for her. She nipped to the side passage, her heart banging away. She fished around for her house keys, but then saw that the door was actually open. Some of the still falling snow had collected on her welcome mat.

She stopped dead in her tracks. Someone was in there. Someone was home.

'Who's there? Is there anybody there? What are you doing in my house?'

And from within she could hear the laughter. This horrible chuckle. It took her about three seconds to recognise it. She should have known she would bump into him, now she was down here in hell.

Sure enough. The front door swung back and suddenly she could see him in the glare from the streetlight at the other end of the alleyway.

'You,' she said, staring levelly at the smirking cadaver.

'Good evening, Brenda,' Count Alucard purred. He gave a suave bow, right there in her dark hallway. 'I do hope you don't mind my making myself at home.'

Shy of Me?

'I was foolish, wasn't I? A foolish old woman.' Effie drank her tea miserably. Robert had made it too strong.

'I don't see why. It seems that anything can happen . . . anything can be true, down here. And we heard them, didn't we? Laughing and talking behind the door.'

'But I was foolish enough to hope that I could just walk through that door and be reunited with them.'

'I can understand that.'

She sighed. She looked down the length of the covered table, as if willing those other presences to manifest themselves again. 'Foolish. The thing is, my aunts are with me every day, in my own home, hovering about me like guardian angels. No, that makes them sound too soppy. You know what I mean. Why should I get so excited about hearing them here? At the thought of being reunited with them, actually touching them . . .'

'But it is different,' Robert said. 'This is a place where all those lives continue, or so it seems. And being here is quite different to communing with ghosts. Perhaps they really were here. Perhaps they are just shy of you . . .'

She looked at him, incredulous. 'Shy of me? I'm their youngest one. Their baby. None of the aunts would be scared of me. Disappointed, perhaps. Ashamed, even.'

'Really, why's that?'

Effie hung her head. 'I've ruined their legacy and everything they passed down to me. They were witches and wise women. They were proud of it. What am I?' For a second he thought there were tears running down her face, but she dabbed them away quickly with the cuffs of her cardigan. 'I'm just an old nosy parker. A dabbler.'

However, Robert wasn't listening properly to her. He had been distracted by a shimmering translucence that had taken over the bare tabletop. 'Look! Look at that!'

A weird shivery noise filled the air, and the two of them stared as silver platters and dishes faded into view. Cutlery and bowls of steaming vegetables; a huge roasted goose; a hock of spiced ham. Champagne on ice and crystal glasses, glittering in the candlelight that sparked out of nowhere.

'Marvellous!' cried Effie, sobbing. 'This is down to them! My aunts!'

Robert grinned, and dared to hug her. 'Dinner is served, it seems.'

'They're listening!' Effie laughed. 'They're here and they're listening to us!'

Robert was overcome by the gorgeous aroma of the feast laid so beautifully before them. 'Oh, let's eat. It seems like a million years since we last did . . .'

A Whiff of Black Pudding

The last time Brenda had seen Alucard, he was a friend. At least, at the time she had thought he was. It was when Effie had been running about the town with him. He was her man-friend – her suitor, as she insisted on putting it – and it had been a long time since Effie had known one of those. He flattered and courted her like nobody's business and she fell for him dreadfully. Effie signed herself over to him, body and soul, in just a matter of days. And all the while, Brenda had discovered, what he was really after was the arcane knowledge of the old texts she kept in the upper storeys of her house. It was Effie's aunts' dark secrets that Alucard was eager for.

But what good did they do him? The contents of those old texts took him on a hunt for the Bitch's Maw, up in the ruins of the abbey, and thanks to the intervention of the old vampire abbess, he was sent spinning into the underworld, dwindling down, shrieking on the fomenting air . . . down here. To this very place.

So here he was now, in this curious reflection of Brenda's own sitting room. Standing at the window and staring at the pale, snowy rooftops of this otherworldly Whitby, where the party was still going on, ever more raucously, in the twisting, thronging streets.

He turned his thin white face to Brenda again. He'd grown a

'tache, she realised. He smiled at her, with just a flash of fang, and said, 'I had rather hoped that you and Effie would come to my rescue.'

Brenda felt like laughing. The fool thought that was what she was here for. He believed that they had been working on his rescue all this time. 'That isn't quite what happened, Alucard.'

He shrugged his elegant shoulders, and slipped off his cloak. 'I know. Not much escapes me, Brenda. I know how you got here. And why.' He raised a questioning brow. 'Tonight, isn't it? Midnight tonight?'

This surprised her. 'What is?'

He slung his cloak on the green bobbly armchair and sighed at her, as if she was being deliberately obtuse. 'Your wedding, my love. Your much-delayed ceremony. All of Whitby knows about it and we will all be attending. A wedding of monsters. Hell's favourite thing.' He gave her a nasty smile and perched on the arm of the chair.

'Shut up. You're taunting me.'

'Hardly. I'm just saying what's on the cards. Unless you can escape from this place. But I warn you, I've been trying for months. Hell is very selective in who it lets back out.'

The 'tache suited him, she decided. 'We wondered if you would get out. Effie was waiting. Even though I told her you were best forgotten about. That you're no good. She was still holding out hope.'

'Faithful Effryggia.' He smiled softly. 'How is she?'

'As if you care!'

His face darkened. 'Of course I care. I was falling in love with her.'

Brenda clenched her fists. 'You used her. Like you use everyone.' She hadn't moved from her spot, standing rigid in the centre of the room. Glaring down at him. She was a formidable sight. She looked as if she was about to march across the lounge in three steps and punch him out cold.

He frowned up at her. 'What's happened to you, Brenda? What's turned your head, my dear? You sound as if you really hate me, and I thought we had come to some sort of understanding . . .'

She wouldn't soften. She held his gaze and felt the fury rising up in her as she explained to him, 'My memory started to come back. Earlier this year.'

'Oh yes?' he said, with the tiniest of flinches.

She went on: 'I remembered – in full ghastly detail – an earlier meeting with you. Back in the forties. It had been blocked completely from my mind, but suddenly it was all back. And you tried to kill me back then. Remember? In a filthy tunnel under Limehouse. You sucked out all my blood and then you left me for dead.'

Best feign ignorance, he decided. It was often the safest way, with a past as chequered as his. 'Did I?'

'I was there when you did some heinous things,' Brenda thundered.

'Oh dear.' He flicked a piece of fluff off his neatly pressed trousers, avoiding her eye. 'And don't you think a man can change? Repent?'

'Not you. You'll always be the same.'

He shook his head modestly. 'Such a long, illustrious career. Much longer even than yours, Brenda dear. I can't remember every fiddling little bit. If we were enemies back then, some time in the past, let us forget it now, and work together.' He looked up with a simpering smile and she felt like wiping it off his bloodless face.

'Work together?' She could have spat in his eye. 'To what end?'

'Getting out of here. This rotten place. Getting out of hell and back to the world of mortals and hot flesh and blood . . .'

'Ah.' She realised now why he was so keen to get out. No wonder he looked even thinner and more ghastly than ever. 'How starved you must be down here,' she taunted. 'No mortal prey to be had.'

He glowered at her. 'Yes, well. What do you think? I'm sure you can help me. You have a relationship with the Bitch's Maw . . .'

She crossed her arms over her powerful bosom. 'I'm not sure I want to leave. I like it here. I think I might even prefer it to home.'

'Now you are just being perverse.' He leaned forward all of a sudden, and his tone switched to a much more seductive one. A honeyed tone. His eyes were crimson, she saw, and raw with ravenous need. 'Listen to me, Brenda. Yes, gaze into my eyes . . . Let your thoughts drift for a moment. Tell me what it is you really want. You want your home, don't you? In the human world. You love the human world, just as I do . . .'

She tutted at him. 'Hypnotism, Kristoff? That's crude of you. Did you think I was going to fall for that?'

'I suppose not,' he grumbled sulkily. 'I'll just have to work on convincing you.'

Brenda decided. 'I've had enough of you now. Why don't I show you out?' She wanted to explore this underworldly version of her home. Surely there would be hot water still? She could have a nice bath and ease away her hellish cares for a while. She could find out what clothes were here waiting for her to put on. That was what she needed now. What she certainly didn't need was more wheedling from this capricious corpse, this dandified dead man. This satanic smoothie.

But he was still going on. Trying to get to her. To snag her attention. 'Like I said, there's not much that goes on here without my knowing it . . .'

'Bully for you. Get out. Scat.'

Now he looked like he was holding one last card, close to his narrow chest. 'There's something I'm sure you'd like to know.'

'Oh, really? You're just messing with me again. I don't have time for this, Kristoff.'

Alucard grinned at her. She could smell his dead breath, even this far away. It was like sticky black pudding. Rather grandly he announced: 'Your friends are here.'

She couldn't have been more shocked. 'What?'

'They came down here to rescue you.' With one smooth movement he was out of the chair and slipping his cloak back on. With feigned nonchalance he took in Brenda's expression. 'Aha. I see I've got your interest now, my dear.'

The Reek of Incense

Sheila Manchu had been a widow for a very long time. She had been married horribly young, back in the early seventies, when she had been the merest slip of a thing, a nubile glamourpuss who had really known no better. Her husband had filled every iota of her world for the few years of their marriage. And how short that time was. She couldn't help marvelling at the fact that it was only a handful of years that they had spent together.

They had left the dingy lights of London and moved together to Yorkshire. An alien element to her husband, but she had taught him to love the fresh air and the open spaces. He even came to love the moors and, ancient though he had been, would hike for miles with his young wife, bird-watching and having long, rambling conversations with Sheila about the meaning of it all.

Sometimes he would still talk about his need for world domination. He would reflect on his many years as the most feared criminal in all of London, and the world beyond. It had been hard on Mumu, giving all that up with his retirement. Sheila gently tried to remind him that it was probably best that he let other, younger crazed masterminds carry on the good fight, and he should learn to enjoy the peace and quiet in the north. Grudgingly he would agree, and relish the tranquillity that his wife had brought to his megalomaniac's heart.

So for a few brief years they were content at the Hotel Miramar, which he had bought for Sheila, lock, stock and barrel. Of course, he kept his hand in, a little bit, when it came to nefarious crimes and so on. He would sit and stew and plot in the sitting-room office at the back of the Miramar, and Sheila was proud of her elderly hubby, proud possessor of all his Machiavellian marbles.

But he had died before Sheila was even thirty. And she had been a widow for another thirty years after that. Learning to live alone. Keeping the hotel afloat. Still doing honour to Mumu's name. He had become for her more than the fading memory of a once-vital one-hundred-and-twenty-year old man. He had become a god. She kept belongings of his – the few pieces that his earthly remains distilled down to – in a lacquered cabinet in the basement of the Miramar, and it would be fair to say that she worshipped them, with a kind of dutiful, if habitual, reverence and awe.

So it was heart-stoppingly strange and exciting for Sheila to enter into that half-familiar sitting room office of the Hotel Miramar and find it shrouded in incense-laden gloom. It was overwhelming and nightmarish for her to advance into the room and to hear the strangely familiar rustle of ornate silken robes, and the whispering, fluting breaths of a very old man sitting in the darkest, furthest corner. Sheila could feel his burning golden eyes upon her. She could sense the presence of that fiercely wicked intellect in the back parlour before her. She was filled, top to toe, with a dreadful sort of delight.

She whispered hoarsely, 'M-M-Mu? Are you here? It's so dusky and dark. I can't see you . . .'

When his voice came, she shivered. She had forgotten its precise timbre, and that shocked her. How could she forget Mumu's sweet, rasping tones? 'I am here, my love.' He clicked on a green shaded desk lamp, and revealed himself to her.

Sheila jumped. 'Christ, it's him. It's you. You're really here!' To her eyes he looked just the same. He was at the writing desk, sitting with utmost elegance and staring up at her. A kind of wary joy in his golden gaze. He was in his most beautiful high-necked robes, and his goatee and long, trailing moustaches were freshly oiled and gleaming. His face had that same pinched, alert expression of sheer malevolent genius that the young Sheila Manchu had adored so much. But he didn't rise and come to her. They didn't rush into each other's arms at once. Mumu had never been given to overt displays of feeling. He simply inclined his gleaming bald skull in a nod of welcome to his one-time wife.

'Where else would I be, Sheila?' he asked, almost tetchily. 'I am here and waiting for you. Knowing you would come.'

She simply stood there, suspended in his fiery gaze. She wanted to run to him, to fall to her knees, to have him stroke her lustrous blond hair like he used to, in the old days. 'I never thought I'd see you again.' But she was unsure of him, unsure of herself. She wasn't sure what the famously inscrutable Mumu was thinking about her, sitting there. Was he repelled by her older self? She was chunky and blowsy, she knew. She wasn't at all the swinging dolly bird he had picked up back in Soho, all that time ago. She was a nervous, fluttery matron of advanced years in a feathery gown, which had become rather ripped and grubby through the night's adventures. She stared at her Mumu and wished she knew what he was thinking.

'But of course you were going to see me again.' He frowned, steepling his long, elegant fingers. 'We are to be rewarded with eternity together. That is the way of these things. Mere death couldn't halt the story of our love.'

She peered at him, taking a couple of timid steps closer. 'You are just the same. You look just the same as you ever did . . .'

A moue of displeasure from the mandarin. 'Did you imagine that my dead self would have grown young again, vigorous and strong?'

Sheila shook her head firmly. 'No . . . this is how I remember you. This is you.'

He smiled. 'This is our place together now, for ever.'

'Yes . . .' said Sheila softly, and her lack of enthusiasm was instantly picked up on by her canny husband.

'Perhaps you are too used to being sole mistress of the Miramar? Perhaps you are quite used to being without your Mumu now?'

'No . . . yes. No. I mean . . .' she stammered, desperate to say the right thing. She remembered this now. Appeasing him. Quailing at his mood swings. Failing his little tests. How could she have forgotten what it was like? She told him, 'Of course, I have had to become used to being a widow. I have had to work alone and live alone and struggle along as I thought you would have wished.'

He nodded stiffly. 'And I have watched you from the shadows, every step of the way. You have honoured me, Sheila. I had never hoped to be honoured like you have done. The shrine, the revenants. I was watching you from the eye sockets of my own dead skull. Each time you came to pray to me, to confide in me . . .'

'I made you my god,' she said, feeling rather queasy.

'And I was watching. Everything you ever did, I was there to share it with you.'

Sheila burst into messy tears. 'I knew it! I just knew it!'

'And now you are rewarded. You are here.' He spread his delicate, beautiful hands like a stage magician. 'In the perfect realisation of our dreams. Our perfected underworld version of the Hotel Miramar.'

She struggled to overcome her emotions and blinked at him. 'And . . . this is our reward, is it? Working still in the same place? The same job.' He frowned at her and she added hurriedly, 'I mean, I'm not complaining, just curious . . .'

'Yes,' he said, still frowning. 'This is what eternity has in store for we two. We are together again. In the home we made for each other.'

She forced herself to smile broadly at him. 'That's smashing. That's really . . . smashing.' Then another thought struck her. Hope thudded rapidly in her chest. 'Thing is, Mumu . . . you see, it's almost embarrassing this, but . . . I'm not dead yet.'

Mumu chuckled drily. 'Not dead? She comes to see me in my sitting room in hell and tries to tell me that she isn't dead? Oh come, my dear. You always were a bit dizzy, you were always a bit confused . . .'

She pulled a face. 'It's, true though. I haven't died. I'm . . . I'm here on a mission. With Effie and . . .'

Mumu looked very unhappy at the mention of Effie's name. 'Yes, I heard you were getting involved with that woman, and the other one . . .' He waved his hands dismissively. 'These connections are not good. I do not approve of some of these friends you have made in recent months.'

Sheila protested impulsively. 'Oh, but you can't say that! When the voodoo bamboo god Goomba possessed me and everyone else at the Miramar, it was Brenda who helped us! She saved all of our lives! And that was your fault, Mumu. You raised that terrible bamboo plant and used it and enslaved it to your will all those years ago, knowing full well that it was a lethal alien intelligence . . .' She stopped, clapping one hand over her runaway mouth. How dare she criticise her godlike husband thus?

'That's as maybe,' said Mumu gruffly. 'But I still don't approve of your friendship with Brenda and Effie.'

Sheila found herself standing up for her friends, and herself. 'You've been gone a long time. You can't tell me who to be friends with.'

His eyes narrowed shrewdly. 'Can't I now? I'm your lord and master, remember. You said it yourself – I am your god.' He looked rather smug about it, Sheila suddenly thought.

'Yes, Mumu, but you passed away in 1977. During the street party for the Queen's Silver Jubilee. You choked on your own venomous tongue when they were singing the National Anthem. You've been gone a long time. A lot has changed.'

'Oh really, Sheila?'

'Yes. I might have . . . worshipped you and honoured your memory, but I like to think that I have become a liberated woman, too.' She was standing her ground. She felt a wash of relief at getting this off her chest.

'You are my wife!' Mumu ranted shrilly. 'You will obey me!'

'No, Mumu. I'm not some ditzy little girl any more. I've run this hotel for years now, all on my tod. I can't go back to being the person I was.'

He thrashed from side to side, knocking his bony elbow against the writing desk and cursing aloud. 'We will see about that. I am Mumu Manchu! Your will is mine. I can bend you to all my desires.'

'Sorry, pet,' she said. 'Couples grow apart.' She turned away from him, heading for the sitting-room door. The reek of incense was making her feel really sickly.

'What? Where are you going?'

'I've left Jessie standing out in the corridor. I'm meeting some friends at seven. I need to go.'

He could hardly believe his ears. 'Wait! Come back! There is something I need you to do for me . . .'

'It'll just have to wait.'

'What?'

'I'm sorry, Mumu. It's been really lovely seeing you again and everything. But you've put my back right up, you have. Fancy shrieking at me and telling me I've got to do your will!'

'But you have!' he groaned, looking somewhat pitiful now. 'I own your eternal soul. You sold it to me, the day we married.'

Sheila waved this awful thought away. Could it be true? She didn't know. She could have signed anything, back then in her younger, sillier days. 'Oh, look. I'll see you later. We can talk about this then. I've got to go.'

'When will you be back?' He sulked.

'Can't say. Bye, pet.' And she hurried out of the sitting room, glad to be away from his presence at last.

Doorstep Reunion

Brenda had changed into something more suitable for the weather in hell. She was in a rollneck black chenille jumper and some comfortable slacks and her best winter coat by the time she dashed round to Effie's. All of these items of clothing were long gone in the everyday world upstairs. But they had been favourites and she was delighted to find them waiting for her in her wardrobe in hell. She hadn't exchanged another word with that ghastly gigolo Alucard. She barged past him, out of her B&B, and hurried off on her business. She was sure she had hurt the vampire's feelings, but, really, she was glad. He deserved much, much worse than that.

He can't be right, she thought, as she reached Effie's antiques emporium door and started banging away like mad. He must have got it wrong. He always told lies. He'd say anything to get you all worked up, Brenda. Anything at all. But what if he's right? She pounded with all her might.

'Effie! Effie! Are you there? Are you in?'

She could hear noises. Her heart leapt at this. There was surely someone in there. Of course! There were gentle amber lights in the shop. And now there were noises on the other side of the door. The jangling of keys, the thunking of the lock. And then the front door was yanked swiftly open.

Effie stood there. Her mouth fell open in shock as she stared at her friend. 'No!'

Brenda grinned. 'It is! It's me!'

It was like they hadn't seen each other in five years. They fell at once into each other's arms. Effie was squashed and dwarfed in the huge embrace of Brenda. Both were screeching and squealing at each other the whole time.

'I thought that was it! I thought we'd never see you again!'

'But what are you doing here? How are you here?'

'It's really you!' Effie drew back and studied Brenda's face. It was the same careworn face she knew so well. It really was her! Her own expression clouded over. 'But he killed you . . . dragged you down to hell.'

Brenda laughed. 'Ex-husbands! That's just the kind of thing they do.'

'He's here as well?'

They were interrupted by a series of thudding footsteps, and more squeals and shouts as Robert came hurrying out on to the front doorstep and grabbed Brenda in a hug of his own.

'Robert!'

'Brenda! You're here!'

Effie clapped her hands. 'Ha! That wasn't so difficult then, our mission to find you. We've really only just got here.'

Brenda nodded, with a shudder, 'This weird place . . .'

'Quite,' Effie said. 'It wasn't how we were expecting hell to be.'

'It seems quite nice, in a way. But it isn't home. Look, can I come in? I feel like everyone's watching . . .' Brenda glanced over her shoulder at the dark, sloping street. A few people had drifted by, casting glances at all the noise and palaver in the doorway of the junk shop.

'Of course! Come in! We're just eating, upstairs. Brenda! I can't believe it! I thought you were gone for good. I thought he had killed you.' Effie hustled them all indoors and clashed the door shut behind them.

The Enchanted Feast

They set about their dinner with some relish. Brenda tucked into goose with delicious spiced crackling, apple stuffing and perfect golden roast potatoes, without stopping to wonder at Effie taking the time to cook such a sumptuous meal. And all the silver and the crystal too, she never questioned. Only Robert paused for a moment as they ate and drank and gabbled away about their recent adventures, and mused worriedly on the wisdom of giving themselves up wholeheartedly to an enchanted feast. But bugger it, he thought. We're starving.

Brenda was swigging a chilled fizzy Pinot Noir and saying, 'What I can't believe is that you – all of you – would take such a ludicrous risk. I mean, what are you doing here?'

'Looking for you!' laughed Effie, as if, quest accomplished now, she could simply be amused at the absurdity of it all.

Robert added, 'We've come to take you home.'

'So you've merrily skipped down to the underworld . . .' Brenda chomped at a goose leg, shaking her head in wonder at her pals.

'Well,' Robert put in, 'that is, with a little help from the abbess and her magic escalator.'

Brenda looked perplexed suddenly. 'How do you know I can leave? Maybe this is my place now . . .'

Effie wasn't having this. 'Uh-huh. The gateway is permeable. We know that more than anyone. Look at Jessie. She's been just about *commuting* between the worlds. We can get out again. Trust us.'

Brenda's tone became urgent. She lowered her food back to the plate. 'Frank wants to keep me here. He thinks I'm going to marry him. Tonight.'

Effie almost choked. 'What?'

'I woke up in the Christmas Hotel and he was there. Waiting for me. Thinking he'd won, by pulling me down here . . .'

'Horrible man,' Effie sighed. 'Men always drag you down. No offence, Robert.'

'None taken,' said Robert. He'd had his own disappointments, but he wasn't about to go into that now. He said to Brenda, 'So, we've got to smuggle you home, past Frank?'

'And there's something else. Something I've got to tell you, Effie. Something you won't like.'

Effie frowned. 'Something I won't like? What is it?'

Brenda paused. There was no getting round it. She started to explain, 'He was holed up at my place. My B and B, the cheeky devil. I walked in on him when I went back there.'

Effie set down her silverware with an awful clatter. 'Who? Who do you mean?'

'It was him who told me you had come looking for me. We should have guessed he'd turn up. We knew he was here in hell.'

Robert felt his hair lifting off his scalp. 'Not . . .'

Brenda nodded firmly. 'Her fancy man.'

Effie felt like screaming, right there at the dinner table. 'Don't call him that!' She felt her pulse racing and she hated herself for that quiver of joy. She fought it down and tried to keep her voice steady as she said, 'But . . . he's here? Kristoff?'

Brenda lowered her voice as if she imagined that they could somehow be overheard, here in the upper levels of Effie's home. 'He's still next door, at mine,' she whispered. 'He reckons he wants to help us.' The three friends looked at each other. 'Can we trust him, though?'

March of the Mods

Some time later, the three of them were hurrying up the hill in the dark. Effie was saying quietly, 'I'm not sure whether he's trustworthy or not. But I don't want to see him yet. Let's just nip past your place, Brenda, and hope he doesn't notice.'

Brenda cast a backward glance at her guest house. 'I think I saw the curtains twitch in my attic.'

Robert said, 'He's there. Dark shape peeping out, look.'

Effie picked up her pace, and refused to look back. 'I can't look! I can't believe he's there!'

Brenda said soothingly, 'If you want to go to him, that's all right.'

The streets around them teemed with the noise of revelry. The singing and shouting was more alarming now, more raucous and drunken. For a second, Effie seemed to consider slipping back over to Brenda's for a one-to-one with her one-time beau. But she said firmly, 'No. We've got to meet the others at seven. We said we would. Kristoff can wait.'

The three of them set off once more, huddled together, up the sloping street. There were gangs of revellers clustered outside the pubs here, sparing the newcomers the most cursory of glances. Music thudded heavily from every pub doorway. Folk, metal,

271

Goth and – weirdly – the rather jaunty 'March of the Mods'.

'Isn't he awful, just moving into my place, without a by-your-leave?' said Brenda.

Effie said, 'He couldn't go to mine. My aunts are there. All of them.'

'You've seen them?' Brenda knew what it would mean to Effie to actually see her aunts again in the flesh, or something approximating it.

'Not yet. We've felt their presence, though, and heard them. They put on that lovely spread for us.'

'Maybe they can help us,' Brenda mused. Now they were at the end of the street of pubs, and tall black trees lined the road on either side. The pavements were coated and slimed with days' old ice, and it was treacherous going as they hurried towards the Miramar.

'Can you believe,' said Effie, 'that this is where we end up? After everything?'

'And it's just the same as home,' Robert added. 'What does that mean?'

Brenda said, 'I was told that this isn't it. It's not the end of it. Beneath this, there is another Whitby. And beneath that, another. Layers and layers of them, getting ever darker and darker, and further away.'

'No . . . That sounds awful,' gasped Effie. 'Who told you that?'

'Mrs Claus. Oh, she's here too, somehow. Quite young and sprightly, and wickeder than ever. It's her who had me captive. She's working with Frank to keep me here.'

Neither Effie nor Robert looked pleased to hear about Mrs Claus's involvement. Effie cursed. 'How can she be in both worlds at once?'

Brenda plunged her hands deep into her old coat pockets and

wondered aloud as they trudged along the snowy streets. 'There's even more to Mrs Claus than we thought. I feel like she's let me go because she knows she can reel me back at any moment. And I also feel like, while we're down here in this reality, she's somehow watching our every move.' The other two felt a prickle of paranoia at this, realising that they felt just the same. With all the snow about them, it was like being inside a glass snow globe, and it was as if Mrs Claus could give them a good shake any time she liked.

Brenda said, 'She rules this town, down below, even more completely than she does the one above . . .'

Ladies in Hades

'Jessie!' Brenda cried, opening her arms. 'Look at you!'

They were all standing by the largest of the bay windows in the bar at the Hotel Miramar. They had arrived at the same time as Jessie, and there had been shrieks and cries of pleasure and surprise. Brenda was astonished to see Jessie so perfectly restored to her former self. It was just as if she had never paid that first, disastrous visit to The Deadly Boutique. Hell had certainly done her some good.

'Look at this! What a reunion!' Jessie whooped with pleasure. Effie glanced at her, not sure if there wasn't something simian in that whoop, but no one else noticed, so she didn't say anything.

They sat down at a table before the dark windows and Robert gallantly took charge. 'I'll go to the bar. I'll get everyone's usual.'

They watched him go, and Jessie said fondly, 'Oh bless him. He's rather shy with his old auntie.'

Effie glanced at Jessie, registering the fact that she was sporting a revealing summer dress, wholly inappropriate for the season (eternal winter) and the occasion (planning an escape from Hades), but in Effie's experience, there were some people you just couldn't ever make listen to sense. She considered this business of Robert's new-found wariness with his born-again aunt. 'You can hardly blame him, Jessie.

It must be quite a shock. You springing back from the dead, yet again.'

Jessie was dismayed. 'But we were best friends! I was his favourite auntie.'

'Poor lad,' Brenda sighed. 'He's come all this way down to hell, just for the sake of a bunch of old biddies like us.'

Jessie was about to point out that she was no kind of old biddy, and in fact she hardly looked old enough to be aunt to a fully grown-up man like Robert, when they were interrupted by the bustling, breathless approach of Sheila Manchu. She had changed into yet another fancy floaty creation, this time in pastel pink and silver. Her hair and make-up were immaculate, but as for her demeanour, Brenda and Effie decided, sharing a significant glance, there was only one word, and that was 'discombobulated'.

But Sheila soon forgot her own worries and concerns when she got close enough to focus on the occupants of their table and clapped eyes on Brenda. Brenda in her black sweater and favourite earrings – lost for many years, then found on her dressing table in hell. Brenda grinning and opening her arms to hug her.

'Brenda!' shrilled Sheila, surrendering herself. 'They've found you!'

Brenda laughed, squeezing her then setting her free with a jangle of theatrical jewellery. 'I found *them*, as it happens. I went knocking at Effie's door because there was a light on. And there they were!'

Sheila was amazed, staring delighted at their gathered party. 'We've done it! We've been here a few hours and we've done what we set out to do in hell! We're brilliant!'

'Hurrah!' cried Effie, only slightly sardonic. 'You make it sound so easy, Sheila.'

Sheila suddenly looked despondent. She lowered her voice and her eyes. The others had to draw in to hear her say, 'I don't think Mumu is going to let me go.'

Brenda stifled her gasp of shock. 'You've seen your Mumu?'

Sheila nodded, a lot less chuffed-looking than any of the others might have expected. 'He's lively as ever. Sitting through in the back parlour. Welcoming me to my new life in hell with him, just assuming that I'm dead and buried and glad to remain here. Being his bloody concubine again.' She clapped her hands over her mouth. She had said something terrible. What if her Mumu could hear her saying things like this?

But she couldn't go on like they used to. She couldn't be the demure and accepting wife. Standing by as the old man advanced his strange plan for world conquest. Assuaging his tears of rage and frustration when it didn't work. Watching him cooking up ludicrously baroque revenges upon his enemies and rivals. Death by drowning and stabbing and surprise smotherings and stranglings. Her heart sank when she thought of him getting up to his old tricks: injecting lethal poison into sponge cakes, and parcelling up hopping-mad scorpions to send through the post. It felt to Sheila that the whole Mumu Manchu period of her life was well and truly over. It had been over for many years, and she couldn't simply go back.

'Oh dear,' said Effie.

Brenda said, 'And you're not very happy about being his wife again?

Jessie made a loud, sarcastic noise, and once more Effie couldn't help but think it a little monkeylike. Jessie said loudly, 'I should think not! Old devil!'

'Oh, I was delighted to see him again,' said Sheila miserably. 'It was amazing. He's exactly the same as he ever was. Brilliant, sardonic . . .

megalomaniacal. But it's not simply the world he wants to take over any more. It's me! He figures I'm down here for good now, and at his beck and call.'

'And you aren't,' said Effie.

'I'm still a youngish woman! I've got years ahead of me yet, up on earth. I've a life to live! I'm not ready for this.'

'Hmm,' said Brenda, wishing Robert would hurry up at the bar. 'Hell's quite seductive, though, in a way, isn't it?'

Jessie nodded firmly, mulling over her own situation – in its way as complex as Sheila's. 'In some ways hell *is* seductive, yes. But apart from my change of form, I'm living much the same life. I'm still a waitress, aren't I? Nowt's changed. And down here I haven't even got my mates with me. No, it's a poor substitution. I want to go home.'

Just then Robert arrived, bearing a loaded silver tray of tinkling glasses and mixer bottles. 'Here we are, ladies. Budge up.'

Brenda burst open the crisp packets and laid them out and urged everyone to help themselves. She was starving again, she realised. She said, thinking aloud through a mouthful of Smoky Bacon, 'I think we all want to go home, don't we? We're all agreed. We get out of here and up to our own world as soon as we can.'

'For some reason,' said Robert dourly, 'I don't think it'll be as easy as that.'

'He's right,' Effie said, taking her first hefty swallow of gin. Bombay Sapphire. She curled her toes inside her warm winter boots.

Robert was saying, 'I've decided this place gives me the creeps. At the bar there, all these people were saying hello. People who've stayed in this hotel before . . . and I've met them. Signed them in, checked them out. And they've died and found themselves here. On holiday for ever.'

Jessie shrugged. 'Doesn't sound so bad when you put it like that.'

Robert shot his aunt a glance. 'But it's like that forced, artificial jollity of the Christmas Hotel. That's what they live in all the time here.'

Jessie looked at him rather blankly, as if she couldn't follow what he was saying. As if forced, artificial jollity was something she was all in favour of.

Brenda detected the silent clash between aunt and nephew and quickly asked, 'Why do you think it'll be hard to get out of hell?'

'It will want to keep us,' Robert said. 'I can feel it.'

'Then we'll just have to fight our way out,' Brenda said happily, deliberately sounding as if she relished the challenge. She knew she had to put on a brave show for the others. They had come all this way for her – for her! She could hardly believe it. And now their spirits were sagging somewhat. She had to exert every fibre of her super- natural being and egg them all on.

Effie was cheered by Brenda's optimism, and she held up her gin and tonic in salute to her friend. 'Good old Brenda. She's always got the straightforward solution.'

'Can we use the escalator again?' asked the pragmatic Sheila.

Effie frowned. 'Since we don't have the abbess with us, we don't know how to call it down.'

Sheila said, 'But surely with your magic, Effie . . .'

Effie threw up both hands, as if to stop Sheila mentioning her supposed magical gifts. 'I can't do things like that! I can do love potions or repulsion cakes, and that't *it*!'

'Well, your aunts then,' Sheila persisted. 'Surely they can help us.'

'Possibly.'

Brenda interceded, 'It can't be easy. Going back the other way. If even Kristoff has been stuck here all this time . . .'

'That's true,' said Robert. 'And he must know far more about this kind of magic than we do.'

Effie glowered at her chilled gin. 'We need to talk to him, don't we? About what to do.'

Brenda patted her hand. 'You don't seem to relish the idea, Effie.'

Effie couldn't keep the scowl off her face. 'I've hoped and prayed for months to see him again. I really have. Oh, I know he was no good for me. I know he was just using me. But I've wanted to see him again, even though I know he's the . . .'

'The quintessence of all evil?' put in Sheila helpfully.

'What, and your bloke isn't?' squawked Effie.

Sheila was stung by Effie's tone. 'Mumu's not my *bloke*. He was my *husband*. And he was a good man really, underneath it all.'

Brenda laughed and shook her head. 'It's all fellas, isn't it?'

'What?'

'Mumu, Kristoff, Frank. Three of us have got fellas in hell.'

They sat in silence for a moment, contemplating the awful truth of this.

The Helpful Seance

Even though, to all intents and purposes, they were already in the afterlife, it was felt that a table-rapping session round Effie's was probably in order. The ladies plus Robert gathered hurriedly in her dining room, reasoning that, since there appeared to be layers and layers of afterlives below them, and since the aunties seemed reluctant to properly show themselves, then a bit of a seance might be just the thing.

It wasn't something Effie was particularly keen on doing, but she could see the use of it on this occasion. She bade them all gather around her table and said it didn't matter about all the hand-holding and jiggery-pokery. They just had to sit there and be ready to listen to whatever she came out with while she was under the influence, or to whatever was said by whichever being she summoned up out of the ether. Brenda helped her light the nightlights and they all sat down to wait.

Secretly Effie was rather gratified to be the one with the necessary skills. She could at least be doing something practical.

'Can you hear me?' she warbled, in her special seance voice, squinting into the gloom. She braced herself and spoke in a loud, clear voice. 'Are you listening? Hello?'

Jessie nudged her nephew. 'Is she getting through?'

'Sssh, Auntie Jessie. She needs to concentrate.'

Brenda tutted worriedly. 'I don't think it's working.'

Sheila was agitated by the whole thing. She hated anything eldritch, but sometimes needs must. 'It has to work. They have to agree to help us. They will, won't they?'

'I don't know,' Brenda sighed. 'I don't really know a lot about Effie's witchy relations. I mean, I've felt their presence. I've even heard them whispering about the place. But I've never felt that they were actually benign or very helpful . . .'

'Oh, great,' said Robert, leaning across. 'Actually, I thought that, when they put that feast out for us before, it was rather more sinister than it was friendly.'

'We're caught here,' said Brenda, feeling claustrophobic suddenly in Effie's crowded dining room. 'Stuck with them. Stuck with the whole lot of it . . .'

Robert smiled, but wasn't sure she could see him. 'Don't be gloomy, Brenda. We're all together, aren't we?'

'But things are pretty desperate. We're home and not home. We're reduced to calling on Effie's relatives for help . . .'

Robert suddenly asked her, 'What was it like, being dead?'

Brenda didn't want to go into it just now. 'It felt no different.'

'At all? It must have done. When you fell off the cliff . . .'

'Oh, that.' Effie's chanting and calling were getting louder and more desperate. Brenda leaned forward and lowered her voice. 'Well, never believe them when they say you pass out before you hit the bottom. I was conscious of every moment of it. And what was worse, there was no one to blame. I couldn't even blame Frank. It was my doing that pitched us over the edge.'

'We assumed it was him . . .'

'No.' She shook her head sadly. 'I'm afraid I *swung* for *him*. And over we both went. To our deaths in the tumultuous sea. Didn't hurt much. I'm more resilient than most people, as you know. I suppose it was a relief to know that death didn't actually hurt that much. And before I knew it, I was reborn into the Christmas Hotel.'

Effie's haunted moans and cries reached fever pitch just at that moment, causing the others to hold their breath and stare. She looked ghastly in the meagre light from the nightlights on the table in front of her. Brenda fretted briefly about her setting light to herself, or splashing hot wax everywhere. But Effie was stock still now.

Robert said, 'I think she's gone into a trance.'

'Maybe she'll get through to them,' said Brenda. 'They were eager enough to show themselves that time we had a TV crew round Effie's house . . .'

'Do you think we'll ever get home?' Robert said suddenly, a tinge of hysteria in his voice.

'Of course I do. We have to.' Brenda tried to be reassuring. 'This isn't our place.'

'It might have to be,' he said.

Brenda shivered. 'I can't stay here for long . . . It's torment. I can hear voices. When I close my eyes, I can hear them.'

'The whole place is full of voices. It's the damned. They can get quite rowdy.'

She shook her head. She wasn't going to tell anyone this. She had decided to keep a tin lid on it. But now she started to describe the weird phenomenon she had experienced every time she closed her eyes since she found herself in the underworld. 'What I mean is, voices within me, Robert. Inside of me. Crowding in on my mind, clamouring for attention. Wanting to be reborn themselves . . . wanting to live in hell . . .'

'Who are they?'

'It's not very nice to say, but it's the voices of my constituent parts. Hands, ears, spleen, feet. The whole shebang. As you know, every bit of me belongs to somebody else. Except the brain, of course. Perhaps you could say that was me and mine. But all the other bits, now we're in the underworld, they're calling out to be reunited with their original owners.'

'That must be horrible.'

'Pretty gruesome, eh? I'm trying not to let it get to me. But they're getting louder, those voices. They have been for the past day or so. I couldn't live with that kind of noise inside my head. I have to get out of here. It's as simple as that.'

'You two! You can stop your conflab right now! Effie's getting through, we think. There's all this ectoplasm or something!'

Jessie was out of her chair and backing away from the table. 'She's covered in it. It's coming out of her eyes and nose and . . .'

They had broken the circle and left Effie alone in her trance. Now she did indeed have a coating of terrible slime. The glistening, colourless matter was weeping and secreting itself out of her and the worst thing about it was that Effie hardly reacted to its presence. Even when it seemed that the alien mucus should be suffocating her, she sat there still and compliant.

Robert gagged. 'Effie!'

'Keep back,' Brenda warned him. 'We can't touch her. She's in communion now. She's broken through. If we break the link or disturb the—'

Effie spoke up, in a loud, panicky voice. But she wasn't talking to her friends. She raised both dripping arms and implored a group of people that the others couldn't see, 'Please . . . not too fast . . . not all of you . . .'

But then they *could* see them. All of a sudden, and with a curious, fluting noise, there materialised in the already crowded dining room several tall, spectral shapes. It was hard to make out any details or specific features, but the party around the dining table were more than aware of being surrounded and hemmed in by the glowing figures. Only one was very distinct. A burly woman with badly cut hair and a prodigious bosom. She was outfitted in something a Victorian matron might have sported and she was glaring so crossly at Effie that the others feared for her.

When Aunt Maud spoke, it was in thunderous tones that raised the hairs on everyone's neck and made the furniture tremble and the pictures quiver on the walls. 'What on earth are you doing down here, girl?'

'Aunt Maud!' Effie cried. Her voice sounded strained and strange, rather like she was gargling with her ectoplasm. 'You're speaking to me!'

'Of course I am, girl. The others aren't happy about it. They say you don't deserve it.'

'But why . . .?'

Aunt Maud was gruff and impatient. 'Many reasons. Not least you coming down here. Messing about between the levels, and with things you patently don't understand.'

Effie protested, 'We came here to help Brenda . . .'

'Brenda!' Maud cried out. She rolled her eyes scornfully. 'Fat lot of use she's been to you. She's always getting you into trouble. Best off without her, I say. You don't need her. The wise women of Whitby —

all your ancestresses – we've never needed anyone. Why do you suddenly need the likes of her?'

Effie looked down at the white damask of the tablecloth. 'She's my friend.'

'We don't need friends,' said Aunt Maud grandly.

'I do.'

'Why, because you're lonely? You're old and powerless?' Aunt Maud's voice rose in a hectoring crescendo. 'And whose fault is that?'

'Mine, I suppose.'

'Yours. Of course it's your fault. We offered you our powers. We offered you everything we know. You were our only hope in the world, our only surviving child. We depended on you to carry our knowledge on into the future.'

'I know.'

Aunt Maud leaned in closer, thrusting her sparsely haired chin right into Effie's face. 'And you refused us. You refused to learn. To accept the power. You wouldn't have any of it. Such a headstrong child.'

'Forgive me, Aunt Maud.'

Suddenly the ghostly woman let out a great cackle of glee. 'But you were still my favourite. I don't know why. Snotty, haughty, irksome little scrap of a thing. I don't know why I bothered with you.'

'You were always good to me.'

'Yes, well. My sisters and my aunts before me aren't best pleased that I've come to you now and fed you and your strange friends. And they don't think I should help you escape from hell. You've made your bed, they think.'

'Oh, please . . .'

'Don't grovel, girl. I will help you. I will do what I can.'

Suddenly Effie was eager. She started to gabble. 'The escalator back through the gateway, up into our own world . . . can we use it again? Can we call it down?'

Maud considered and shook her head sadly. 'I think that is beyond my current capabilities. We never used such a device in the old days.'

'Then what do we do?' gasped Effie, sounding impatient.

Maud turned thoughtful. She looked away and said, in a quieter, troubled tone of voice, 'There is one woman living here in the underworld who will know what to do. She has the required knowledge and the power. If you ask her, she might well help you. If you dare to ask her, that is.'

'Who? Tell me, Aunt Maud!'

'In the past you have underestimated her and reviled her.'

Effie gasped, knowing at once who her aunt must be referring to. 'Not . . . Mrs Claus?'

'You have dismissed her as simply a dangerous, evil woman. But she is more than that. Much, much more. Have you never realised the truth about her? Really, Effie?'

Effie stared at her aunt. 'The truth? What do you mean?'

Aunt Maud thought for a moment. She seemed to be on the brink of bestowing some marvellous secret on her niece. Everybody's eyes widened and they craned forward to listen. But then the ghostly crone cackled. 'No! There's no time to go into all that palaver tonight. All those family squabbles. No time to tell you all that nonsense!'

'Family squabbles?' Effie quavered. 'Are you saying that Mrs Claus is . . . is somehow related? To us?'

'Gah,' cried Aunt Maud. 'Don't let yourself get sidetracked, girl! All of that isn't important now! All you need to know is that Mrs Claus has the power. She has the wherewithal and the knowledge.

And she can, in fact, I believe, help you tonight to find your way home.' Then her face grew dark with horrible foreboding. 'But if you ask her, I imagine that she will require a forfeit.'

'I imagine she will . . .' Effie shivered.

Aunt Maud shrugged. 'But she is your best hope.' Now the gruff old woman looked tired, as if the psychic energy supplied by her niece was leaking out of her. Her image flickered and faded for a moment, as did the more shapeless forms of her glowing witchy lieutenants. Then she reappeared, saying, 'Goodbye, Effryggia. Promise me, if you manage to get home again, you will try harder to learn our ways. To honour our memory and to protect our secrets . . .'

'I will!' promised Effie.

'I'm fading away now . . . I've used all my power to speak with you for this long. There is one more thing . . .'

'Yes?'

Her aunt suddenly looked very severe indeed. 'Alucard.'

Effie glanced away, as if thoroughly ashamed of herself. 'Ohh . . .'

'He is very near. Very close.' Aunt Maud's voice was harder to hear, harder to focus on. She quivered on the air, turning blue and two-dimensional. 'He will come after you, Effie. You have been foolish. You invited him into your heart. Your home. Our home.'

'I know.'

'You must . . .'

'I can hardly hear you, Aunt Maud . . .'

For a moment Aunt Maud was standing there solidly before them again. She was standing in four dimensions and technicolour, and her voice boomed at them all. 'I said, you must kill him. Only you can destroy him for good, Effie. You must get rid of him!'

And with that, she and her sisters vanished completely.

Effie sat in silence for a moment and then looked at her friends. They all appeared shocked at this rather spectacularly successful seance. 'Did you lot hear all of that?'

Sheila squeaked, 'I think so . . .'

Brenda tried to be calm and sensible. 'Sounds straightforward enough. Erm, let's see. Don't, whatever you do, let yourself trust me, because I'm an abomination. And you should beg Mrs Claus, about whom there is some considerable mystery – not least how she lives in two different incarnations in separate worlds simultaneously – for help, which, knowing her, will come at some ghastly price. And while we're on with that little lot, find a spare mo to stake that bothersome Alucard through his fat black heart.'

Robert gave a grim laugh. 'Easy night's work, eh?'

'Oh, Brenda,' Effie said, sounding defeated and disappointed. 'She wasn't much help at all. She was so bitter and cold . . .'

Jessie tutted, scratching herself. 'Witches. That's what they're like.'

'Well,' said Brenda, standing up brusquely and reaching for the light switch. 'We'd better get on with things. Time's pressing on. There's the small matter of my wedding at midnight, if you remember. I'd like to be away from here before that, if at all possible . . .'

Hellish Ablutions

Effie found that even the bathroom in this version of her house was nicer than the one she used at home. It was larger and more luxurious, as she discovered when she went to clean herself up. She set a hot shower running and bundled up her ectoplasm-sodden clothes. She washed her hair several times and scrubbed her skin thoroughly, to get the weird, unearthly scent off her body. There had been oodles of the vile stuff hanging off her.

She was in a dressing gown and had a towel turbaned round her head, peering into a misty mirror, when Alucard came to her. He stepped up behind her with a delighted grin on his pallid face.

She suppressed a shriek. 'What do you think you're doing?'

'Hardly a warm welcome.' He was exactly as she remembered. How she had pictured him, during all of the months since his banishment. She stared at him in his evening dress and cloak, looming out of the steam and training his sore-looking pink eyes on her obvious distress.

'Kristoff, I . . .'

'How long is it since we clapped eyes on each other? Over a year, isn't it? Time moves differently here, of course. Here in hell.' He let the self-pity creep into his dulcet tones. Let her hear that he had suffered, too.

'A long time, anyway,' Effie said awkwardly.

'Won't you kiss me, my dear?'

She shuffled backwards, coming up against the sink unit. She had nowhere to run, even in this more spacious bathroom. 'Stay back. Keep away from me.'

'You disappoint me. You've been listening to Brenda. To her horror stories about me.'

Effie whispered, 'What do you want with me?'

'I want you to trust me. To believe in me. I need your help.'

She shook her head. The things she had intended to say to him were welling up inside her now. Now that she was face to face with his slightly grey, pearly complexion. Now that his strange, not unpleasant scent was coming to her in waves on the mist. All of the things she had thought about him in this past year and saved up to tell him were ready to burst out of her. She took a deep, measured breath. She couldn't lose her temper, or her composure. She had to keep calm. 'You. You were so keen on finding your way into hell.' She glared at him accusingly and was pleased to see him flinch. 'You used me to find the charts and the maps and everything you needed. And now you want out.'

'I thought there was something down here. Something that could help me.'

'Oh yes? You abandoned me, Kristoff. You would have flung yourself down here, even without the abbess's help. You were quite prepared to leave me up there, alone. You never really gave two hoots about me.'

'Not true.' She had never seen him look so earnest and hurt. This brought her up short. He added, 'I was falling for you.'

She gulped, and shook her head. 'Rubbish. No one's ever fallen for me. I'm unlovable.'

He pulled a face. 'Self-pity ill suits you. But you must believe me. You felt it yourself. We were falling in love.'

'Perhaps. But you were keen to leave me.'

'I came here because I thought there was something here that could cure me of my . . . disease.'

Her eyes widened at this. 'Really?'

He nodded, and half turned away, as if ashamed of his condition. 'Hints and rumours. Down the centuries. They said that vampirism could be reversed. Even mine.'

'And you haven't found it, whatever it is?'

'A foolish errand,' he said curtly, his voice blunt with disappointment. 'I was blind. I had no idea what I was coming to. Hell is just the same as the everyday world. Oh, it's darker. It's night-time almost all day long. Maybe that's what the old legends meant. In hell, the vampire will feel as if he is more human. Not a cure at all. He just feels more at home.'

Effie felt something shift in her chest. Her vision blurred with tears for him. 'Oh, Kristoff. I'm sorry.'

'Are you?' he snapped. I came here thinking I might turn human again. I might become real. My coagulated blood might start to thump again, fresh in my veins. My pallor might vanish. I might grow warm. All for you, Effie. I wanted to return to you, alive and mortal.'

She hung her head. 'I wish I could believe you.'

'Please believe me. And I wish you could accept me as I am. As a vampire still.'

She felt herself getting angry at him now. 'Did I ask you to change? Did I say go down to hell? Put yourself in danger and get stuck down here? Did I send you on that fool's errand?'

He had to admit it: 'No.'

'I was happy how we were, Kristoff. I was falling in love with you, as you were . . .'

Just at that moment, Effie became aware of the rising noise outside. Down below, out in the sloping street, the revellers were becoming more rowdy and excited. It was as if some kind of parade was passing by. She paused to listen, pursing her lips worriedly.

Alucard was still fixed on their private talk, however, saying, 'I heard your Aunt Maud. I was listening. When she came to you. Telling you to kill me.'

'I was a fool,' Effie said. 'Thinking my aunts would help me. Thinking they loved me. I've never felt more alone. Even Maud . . . sounding so brusque with me.'

He smiled sadly and told her, 'You've still got a bit of ectoplasm in your ear.'

She shrugged unhappily. 'That's the least of it.'

Now there was a ragged chanting out in the street. Many voices were raised together and Effie tried to piece together the words, while still focusing on what Alucard had to say.

'I heard your Aunt Maud tell you that you must . . . stake me. Was she like that with all your boyfriends?'

'Yes.' She nodded, frowning. 'Not very nice for you to hear.'

He seemed so earnest and trusting all of a sudden. Effie felt a bit dizzy with the power of it. He was like putty – or ectoplasm – in her hands. 'Will you turn against me, Effie? Will you obey your aunts?'

'Of course not. I couldn't stake you . . .'

'Well, that's something, at least. But your aunts . . .'

She was resolute. 'I don't have to do anything for their sakes. Never again.'

'And this business of asking Mrs Claus for help? Will you?'

Effie began, 'That's . . .' But then she had to stop, because the noise from outside had become so fierce that she could hardly hear herself think. She gasped. 'What *is* that bloody awful racket out there? It sounds like . . . like . . .'

Alucard listened, and his face fell. 'Like a lynch mob. Like a mob of torch-waving peasants.'

'Oh no.'

She watched as he hurried to the high bathroom window and creaked it open. The steam filtered out, as the outside cold and boisterous noise crept in. Both made Effie shiver in her dressing gown. She had to get dressed. She had to get ready to run, she just knew it.

'They're right at the door,' Alucard told her, sounding urgent. 'They're shouting up at these windows.' He looked like he didn't know what to do. 'I think it's us they're after.'

Then Brenda was pounding on the other side of the bathroom door. 'Effie! Finish up in there! Quickly! Have you heard them outside? They've come for us, Effie!'

Effie started rifling through the clean clothes she had taken in with her. Panic was clawing at her as she struggled to sort her garments out. 'Brenda, hang on . . .!'

'What are you doing in there?' her friend cried impatiently. 'You've been in there for hours! We're waiting for you! We have to get away . . . now!'

Effie whirled round to face her beau. She could see him more vividly, now that the steam had frittered off into the night. He looked terrible and handsome, and her heart jumped in her rattled chest. 'Kristoff . . . you're coming with us.'

He shook his head sadly. 'No. But I will be nearby, Effryggia.'

His whole being shivered and shook then, forcing Effie to step back and gag in astonishment. She had never before witnessed him transform himself like this. His arms went up in the air with his cloak swishing around him. His fangs suddenly grew to absurd proportions, as did his ears and his wings. His wings? And then he was shrinking and hovering and flapping in mid-air. His eyes glowed scarlet at her, and Effie felt silly for realising so belatedly that he was turning himself into a long-eared bat. Of course. It was just one of the many tricks of the trade. Lucky him, she thought dismally, as he flapped his way out of the bathroom window. A whoop of displeasure greeted him as the chanting mob noticed his escape. At least he could flutter away safely, Effie thought. Unlike the rest of us, who can't turn ourselves into anything much, more's the bloody pity.

Brenda was still banging on the bathroom door, rather alarmed by the squealing bat noises. 'Effie! What's going on?'

She broke the lock with one of her hefty thumps and the door swung open on splintered hinges. She found Effie in her dressing gown, clutching her fresh clothes. 'He's shot out of the window!'

Brenda knew at once what had been going on. 'Who, Alucard?' She had suspected as much. That conniving zombie had been sniffing round her friend again. 'What was he doing? Attacking you?'

'Of course not!'

There wasn't time for the ins and outs of Effie's love life right now, Brenda thought crossly. 'Look, forget him. We've got to get away. The others have decided to try slipping out the back way . . .'

Effie jolted herself into the present moment and its dangers. 'What's happening? What are all those dreadful people going on about?'

'They're after our blood,' Brenda told her, almost apologetically.

'Seriously? That's why they're chanting out there?'

Brenda nodded. 'It's the mob. They've come for us.'

'What do they want?'

Brenda squinched up her face thoughtfully. 'I've got my suspicions. Come on. We don't want to hang around here.'

But first Effie had to whizz her new outfit on. Brenda left her for a moment as she tussled with her clothes, while the mob's chanting echoed horribly in their ears.

Here Comes . . .

The others were waiting for them by the back door. Even though the situation was desperate, Effie reflected that she felt a lot better for being clean and neatly attired.

Robert said, 'Brenda . . . you've got her. What was it?'

'Alucard,' Brenda told him. 'He's gone now. What's the matter? Can't you get the back door open?'

Sheila said, 'It's not that.'

'They're round the back as well,' said Robert.

Effie sighed heavily. 'Oh no. This is my fault. You could all have run away in time.'

Brenda put on a determined expression. 'We just have to face them. Ask them what they want.'

Jessie had a wild and panicky look in her eye as they stood there together in the fusty back hallway. 'Oh my God, they want to torch us . . . murder us . . .'

Brenda mused. 'No. I don't think so.' She stepped forward and unlocked the back door. Then she took a deep breath and threw it open on to the noisy alleyway.

The mob cried out as one at the sight of her.

Brenda wasn't going to be cowed by that. She stared back at them.

Night-time revellers in carnival dress. Fierce white faces looking crazed in the blazing torchlight.

'What is it?' she shouted at them. 'What is it you want from us?'

The mob muttered and laughed at her, but no one stepped forward to answer.

'Tell me!' Brenda demanded. 'Or let us go our own way in peace!'

The mob continued to mumble and jeer. Brenda was just about to lose her temper when one voice rose above their agitating. A single, imperious female voice suddenly made itself plain silencing the crowd at once. 'All of you. Cease and desist! Be quiet!'

After a pause, a figure in a white fur coat stepped out from behind the crowd. She stood in the lamplight, and Brenda and her friends could see that she was wearing a kind of tiara woven from mistletoe and holly.

'Mrs Claus,' Brenda growled.

Mrs Claus laughed merrily. 'They are here at my behest, Brenda.'

'I've always thought "behest" was a very silly-sounding word.' Brenda was still gobsmacked at the sight of this svelte and gorgeous Mrs Claus. It wasn't what she was used to at all. Somehow the woman seemed even more dangerous in this beguiling incarnation.

Mrs Claus went on, 'This mob is your entourage, Brenda. This motley assembled crowd. They are here – we are here – to escort you and your friends back to my Christmas Hotel.'

'I see,' said Brenda stiffly. There isn't anywhere to run, she thought unhappily. If we dash back indoors and seal ourselves into Effie's house, they'll simply bash down the doors and smash in the windows. They'll drag us out and there'll be violence. Look at how many of them there are. It will be carnage if we even try to put up a fight. What can we do? She was playing for time, but she knew they had no choice. They would have to give in. She asked Mrs Claus, 'And why's that? Why would we want to go willingly to that horrible hotel of yours?'

Mrs Claus smiled beatifically, savouring the moment. She knew she had everybody's eyes on her as she stood in that becoming lamplight, the snow falling on the mob scene around her. She explained in breathlessly dramatic fashion, relishing every syllable of this triumphant announcement, 'Because your groom is waiting, Brenda. Midnight approaches and we have much to prepare. The bride must be ready! Your wedding is nigh!'

An Awful Jamboree

As the mob escorted them through the winding streets to the West Cliff and the Christmas Hotel, the atmosphere was celebratory. They sang and chanted as if Brenda was their queen.

Plodding along in their midst, she wondered miserably why it was they sounded so pleased that she was giving in and coming with them like this. But what choice did she have? They were in a carnivalesque mood. It was like everyone was in on some joke she just didn't get. She also felt that if she disobeyed them, or put one foot out of line, they would tear her limb from limb. Underneath all the singing and laughing there was an ugly mood. A palpable sense of danger and threat. Carnival, she thought. It meant the rending of the flesh, didn't it? And she was the sacrificial bride, one way or another.

'I recognise faces here and there, don't you?' Effie asked her, as they were shuffled along the cobbled lanes.

'Can't say I do.'

Effie looked haggard and scared now. 'I've lived in Whitby all my life. And I'm telling you, these are the faces of the dead . . .'

At first Brenda had thought it was fancy dress, but now she could see that Effie was right. These dead souls hailed from different eras. Here were the Edwardian bathers in their candy-striped cossies, here the Victorian patriarchs in frock coats and tall hats, and here were the drowned sailors wreathed in rotting weed and all pearly about the eyes.

'I wish we could do something,' Robert hissed. 'Give them the slip somehow . . .'

'*You* could,' Effie pointed out. 'I think it's us two that are wanted, really. You could nip off into the crowd if you wanted, Robert.'

He looked amazed she could even suggest such a thing. 'No, I'm here with you two. I'm not abandoning you.'

Jessie was clingy. 'Don't leave us, Robert!'

'Of course I won't, Aunt Jessie.'

She hung her head. 'I'm scared you'll abandon me down here. I want to be home again . . . real home . . . alive once more.' And then she said something that caused Robert to shiver. 'Glooop,' she said unhappily. 'GloooOOOoooppp.' It was the haunting moan of the womanzee. The terrible beast his aunt had once become. Was she reverting? wondered Robert. That was all they needed.

'We'll all get safely home,' Robert said reassuringly. 'You will be fine, Aunt Jessie. You'll see.'

'What's all this, though? This hair, growing on my arms, on my wrists. I feel so hot . . . so mithered . . . What is happening to me?' She itched and scratched at herself and tore at her clothes, as they were bustled along through the narrowing streets.

'Oh God. I'm sure it's nothing, Auntie Jessie. You'll be all right.' But Robert wasn't so sure at all.

Up ahead, they could hear Mrs Claus laughing jubilantly as she led the crowd through the streets. People were hanging out of windows to cheer the parade. As the alleyways bottlenecked, the faces loomed out over the prisoners, trying to get a look. Mrs Claus led them in a ragged, rousing chorus of 'Here Comes the Bride'. Brenda thought: Nothing's going to save me from this, is it?

They toiled up the hill to the grand West Cliff, where the sea winds were battering the cliffs and dark purple clouds were roiling and massing on the horizon.

Brenda stared beyond the town and wondered if the whole world was down here in hell. Was it all a carbon copy of the world she knew, only steeped in near-perpetual night and populated by the dead? In some ways she was hungry to know the secrets of this world below. She had spent much of her life wondering what lay beyond life for the likes of her, and now here she was, sampling the first of those secrets. She was on the threshold of all kinds of knowledge at last.

But actually, when it came down to it – there on the brink of those almighty mysteries – all she really wanted to do was go home. She wanted to be back in her nice home, with her swollen feet up on a pouffe, and a record playing, sipping her spicy tea and thinking about everyday things.

Effie cried out: 'Oh, look at the place, all lit up!'

Mrs Claus shouted, 'Magnificent, isn't it? It's been a long time since we held a wedding here.'

They really had gone to town. The Christmas Hotel was festooned with baubles and glowing lights. It blazed white and gold like some weird kind of lighthouse, right out on the edge of the cliff. And the music, of course, was a strangely discordant version of the wedding march.

Brenda was borne inside, through the foyer of the hotel. Her friends were all about her, looking as scared as she must look. Inside she was rather calm. She wasn't dressed properly. She must look terrible. But here were crowds eager to see her. Everyone was gathered there to honour her. She was filthy and bedraggled. She had been through hell. And the dead were assembled to see her.

They were solemn now, watching on as Mrs Claus led a stately procession to the grandest of her hotel's downstairs rooms, where twelve tall Christmas trees touched the ceiling and a black jet altar dominated one end of the room.

The dead and Brenda's friends were ordered to sit. Pews had been arranged for them. Brenda was alone in the aisle, following on behind Mrs Claus.

Had she been drugged? That incense they were burning, had its fumes somehow infiltrated her good sense? Made her passive and pliable? Why wasn't she resisting at all? The fumes were of cinammon, nutmeg, spices, fir trees, hard frost. Every kind of seductively Christmassy scent. They combined to remind her of a childhood she had never known.

There he was, up ahead. Her husband-to-be. Dapper and impassive in his grey morning suit. Setting off his greenish tan to perfection. He looked nervous too, she could see, as she approached, jerking her limbs stiffly, puppetlike, drained of all volition. He was staring at her as though he couldn't comprehend that she had come, like a man who couldn't believe his good fortune.

She stepped closer, advancing down the makeshift aisle, and she was less and less aware of the crowd around her, even of her friends.

They were all holding their breath. Everyone within the Christmas Hotel was holding their breath.

Brenda stepped closer and closer to her destiny.

Her groom smiled. A ragged, lopsided smile. His inky black eyes were twinkling. His fetid breath rolled out to meet her, and he held out one huge hand for her to take. Each scarred finger was trembling.

She looked up into his face and saw how carefully he must have combed down his blue-black hair across his flattened skull.

She felt a twinge of . . . What? Compassion? Fellow feeling? Surely not love.

But she saw in a flash that this was a moment she had spent two centuries and more avoiding. It was this moment that she had been running from. She had thought she was making a way in the world. Becoming a liberated woman and deciding for herself what shape her life might take. When all the while this was what was really awaiting her.

Matrimony. Love. The man of her dreams.

Brenda lowered her head and just gave in to it.

Mrs Claus stepped forward, beaming in triumph. 'Dearly beloved. We are gathered here today in the Christmas Hotel to witness the marriage of Frank and Brenda.'

Suddenly Effie was on her feet, screeching above the heads of the congregation. 'I do!'

There were startled murmurs and chuckles.

She yelled again, 'I mean, I have just cause and impediment!'

Robert joined her, adding, 'So do I!'

'Erm . . .' said Sheila shrilly. 'And me!'

Robert cried, 'She's been brought here against her will! She doesn't want to marry him!'

'This is a farce!' Effie snarled. 'She's been kidnapped! Ask her!'

Mrs Claus turned, bemused, to the passive bride. 'Brenda?'

Brenda blinked. She stared down at the sparkling bouquet someone had thrust into her hands, somewhere along the way. She didn't have a clue what was going on. How had she got here? Who was she supposed to be now? She had been shaken out of her own life, and set up here on this jet-black altar. She struggled to say something, staring around for familiar faces. 'I . . . Effie, I . . .'

'What? Brenda! Snap out of it, woman!'

'She's in a trance!' Robert said.

'Wake up! You don't want to get married. You told me that!'

Brenda sobbed, 'I don't know any more . . .'

Mrs Claus interposed herself between Brenda and the noisy congregation. 'Brenda, you must make up your own mind. But this is your chance. This is what you were made for. You know that. This is the fulfilment of all your desires. The realisation of all your hopes . . .'

Effie wasn't having any more of this. She took a deep breath and bellowed with all her might: 'COCK!'

Mrs Claus flinched. The congregation muttered and giggled. Effie yelled again, stepping out into the aisle: 'She's talking a load of old cock, Brenda, and you know it!'

Now Frank came to life, turning to his bride-to-be with a pleading look in his eye. 'Brenda . . . please. Listen to Frank. Marry Frank, Brenda. Stay with Frank. Don't listen to them. You know what you really want. Only Frank. You only need your Frank . . .'

It wasn't actually the protestations of Brenda's friends that brought a temporary halt to the proceedings. Something else was going on in the congregation. Something was starting to cause an even bigger stir. And although afterwards Brenda would think: Poor Jessie, she was also glad that Jessie chose that precise moment to *revert*.

For a while Robert's aunt had been watching the hairs on the back of her hands turn coarse and black. She had felt her ears, her nose, all her extremities tingle and burn horribly. And now she felt herself in the throes of a truly terrible – and not unfamiliar – transformation.

Jessie was turning back into a womanzee.

Who knew what combination of hormones, sorcery, karma and bad timing had triggered her awful metamorphosis?

Oh, but Brenda was glad.

She felt her husband-to-be stiffen beside her. Tense, alert, braced for action. She heard Mrs Claus give a strangulated shout. She saw members of that raggle-taggle crowd, gathered there to watch the rites, go up and down in a Mexican wave of appalled dismay. Torrents of panic ran through them. She could hear Effie's distinctive fearful shrieking. A noise that somehow always managed to contain a note of reproach.

And then . . . then she could hear the ghastly sound of Jessie on the rampage.

GlloooOOOOoooopppp! GGGgggglllooooOOOOOoooopppp!

Jessie's waitress's uniform hung in tatters about her powerfully compact body. She shucked these rags off her as she lurched into the aisle. The primitive womanzee was well nigh nude as she scattered revellers about her. She lashed out – *ssszzhh, whizzsshhh* – with her gnarled and filthy claws, and a great space opened up in the middle of the ballroom. She snarled to keep them all at bay and then she fixed her yellow eyes on Brenda and her groom, transfixing them with an ancient, alien gaze.

They were frozen there for a moment, under the glittering brilliance of the chandeliers in Mrs Claus's ballroom.

Jessie growled low in her wattled throat. Brenda knew then it was Frank's presence she was responding to. Perhaps, as the most obviously powerful figure there, he had attracted her attention and enmity, and put her hackles up. His very presence was a challenge to her. Whatever the cause, she had started squaring up to him and shuffling towards the dais where he and Brenda were supposed, by now, to be exchanging their vows. Frank could see as well as Brenda that the womanzee was advancing on him with intent. He flushed a deep, excited jade green. He took one step forward.

He liked a good punch-up, did Frank. He always had.

Deadly Bargain

In all the kerfuffle, Brenda's friends managed to seize hold of her and drag her away into a side corridor, near the ballroom toilets.

'Come on!' yelled Effie. 'While no one's looking . . .'

'You can't!' Robert protested. 'We can't leave Jessie!'

'Just look at her, man. She's gone back into her primitive past. We can't do anything for her.'

'Probably triggered by wedding envy. Jessie's always fancied herself as a bride.' Sheila looked extremely worried by the noise at their backs. 'They're going to rip each other to pieces in there . . .'

Effie was practical as ever. 'Well then, they've bought us some time. We can get away.'

Brenda looked gloomy. 'They'll never let us get away.'

'Come on,' Effie barked, sounding rather like her own Aunt Maud. 'There's no use moping about.'

'Don't you see, Effie?' Brenda was shaking herself out of her weird trance, and now she could see things with dreadful clarity. 'They'll never let us go. Mrs Claus, all of them. This whole place. We're stuck here now.'

Effie scoffed, trying to snap her friend out of this passive mood.

'She's turned you funny. Anyone would think you'd changed your mind about getting married.'

'What I thought was . . . if I just let him marry me . . . if I did what they said . . . maybe they would let you lot go home. There could be a kind of bargain.' She looked hopefully at Effie.

'No way!' Effie was furious. 'Come on! We're going.'

'You're coming with us.' Robert caught hold of Brenda's arm. 'It looks like we've lost Jessie again. We're not losing you, Brenda.'

Now the congregation was massing in the smaller corridors and it was harder for the four friends to struggle their way towards the main entrance. They clasped hold of each other and were jostled and tugged along in the seething mêlée. Voices cried out as people recognised the bride being dragged away from the ballroom: 'It's her! That's Brenda! Stop her . . .'

Effie rolled up her sleeves. 'Looks like we've got a fight on our hands . . .'

Sheila Manchu was never any good in a punch-up, and so they tried their best to defend her in the ensuing disturbance. She was yelling at them about how her Mumu would make them all suffer the boiling plagues of Egypt if they hurt one hair on her friends' heads, but they weren't listening, the mob. Effie and Robert and Brenda put their dukes up and landed a few good punches on the marauding dead. Why is it, Brenda mused, as she picked up a chair and whirled it about her head, that people feel they can misbehave so badly at weddings?

'Oh, hang on,' Effie suddenly called. 'There she is, look . . .'

Striding across the plush carpets of the foyer, looking cool as anything as she approached them, came the slinky form of Mrs Claus. In full command of the situation as usual.

'STOP! Stop this ludicrous furore at once.'

'Let us out of this place,' demanded Effie.

Mrs Claus said, with heavy irony, 'You're always running away from my Christmas Hotel.'

'I don't just mean this dump,' said Effie. 'I mean this . . . underworld. Hell. Whatever you want to call it.'

'I think you credit me with far more power than I actually have, my dear.'

'I don't think so. My Aunt Maud told me. You know the ways out. You always know more than anyone else.'

'Talking with old Aunt Maud, eh?' Mrs Claus grinned savagely. 'She was taking a risk, speaking to you.'

'What does that mean?' snapped Effie.

'And Brenda . . .' said Mrs Claus, tutting, 'Surely you don't think I'd help you to leave? Not when the ceremony was so close to completion?'

'I don't understand,' Brenda moaned unhappily. 'What is it to you if I get married or not? Why are you bothered?'

They were interrupted by the huge noise of the main doors to the ballroom crashing open. A sudden gap opened up in the murmurous crowd. Battered and bloody, Frank came striding towards Brenda's party.

'I'm here. I have defeated her . . .'

Robert yelled out, 'No!'

'What have you done to her?' shouted Effie, staring at the blood on his hands.

Mrs Claus laughed. 'The womanzee felled at last. Nice work, Frank. That apewoman was becoming a pest. Now, we're all here. Shall we continue with this wedding?'

'What?' said Brenda. 'No!'

'You said it yourself, Brenda,' Mrs Claus told her. 'There's a bargain to be struck. I know the ways and means to get your friends back to your own world. You marry Frank and stay here, and I'll send them back.'

'No way,' Effie said. 'You're not splitting us up.'

'Sweet. But doomed. Brenda will give in anyway. It is her destiny to marry Frank. She's been running away for two hundred years. Tonight she has been caught at last.'

Brenda looked from one to another of her friends. She stared at Mrs Claus and realised that it was useless to struggle. She nodded. 'Yes. That's just what it feels like. Like I've run out of places to run away to and hide in.'

'Brenda, no! You can't give in like that! Look at him. A killer. Look what he did to—'

Just then Robert lunged into action. He sprinted straight at Frank without a thought in his head but vengeance for his poor, transformed auntie. Frank noticed him in time, and swatted the boy away easily. Robert flew backwards, reeling dazedly into the crowd.

'Robert!' Brenda yelled at Frank: 'If you've hurt him . . .'

'He's all right,' said the impatient Frank. 'Look, Brenda. Frank has had enough of this standing around, and all these delays. Are we going to do this or not?'

Brenda considered. This was it. 'And you'll let them go? My friends?'

'Believe me,' Mrs Claus told her, 'I have no desire to keep them here.'

'Then I'll do it,' said Brenda.

Forced Nuptials

'I do,' said Frank.

    'And do you, Brenda—'

    'Yes, yes, just get it over with.'

    'Brenda, no!' Effie squawked, distantly.

Effie and Robert

'I can't believe she just gave in like that,' said Robert. He winced with bruises and misgivings. The snow crunched noisily underfoot as they wandered along the cliff path.

Effie was gloomy. 'We've lost her for ever, haven't we?'

'And we've lost Jessie, as well,' Robert added. 'Brenda's gone and married the man who murdered my aunt. Did you see the blood on his hands?'

Effie linked her arm with his. 'We don't know about that. There's no sign of Jessie. She might have fled. There's no body . . .'

They walked for some time in silence, all sounds deadened by the thick-falling snow. The sea sounded muted and mournful, even though it was very close.

Robert said, 'I've had enough of this place. I want to go home.'

'Well, quite.'

'Do you think Mrs Claus is going to be true to her word?'

Effie looked at him. Her face was pinched and cold. 'Oh, I hope so. We're running out of options.' Why am I clutching Brenda's bouquet? she thought. She didn't even remember catching it.

Mumu's Revenge

Thinking that her time in this underworld Whitby was about to come to an end, Sheila Manchu felt that she had to return to the Miramar. Her friends had warned her: they shouldn't split up. Effie had become quite heated on the subject. 'Anything could go wrong at this delicate stage,' she said. 'If we split up now, then we might never get home. We're waiting on Mrs Claus and her whims. What if she decides to help us, and you're away across town? What do we do then?'

But Sheila couldn't help it. She could see the sense in what Effie said, but there were things she had to do. Nothing she said would make Effie understand. Effie didn't have a husband. She had never had one. She had never felt like this. Like she had to leave her friends for a while and hurry through the weirdly empty streets of the town, seeking some final words, some final sense of closure with Mumu.

Sheila said goodbye to Effie and Robert in the downstairs of the Christmas Hotel, and her promises to catch up with them later seemed hollow even in her own ears. But she meant it! She'd come back with them. She wasn't staying here! Her friends stared at her like they didn't believe a word of it.

I'll show them, thought Sheila – and fled.

She lost track of time. She tottered on her unsuitable shoes. Soon she was creeping into her own home.

Into the sepulchral sitting room, where Mumu was waiting for her.

'I couldn't keep away. Once I knew we were staying at least this night.'

Mumu nodded. 'I understand. And love is in the air, is it not, at the Christmas Hotel?'

'That's not funny.'

'Are you saying that Brenda doesn't love her groom?' He turned his chillingly handsome face to examine his wife. Sheila dithered before him. She was annoyed now that Mumu had hardly fretted that she had left him for good. He seemed sanguine about this return of hers. He seemed even less bothered that she had made it plain she would leave him again, for her own world, as soon as she could.

'Of course Brenda didn't really want him,' she said. 'It's a ploy.'

Mumu sighed. 'A ploy? You say it like it's some everyday thing. Women with ploys, trapping men. Foolish men. Is that how it was with us, Sheila?'

'Oh no, Mu. You know it wasn't.'

'Good.'

And then they were kissing. He was as gentle as she remembered. Then, as urgent. He slid off his chair and guided her to the day bed.

'I'm so old, Sheila. Do I seem older? Older than I ever was in the world above?'

'Not at all. You seem just the same to me. Younger even. More sprightly. Vigorous.'

The room was mostly in darkness. She was hardly aware that he was undressing her and kissing her bare skin where it was revealed to the night.

'Ha. Vigorous.' He laughed. 'You always knew how to flatter an old fool. Vigorous indeed.'

'Hush now, Mumu. I want you to hold me.' She quivered under his kisses, and reached out her bare arms to take hold of him.

'You are still planning, aren't you? All you lot. You're planning to leave, to abscond tomorrow. You're not going to stay here with me.'

She let him lay her down on the silken day bed. 'Of course . . . of course I'm going to stay . . .'

'There is too much life in you. You are in your prime, Sheila. Why should you stay here, in amongst all the dead things?'

'But Mumu . . .'

'Hold me, Sheila. I'm as light as a bird, aren't I? There's nothing *to* me these days.'

He was laughing at her, low in his throat. He was so close she could hardly see him now. His robes whispered as he lay with her and she held him to her. Sheila kissed him again and his lips were dry. Not just dry. Powdery. Salty. She touched his face and found it was socketed and toothy. A skull. She made a strangled noise and stiffened up. She squealed and started thrashing around.

Mumu was falling to dust in her grasp. His laughter still filled her ears. The robes fell into folds in her arms. She was left hugging a clattering heap of old bones. Nothing much was left of him. As she gasped for breath between her screams, she found she was inhaling much of what remained of her husband, and she felt his laughter tickling her and scratching at her from within.

And then – for a good long time – Sheila lost all sense of herself.

She wouldn't be leaving the Hotel Miramar any time soon. Mumu had seen to that.

315

In the Honeymoon Suite

Brenda still had the hectoring jeers and the catcalls of the congregation ringing in her ears. Vile confetti – snowflake-shaped, Christmas-themed – was in all her clothes.

And now she was left alone with him.

Mrs Claus had given them her best suite. In the topmost turret of her grand sea-front hotel. The bridal suite.

'Now, my love. Can you believe it? After all this time.' Frank thrust the French windows open and revelled in the noise and the blustery snow. 'Listen to the sea tonight. Wild, wild. The sea is going wild for us. It is like applause.'

'Don't go all lyrical on me, Frank.'

'Let me have my moment, will you? This is my moment . . .'

'Of triumph?' She wasn't frightened of him. She wasn't nervous or bitter. Brenda felt simply numbed and resigned to her fate.

'Oh yes. This is what I asked our father for, all that time ago. A bride of my own. This is what I desired most of all. To make me like other men. To make me natural and real.' He smiled at her.

'Pah.' She sat on a chair to remove her shoes, and rubbed her feet. 'And isn't that just like a bloke? Depending on someone else to back up his idea of himself.'

He held out his arms, still smiling. 'Come here. Kiss me.'

'Not on your nelly. I'm here in order to save my friends, that's all.'

'Yes. So you trust her then, Mrs Claus? To send them back to the world?'

'I have to. She can do it, can't she?'

'Oh, certainly. She's more powerful than anyone realised.'

Brenda frowned at him. Immaculate in his tuxedo. Suddenly Frank seemed a lot better informed than she had ever imagined. 'How, though? Why is she so powerful?'

'Didn't you know? She's one of the witches. The greatest of them.'

'What?'

'One of Effie's lot. One of Effie's own family. Doesn't Effie know?' Frank looked surprised.

'No! I'm sure she doesn't.'

'How funny. They're related. Quite closely.'

'I see,' said Brenda, resuming her foot-rub, her mind racing. Effie related to Mrs Claus? Surely Effie would know if that were the case. But hadn't the ghostly Aunt Maud hinted at something similar? And what would Effie think about all this? She couldn't stand that enigmatic old bag. What was she? Another aunt? A sister?

Frank coughed gently. 'Stop prevaricating. Come on, Brenda.' He was sitting on the bed now, grinning at her foolishly. 'Frank's keeping the bed warm. Come over here. Kiss me.'

'Frank . . . I'm too old for all this nonsense.'

'We're the same age. We're all right.' He patted the continental quilt invitingly. He didn't seem to mind the chill in the room; the snow swirling on to the carpet.

'I can't say I'm not flattered. I didn't think . . .'

'Brenda didn't think what?'

She looked away. 'I never thought I'd be wanted again. By anyone.'

'I always wanted you. I always will.'

Brenda paused to absorb this. He was different to what she had expected. This wasn't the monster, the rapacious beast she had always suspected. 'It's a seductive thing. Being wanted.'

He went on, 'We should cling together. The world doesn't want us. If we don't want each other, who will?'

'I don't know.'

'Come to Frank, Brenda.'

'I . . .'

'It's midnight now. Listen.'

Somewhere in the Christmas Hotel, a clock was chiming.

'Bong bong bong. Can't you hear? It's destiny.'

Brenda shook her head. Cobwebs. She was full of cobwebs and couldn't think straight. She was letting her body and its wayward parts make up her mind for her. Then she burst out, 'But you . . . I can't . . . You've got Jessie's blood on your hands.'

'Don't be daft. I never hurt a hair on her head. Mind, she gave me a pretty good walloping.'

Brenda's heart raced, 'Jessie's all right?'

'She loped off into the night.'

'That's good.'

Now he fixed her with a warm, ironic smile, and took off his cravat. He started to unbutton his shirt. 'You're changing the subject. Come on.'

She watched him thoughtfully as he stripped for her. She let him get on with it for quite a while before telling him, 'You're still a good-looking fella.' But he's *green!* she was thinking all the while. *Green!*

Frank had no shame. He was proud of himself, of his whole scarred body, as he stripped it naked for her to see. 'I'm still exactly the same. We don't get any older, us old monsters. It's true, isn't it? We just get better. Come here.'

Brenda thought it over for a moment. 'I . . .' And then she shrugged, and started to wrestle her way out of her turtleneck jumper. 'All right,' she said.

Christmas Wishes

Effie and Robert were sitting in the bar at the Christmas Hotel. The celebrations had calmed somewhat, with most of the crowd drifting back out into the streets. From her vantage point in one of the bay windows, Effie watched them surging along the prom. Both she and Robert felt like they had been left at something of a loose end.

'What are we supposed to do?' she asked him. 'Hang around here until they've done the dirty deed?'

'I don't know,' he said despondently. He wondered if they should return to their homes, to rest, until Mrs Claus saw fit to return them to their real homes. But he decided he didn't want to move from their spot. 'I'm not tired. I couldn't sleep.' All they could do was wait on the whims of their wicked hostess.

Suddenly Effie turned to him, and she had a curious glint in her eye. 'There's one thing we haven't tried. We might not have to depend on Mrs Claus . . .' She leapt upon her bulky handbag and started to rustle about in its darkest recesses.

Robert knew at once what it was she was fetching out. They both studied the nasty shrivelled thing as she dangled it like a horrid tree decoration before their eyes. 'The monkey's paw,' Robert whispered. They looked around, suddenly alert to the other late drinkers in the hotel bar. It wouldn't do to be seen swinging such a supposedly powerful object about in a place like this.

Effie pursed her lips worriedly. 'It's worth a try, surely? It might just be an old legend, though.'

'But so many things are, and still turn out to be true. Be careful, Effie . . .'

She smiled at him. 'Be careful what you wish for, you mean? Ha. Too late for that.'

'And what about Sheila? Shouldn't we wait till she comes back?'

Effie tossed her head. 'Do you really think she will? She should have been back by now if she was coming home again with us. If she'd just been saying goodbye to that rancid old bloke of hers she'd be here right now. No, I reckon that Sheila has decided that she's staying. I bet you any money.'

'No!' gasped Robert. But he thought on. He had worked with Sheila. He had seen the shrine she had tended all these years, devoted to her beloved wrinkled mandarin. Surely, given a choice, Sheila would stay by his side? Even in hell? Effie certainly seemed to think so. But wasn't Effie – keen to be home, keen to be out of this terrible place – wasn't she jumping the gun? Now they were both gazing at the dangling monkey's paw in awe.

'Horrible-looking thing,' he said, as the hairy pendant twirled about on its golden chain.

'What shall I say?'

He closed his eyes to think better. 'I wish . . . I wish . . . Oh, this is daft. Like a game.'

'Wishes can be powerful things. Sometimes I think they are all that holds us together.' Effie concentrated hard for a moment. 'Look, let's wish that we could get Brenda away from Frank.'

321

'How?' By now, he wasn't even sure that was such a good idea. He felt that Effie was meddling, and who knew where that could end up?

'We need someone to help us,' Effie said decisively. 'Someone strong.' She nodded quickly. '*I know . . .*'

Monster Mash

All was quiet in the grand bridal suite at the top of the Christmas Hotel. Some hours had passed, and now Brenda was sitting on the bed, flopped out on the sumptuous pillows, sleepless and letting her busy mind wander where it would. The blue muslin curtains billowed madly at the French windows, but she hardly noticed the chilly breeze, or the snow pattering noisily on the stone terrace of their turret.

Beside her, Frank, exhausted, was snoring quietly. His vast body was completely at rest, arms and legs flung out with touching abandon. Brenda felt a spasm of pure tenderness expand through her chest.

It had been a long time since she had felt anything like this. She felt weirdly calm and vulnerable and open to this world in which she found herself. Even here, in a tower belonging to her enemy, she felt at rest and content to be still.

And then the moment was utterly ruined.

Her peace was shattered by one noise, very quiet at first, and then growing louder, as the maker of the noise flapped closer and closer through the moonlight.

It was the squeaking of a bat.

She had to warn her husband. She turned to shake his massive shoulder. 'Frank?'

The shrill squeaking grew louder. Then the curtains were whipped about and parted abruptly as the creature found its way into the suite. Brenda was about to swing for it; to wrench it out of the air. What was a bat doing in here? Spoiling her honeymoon peacefulness? But she knew. She knew who it was, even before the strange whooshing noise of his transmogrification filled the air.

'Not you . . .' Brenda groaned, at a dense patch of silver mist gradually solidifying at the foot of the bed.

Frank was stirring. 'Uhhh . . .? Whuzzat? Brenda?'

'Go back to sleep, Frank.'

She thought that he was better off not seeing this. Not being aware that the bat had turned into mist, which in turn was shimmering wildly and forming itself into the suave and smug figure of Alucard, who looked most amused at the spectacle of Brenda in bed with Frank.

'What are you doing here?' she asked crossly.

Alucard purred, 'I've come to rescue you.' He nodded towards the recumbent brute. 'From him.'

'What?' Now Brenda was struggling into her clothes, under the cover of the quilt.

'Effie sent me.'

This brought Brenda up short, with her head half inside her turtleneck. 'She what?'

Alucard was looking miffed at this lukewarm reception from his damsel in distress. 'Well, you might look more pleased, Brenda. I'm putting myself out here.'

'Just go! Leave me alone!' she burst out. 'I don't need the likes of you.'

The vampire spread his hands and shrugged helplessly. 'Ah . . . it's not as easy as that. I'm being coerced, you see. Effie has invoked a very powerful spell.'

'She can't! Even her fairy cakes don't work.'

Her rescuer sighed with infinite patience. He was enjoying this muddle a great deal, coercion spell notwithstanding. 'She's using the monkey paw from your safe,' he explained.

Brenda couldn't believe it. 'What?'

'And now I'm committed to saving your sorry behind from this great brute.'

Brenda's agitation had woken Frank. 'Uhhhh . . . Brenda?'

'You've woken him up, you fool!'

'Oh dear. Never mind.' Alucard grinned. His fangs glinted at her.

'Every time!' Brenda fumed. 'Every single time our paths cross, you cause a disaster, Alucard. I could swing for you!'

Alucard studied her with relish as she wriggled into the last of her clothes. 'By the looks of it . . . your dishevelled state and so on . . . I'd guess you've already gone past the conjugals.'

'None of your bloody business!' Brenda bellowed.

Then Frank was fully awake, sitting bolt upright in bed. 'Brenda! What's happening?'

She sighed. 'We've got company, Frank.'

'Whuh?'

'It's only me,' Alucard told him.

There was a click as Frank switched on his bedside lamp. A warm pink glow filled that side of the room. Frank struggled to pull his muzzy thoughts together, and at last he focused on the triumphant form of Alucard.

'You! Fiend! Where did you spring from?'

'It's been a long time, Frank,' Alucard said, studying the

unchanged monster. 'When was it I last had the mastery of you?'

Brenda knew where this was heading. The two old enemies were squaring up to each other. She stood up off the bed. 'Oh no.'

Frank clambered out, heavy-limbed and trying to find his dressing gown. 'I've waited a long while to get you, Alucard. It's time for Frank's revenge . . .'

Brenda shook her head in despair. 'You can't resist it, can you? Doesn't matter what's going on, does it? You *men*.'

'I'm ready for you, Alucard,' Frank shouted, bounding fully out of bed and bouncing on his heels like a boxer.

Alucard rolled his eyes with elegant disdain. '*En garde*, monster,' he said.

And then they went for each other, Frank half out of his dressing gown, which was rather unfortunate. The two monsters grappled together, clashing and bashing and bellowing. Hands reached for necks, throttling each other as they swayed and rocked in the most terrible dance to the death, smashing the dressing table, a chair, bringing down all the pictures as they tottered and tumbled about the place.

Brenda backed away. 'Always the same. Monster slugfest. They can't help themselves.' She couldn't see how she was going to stop them.

Then there came a banging on the main door to the bridal suite, at first hardly noticeable above the noise of the punch-up. At first Brenda thought it was just other guests complaining about the awful rumpus, but then she heard Effie's voice out in the corridor. 'Brenda! It's us! Are you all right? What's going on?'

She hurried to unbolt the door and let her friends in.

'What were you thinking of?' she shouted at Effie.

'What?'

Brenda flung out her arm, pointing at Frank and Alucard, locked in passionate combat. Both were choking and squeezing their fingers round each other's windpipes. 'What were you doing, sending Alucard in here after Frank? Look at them! They'll do each other in!'

'Oh my God,' said Robert. The hotel room was being systematically smashed and shaken to pieces. Plaster was falling out of the ceiling as the monsters struggled against each other.

Brenda said, 'They won't stop until they've torn each other to shreds . . . It's what they're always like.'

Effie looked very sanguine about the whole disastrous affair. 'Good. Just what I intended. They'll buy us time. Come on! We're leaving!'

Brenda stared at her. 'And where are we going, exactly?'

The noise of battle increased then, as Frank wrenched the vampire away from him and shook him like a dishrag. Alucard slipped out of his grasp and twined about him sinuously, reaching for his neck and his deliciously throbbing veins . . .

Robert said, 'We thought we could make Mrs Claus tell us how to get home.'

Brenda shook her head. 'That's only if I stay here, with him . . . Where's Sheila?'

'We don't know!' said Effie. 'She sloped off to the Miramar and she hasn't come back.'

'She'll be with that old Mumu of hers,' Brenda mused.

'Shouldn't we get out of here?' shouted Robert, wincing as Frank slapped Alucard about between his great pan-shovel hands. The count howled.

Brenda turned to them furiously. 'Frank! Kristoff! Stop it! We've got to put our heads together . . .'

'They're not going to listen to you,' said Effie.

Brenda turned on her. 'I can't believe you used my monkey's paw! I was saving that for a really dire situation . . .'

Effie squawked with laughter. 'How much more dire do you want?'

Robert examined the magical revenant. 'How many wishes do you get on these things?'

'Well, usually three,' said Brenda, 'but it's been in the cupboard so long, it might have run down some . . . Look, give me it here.'

'Horrible thing,' Effie said. 'I'm glad it worked, though.'

Brenda scowled at her friend. 'Wasting my wishes indeed . . . Look. The two of you. Get on the bed.'

Effie cast a glance at the mussed-up bedclothes. 'What?'

Robert was confused too. 'Eh?'

Brenda grabbed at their arms. 'No time for messing about. Come on!'

The monsters had moved away, towards the en suite, where they were still knocking seven shades out of each other. The bidet had come away from the wall, where Alucard had been flung at it, and now smashed pipes were gushing freezing-cold water on to the tiled floor. Frank was shouting incoherently and beating his enemy soundly about the chops.

Effie was doing what she was told, grimacing as the bedsprings jangled underneath Brenda and Robert and her own horrified self. 'I'm not sure I'm keen on getting into your marital bed . . .'

'Oh, shush. I'm just saying sit on it, while I do this wish thing . . .'

There was a strange noise – an exotic distant drumming sound –

as Brenda held the monkey's paw aloft in the dusky, noisome air. The three occupants of the bed stared in dismay as the withered hand twitched and came instantly to life. It flexed its nasty fingers.

The unperturbed Brenda coughed and commanded it in a voice that brooked no refusal: 'Monkey's paw! Take us away from here! Get us out of this place! Take us home again, to the land of the living!'

'Hear, hear!' Robert added.

The faraway sound of drumming increased then, as the paw glowed. The bed gave a sudden jolt against the floor. Its iron frame vibrated with a life of its own. Brenda, Effie and Robert shrieked.

'What the devil?' Effie gasped.

Robert seized hold of the mattress. He could hardly believe what was happening to the bed. 'It's rising up . . . off the ground!'

Even in the throes of his battle, Alucard had clocked what was happening. 'What are you doing?'

Brenda was grim-faced, holding on to the bedposts for dear life. 'Getting out of here! And I suggest, if you two want to join us, you hop on board.'

Frank was confused. 'What . . . what?'

The bed seemed to give a strange kind of revving noise, as it rose several feet above the carpet.

'It's powering up!' Brenda cried, and everyone screamed. 'Get your heads down!' she added, just as Alucard and Frank clambered aboard and the bed flung itself towards the open French windows.

They weren't open wide enough for a whole king-sized bed to escape. There came a great shattering and splintering of glass panes and wooden frames, but eventually the bed broke free of its confines within the suite at the top of the turret. Everyone kept their heads down through the chaotic hullabaloo of crunching and rending and the distant crash of debris on the street far below.

Then there was sudden, shocking quiet as the bed broke free and flew.

The black night air and the swirling snow took hold of it as it shot clear of the Christmas Hotel. The bed soared far above the cliffs and the thrashing sea, and some moments passed before anyone would look up to see what was happening to them, and why it was suddenly so cold.

The first person to look was Brenda. 'Hold on! Hold on tight, everyone!'

Effie opened her eyes a crack and screamed like a maniac. Robert joined her when he realised that they were streaking through the night above the shoreline.

'Brenda, I'm slipping! I'm falling off the bed!' Frank had twisted one corner of the quilt into a rope. His feet had no purchase and he was indeed slipping inch by inch off the bed.

'Here, give me your hand ...' Brenda tried to wedge her feet between the brass rungs of the bedstead. If she could only keep a hold and grab his arms ...

Effie stopped screaming and tried to lend a hand. She jabbed Alucard hard in the ribs. He had to help them. 'Kristoff ... turn yourself into a bat! You can fly alongside us and make more room ...'

Alucard saw at once what she meant. With a loud *pouff* noise, he turned himself back into a bat and fluttered about them as they soared, squeaking madly and not much use to anyone.

Robert clung to the mattress, his hair whipping up and his eyes streaming in the lashing wind. 'I don't believe this!'

Brenda was saying, 'Ah, we're going over the cliffs. You've really got to hold on now, everyone.'

Effie laughed hysterically. 'We're doing it! We're leaving the hotel behind! Look!' She howled crazily. 'We're FLYING!'

'Yes,' Brenda reminded her, 'and look at the sea below us. If you drop off, that's the end of you.'

Effie grasped at Brenda's arm. Her friend looked like the most solidly reliable thing on the bed. 'Where are we going?'

'Give me a hand with Frank, will you? He's slipping off!' She turned to see Frank's anguished face glaring at her from the corner of the bed.

Effie was aghast at the sight of him. 'He's nude! I can't touch him!'

Frank heaved himself up on the makeshift rope of bedclothes. He was grunting with effort, snow stinging his eyes, 'It's all right . . . I'm up . . .'

Then Robert's voice came to them. He shouted, 'Look! Look – above the abbey!' And his voice was filled with awe. The bed bucked and jounced again, the far end rising up like a car on a rollercoaster as it moved towards the top.

Ahead of them a tumbling morass of colour and light was opening up, above the pale remains of the abbey.

'The Bitch's Maw,' said Brenda, as the bed swooshed automatically towards the vortex. 'In all its glory. My wish must have brought it into being. Just look at it!'

'That's where we're going?' Effie shrilled.

They juddered and shook. The bed swooped and flung itself up to a terrible height. The brilliant, coruscating gateway of the Maw drew them ever closer, like a whirlpool suspended in the night.

'We're all going to die!' Effie screamed.

Brenda was laughing, hugging her, and clinging on to her husband. 'But at least we won't go to hell! We've already been! Wheeeee!'

Robert heard Effie tell him, 'She's gone crackers, Robert. It's all the sex.'

And all Robert could say was, 'AAAAGGGHHH!'

At that point, the bed and its occupants were swallowed up by the Maw. It was too noisy to tell if there was a bat fluttering alongside them, and whether he managed to make it through the gaping vortex before it sealed itself up behind them.

In a matter of seconds it was all over. The Maw was gone. The flying bed was gone. The snow continued to fall, and for a while at least there was relative silence over Whitby. The hellish Whitby somewhere underneath the one that Brenda and Effie knew.

Somehow, and in the most improbable fashion, they had managed to escape.

Mrs Claus is Informed

'Madam! Madam!'

She was stewing in her early morning bath, ripping up rose petals, when Martin the elf came running with the news. 'I know. I already know.'

'But you've lost them for ever now,' he gabbled. 'If they've managed to fly that bed home . . .'

She stared at him, fury in her eyes. 'No. I refuse to believe that. There'll be another way. I know there will be another way . . .'

Bedwrecked

It was bright daylight when they woke. The creamy sounds of the surf greeted them with the spangling sunshine, and it took some moments for their party to orient themselves.

They had been flung off the bed, into the damp golden-brown sand. They were on a small beach, somewhere along the coast from Robin Hood's Bay, from what Brenda could make out when she sat up.

The twisted, buckled ruin of the bed lay in the sand beside them, looking the worse for its ride through the skies and the Bitch's Maw. Luckily, none of its occupants – human or otherwise – were injured at all, apart from bruises and aching heads and bones.

Brenda shook them awake. 'Everyone? Are you all right?'

Robert sat up with a jolt. 'Are we home? Where is this?'

'I think we're home . . .' said Effie, squinting at the clifftops, and trying to figure them out.

'Frank!' Brenda burst out, and hurried to where her naked husband was tangled in the shredded bedclothes.

'I think I'm all right. I think I'm in one piece.' He patted at his substantial parts ruefully.

Suddenly Effie froze. 'Where's Kristoff?'

'I can't see him . . .'

'It's broad daylight!' cried Effie, with a tinge of panic. Alucard was never any good in the daylight. 'Where is he?'

'He's not here,' said Brenda. 'He . . .'

Effie's voice was dull. 'He didn't make it out of hell, did he?'

Frank was brusque, wrapping himself in the sand-filled duvet. 'Bugger him. We made it, didn't we? That's all that counts. We're back! We're home!'

Effie turned away from him. 'Brenda, I'd appreciate it if you got your man friend to shut up.'

Frank chuckled. '*Husband*, Effie. Not *man friend*. I'm her husband. Whether you like it or not.'

Effie stood up shakily. 'Whatever. I'm going home. Are you coming, Robert?'

Robert stared at his friends. There were a couple of others missing too, he had realised. 'We left Jessie behind. And Sheila . . . she's still in hell too. I can't believe we did that. Saved our own skins.'

Effie pulled a face. 'Obviously Sheila decided that she wanted to be with her husband too.' She cast a sardonic look at Brenda and Frank. 'Man mad, all these daft women.' She brushed the sand off her clothes. 'I reckon we're somewhere out near Ravenscar. Only a couple of miles. We can catch a bus back home. Come on, everyone.'

Coffee and Walnut Cake at the End

A couple of days later, at the front table of The Walrus and the Carpenter, the young waitress was infuriating Effie again with unwanted attention. 'Haven't heard you on *The Night Owls* for a little while,' she said. 'Have you been away?'

Effie scowled. 'You could say that. But I'd gone off that silly radio show anyway. At the end of the day, I didn't like the way he talked to people.'

The waitress sighed, slowly and unskilfully unloading her tray of its freight of coffee cups, cafetiere and sugar bowl. 'It's gone right downhill, actually. Not as spicy as it was. All the life seems to have gone out of whatsit, Mr Danby.'

'Good,' said Effie, with some satisfaction. 'Horrid little man.'

'Ooh!'

Effie relented. 'Sorry. I'm a bit snappish. I've had a trying few days.'

'Never mind. Happens to all of us.'

'I very much doubt that.'

The main door tinged and in came Brenda. Glowing.

'Here's your friend,' the waitress said, intrigued by the spring in the larger woman's step. 'Will you have walnut cake?'

'Just coffee for me,' Effie said, and the waitress bustled away. Brenda plumped herself down on the banquette and Effie narrowed her eyes. 'Well?'

Brenda smiled at her. 'Good morning, Effie. You've been quiet recently.'

'I've been recuperating. Having a restful time at home.'

Brenda started sorting out the coffee cups. 'That's all right then. I thought you were . . . you know. In a huff or something.'

'A huff! Since when do I go into huffs?'

'Pfft,' Brenda scoffed.

'Are we shopping together and having lunch after?' Effie wanted to know. It was what they often did on these mornings together.

'Oh, Effie, I can't. Frank's—'

'All right.' Effie held up a hand. 'It doesn't matter.'

'It's just that we—'

'That's okay.'

'We're going off for a long weekend. To the Lake District. Grasmere.'

Effie stared at her, very hard. 'That'll be nice for you.'

There was a pause. Then Brenda said, 'Don't be nasty, Effie.'

'Nasty!'

'I don't want this to come between us. Frank and I are talking things over. Discussing our future.'

Suddenly the rush of words inside Effie was too much for her. They all came tumbling out. 'But you can't stand the man! You said he was a brute! A monster!' She sank the plunger of the cafetiere, and spilled coffee on the cloth.

'That's as maybe,' Brenda said crossly. 'But we've got stuff to talk about, me and Frank.'

Effie huffed. 'You only married him because you were forced to.'

'Hmm,' Brenda said. 'And why did I allow that to happen? I did it to save you and Robert. I did it to save your skinny old arse.'

Effie gaped at her. 'Brenda! How dare you!'

'Don't go sniffy with me, lady.'

'Pah.'

Brenda took charge and poured their coffee, pushing Effie's towards her. 'Look. He's different to how I expected.'

Effie shook her head sadly. She looked as if she expected rather better of her friend. 'You sound like any other silly old woman. Settling for second best. Hoping against hope. Putting up with some loutish, boorish old man.'

Brenda lowered her voice as she stirred her sugar in. 'We were . . . at least we know that we were . . . actually *made for each other*. Perhaps we should give it a try.'

Effie was exasperated. 'I can't believe I'm hearing this. I thought you were a clever woman. He's a monster, Brenda! A killer!'

Brenda looked away. 'I wanted to have your support in this.'

'I'm sorry. I can't give it.'

'All right,' said Brenda. She sipped her tepid, bitter coffee and frowned. 'I'll just have to live with that.'

The waitress came trundling over with the cake trolley. 'Sure I can't tempt you?'

They both glared at her. She went away.

Then Brenda broke their silence, asking, 'Have you heard anything from Kristoff?'

'Not a sausage.'

Brenda sighed. She couldn't think of anything else to say. 'I never thought we'd let men get in the way of our friendship.'

'Me neither.'

Brenda suggested, with forced brightness, 'Let's just not talk about them when we're together.'

Effie looked up at her. 'I'm not . . . envious, you know. Because you've got Frank and Kristoff has done a runner again.'

'I never thought you were.'

Effie sagged down, all of the dignity and fury going out of her as she admitted, 'Well, maybe I *am* envious, a little. But I'll just have to get over that.'

'Look, let's get that silly waitress back and order some cake. Walnut cake.'

Effie gave her a guarded smile and gestured to the girl. She had a sudden thought. 'Did you ever find out why Mrs Claus was so keen for your wedding to happen?'

'No, I never did. I still have no idea. But everything was so weird there, wasn't it? So distorted and strange. Like some kind of . . . you know, those continental films.'

'I'm not sure I've seen that kind of film.'

'Whatever she was after, it'll have been something nasty. Two slices of walnut cake, please.' The waitress nodded in triumph and hurried away.

'Have you thought,' Effie began warily, 'that by being together, you and Frank might be playing into her hands?'

'I suppose so.' Brenda nodded. 'But . . . if it's what we want, then we can't let that stop us.'

The waitress was dragging her trolley up to their table again.

Brenda leaned across and patted her friend's hand warmly. 'I'm sorry, Effie. I've put you through hell again. These little adventures of ours . . .' She smiled and shook her head.

Effie grasped her hand. 'They are *ours*. That's what counts, ducky.' She grinned at Brenda. 'And I wouldn't miss them for the world.'

'You wouldn't?' Brenda shooed the poor waitress away again.

'Of course not.' Effie laughed. 'I love what we do. All of it. Just . . .'

'Yes?'

'Don't let that Frank spoil it or bring it to an end.'

'Of course not,' Brenda promised. 'He wouldn't do that anyway.'

Effie studied her best friend carefully. She really did look happy. Maybe as happy as Effie had ever seen her. 'We're a team, aren't we, Brenda?' she said.

Brenda nodded firmly. 'We're the best. And we've got a job to do.' She looked at the table in front of her, frowning. 'Where's that cake? Call the silly waitress back. What was I saying? Oh yes. We've got a very important job to do in this spooky old town. And do you know? I've got a feeling in my water that it isn't over yet.'